Senhor Albasini's Secret

SENHOR ALBASINI'S SECRET

E. Lombard

To my mother Christina Helena Lombard (nee Albasini), who told me the stories. Sadly, she had to say Hamba Gahshle (goodbye) when I had just turned twelve, leaving me, a motherless daughter, to tell the Albasini tale.

Join our free Facebook group for additional historic photos, maps, family trees, discussions and more at: www.facebook.com/groups/albasinibook

Preface

Some of the characters in this book are purely fictitious. Others are based on persons long since dead. No disrespect is intended to any of them. If there is any person who feels offended by the contents of this book, I apologise in advance.

My aim was to make this illustrious great-great grandfather of mine a romantic figure while keeping the historical facts as close as possible to the truth. I also set out to make this an easily readable story for his descendants and any others interested in the life of a brave and remarkable man.

The historical setting is based on actual events with the real names of people and place researched from various sources listed in the Bibliography. Some artistic lenience has been taken to create Stephanus Schoeman as the antagonist in the romantic triangle. Artistic lenience came to my rescue again to create Gertina, the heroine. Some of the Albasini cousins have suggested that she could have been the orphaned child of Lang Hans van Rensburg who was saved by a Zulu warrior. I took my cue from them and created Gertina.

Writing a historical novel made me realise that juggling the uncertainties of the past is not an easy task. The first uncertainty is the physical past; the second is the psychological past. And the third? Working out how much of them the reader actually wants to know.

Contents

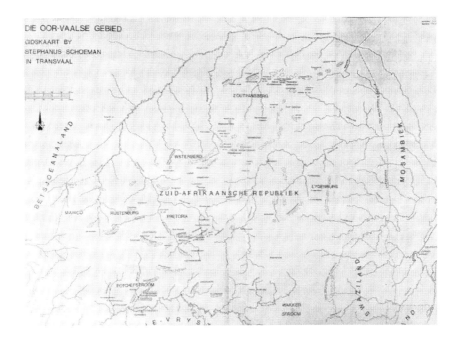

Figure 1 - *A map drawn by Stephanus Schoeman of what the Transvaal looked like during the mid 1800's. Mpumalanga is the modern-day naming of the region in the Republic of South Africa.*

i

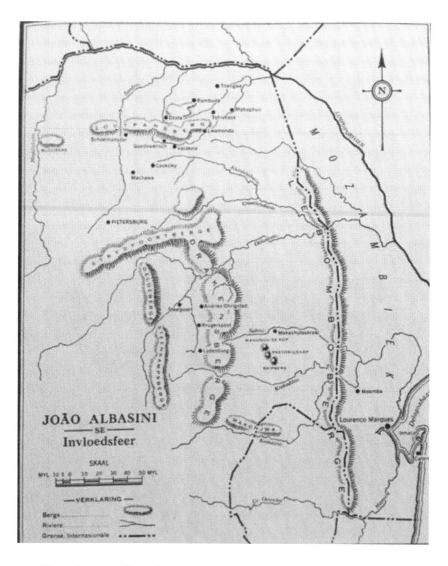

Figure 2 - *Joao Albasini's influence sphere in the Transvaal and the Lowveld.*

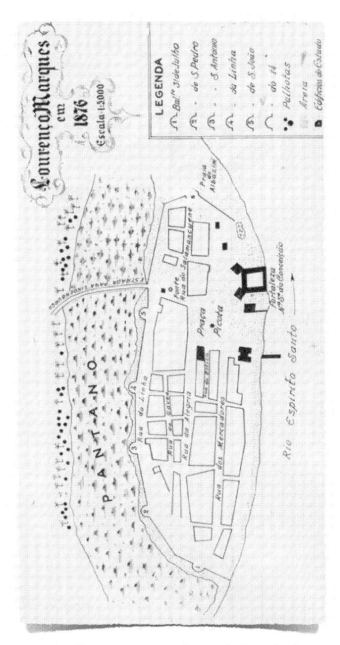

Figure 3 - *Albasini property towards top right (Praia do Albazini)*

iii

*"Like measles, love is most dangerous
when it comes late in life."*

Lord Byron

Introduction

Antonio Augusto Albasini, a political refugee, came from humble means. His first marriage in 1805 was to Luisa da Silva who associated with members of the Portuguese aristocracy, such as the Marquis of Alorna and the Earl of Ribeira Grande. They were two of the highest-ranking aristocrats of the Royal Court and were witnesses at their marriage. Consequently, when Antonio lost Luisa and their son Cesario early in their marriage, he was well connected to the higher social hierarchy of Lisbon.

It might be that Antonio, still young and eligible, moved on quickly to court Maria, the reigning beauty in Portuguese Court circles, who was thought to be of noble Spanish blood with Basque ancestry. Maria succumbed to Antonio's charms and became the second Senhora Albasini in 1809. She gave birth to Maria and, later, João the lionhearted, who emerged later in his life as the Safari King of the ivory trade in South East Africa.

Although this book is a fictional account based around true events, the following is an extract from the diary of Maria de Purificaçao Garcia, the mother of João Albasini:

Diary of Maria de Purificaçao Garcia

My name is Maria de Purificaçao from the Royal House of Spain. But I am a woman with a big heartache. This husband of mine, this Antonio Albasini, he take my son, my bambino

João - he send him to a far place in Africa to make business with the wild Tribes peoples – my son to get lots of ivory.

Tribes people catch him and friend him tie hands and take him into bush far, far away. Then comes the Tribes peoples, him kill friend cook him on fire.

Eat him!!!

My son my João - he think tomorrow Tribes peoples eat me!!

He clever my son. He play him wild animal he sits on haunches cries like jackal fight dog - loose ropes on hands and leave feet and fight mad dog. My son my João fight mad dog bare hands. He put hands over dogs neck - he strangles mad dog.

Tribes people say [non-legible] not this one… We no eat - we just let go back.

In time, João became a legend of courage and forthrightness, emerging as a Chief to amalgamate the splintered groups from the small tribes who fled Sosangane, an exiled impi of Chaka. These groups took refuge under João's strong personality, sharp intellect and perseverance to carve an indelible niche in the history of South Africa and South East Africa.

This story needs to be told to all the Albasini descendants to fulfil the wish of João's daughter, Maria Machdelena Biccard, who said in a letter to one of her children: "Tell the descendants of João Albasini where their roots come from and who and what their ancestor was. In order to keep their heads high when adversity strikes and to say, I am an Albasini and there are things that you can do and there are things you can't do. To tell the Afrikaners that not all natives are your enemies. To tell the Shangaans that they should build on the foundation Juwawa, King of the Knopneuse, had set for them and become a proud nation."

It is impossible to erase the deeds of João and his followers who stood as a bastion safeguarding the safety of the Zoutpanzberg district.

So together with the Shangaans and João's family we greet him with the Shangaan greeting, 'Hosi!'

Chapter 1

Puta Merda (Holy Shit)!

João expressed the expletive, ignoring his gentlemanly upbringing. The surge of excitement stemming from the possibilities of a new beginning, new challenges and opportunities to be explored was unstoppable.

This hunger for adventure was the same driving force which led him to withstand his mother's pleading eyes which implored him to become a lawyer. Later, his uncle's dark accusing eyes, the eyes of a Jesuit priest, exhorted him to take up a career in divinity. But no such safe career paths could compare with the exhilaration of standing, fearless, a few feet away from a charging elephant, lifting the heavy front loader muzzle gun, and shooting. Nothing could surpass the feeling of having conquered fear itself when the beast thudded to the ground and exhaled its last breath. The *Bambino's* near-sightedness left him no choice other than to approach his prey to point-blank range before he was able to shoot. He could stare down a lion, block out the foul breath, and still have the thrill of showing just who was the boss. He liked ruffling the lion's mane to show that there was no ill-filling but, needless to say, a dead lion cannot respond.

N'wamanungu, his companion, shared this indomitable lust for life. The ancestry of the Royal House of Vankomati pumped in his blood. We do not know how many cows were paid as ransom for his mother. Nor do we know if she associated with other royals to attract the attention of

N'wamanungu's father, King Mavungwani. We do know, however, that in the matter of bravery N'wamanungu's and that of João were equal.

They also shared the tell-tale, tiny holes on their ears of caul-bearing babies. João's was removed by a midwife whereas N'wamanungu's was removed from his face by his mother. It was believed that this phenomenon of nature gave both men an extra-ordinary sixth sense.

The trio who sat on the escarpment looking down over the plains below was completed by Tom Albach who was not yet a man but neither was he a child. The two older men called him Tommy. At the age of fourteen he already showed the promise of a remarkable physique. He inherited his ginger-biscuit complexion and coir-looking hair from his mulatto mother and his fierce blue eyes from his father. Neither of his parents had mingled with the elite. He hero-worshiped João and was proud that his rank as 'button and boots polisher' had been elevated to interpreter. He spoke both Zulu and Kitchen-Dutch fluently.

João took out his looking glass to confirm what his spies told him about the influx of people who looked similar to him. They reported that these people were like an army of ants. They wore baskets on their heads and sat on zebras without stripes. Like the ants, they travelled in convoy with their white houses pulled by oxen. The cattle, sheep and goats were so many that they left a wide path for people to follow.

João knew they were called the *Voortrekkers* (pioneers). He gained this knowledge from Louis Trichardt's son Carolus, better known as Karl, whom João had met while on a trip to Lorenço Marques. Karl informed him that his father and his father's cousin, Lang Hans van Rensburg, were considered to be the *Voorste* (the first ones) pioneers to venture north, away from the Cape Colony in the South. They were looking for fresh pastures and independence and were to inform Andries Potgieter, a prominent leader amongst the *Voortrekkers*, and other leaders if circumstances were favourable to establish new settlements. Karl explained that his people were sick and tired of the oppression imposed on these tough and free-spirited people by the English.

As a result, a mass exodus had taken place between 1830 and 1840. These people lived a life of high moral standards based on the Bible which also instilled in them a belief that they were a chosen nation. Karl mentioned that his father kept a diary in which he noted the details of everyday living, meticulously including his meetings with native tribes, and nominating which were friendly and those who might pose a threat.

João wondered what would happen when these basket-wearing ants with their moving houses met up with the vast numbers of another kind of ant. These were the likes of Soshangane, of whom João had first-hand experience, who had fled the tyranny of Chaka, the Zulu king, and established a rule of terror in the south-eastern parts of Mozambique. The spies also told him of other groups of natives who were moving deeper inland to look for greener pastures and a place to live. They told him about the Macatese tribe at Beja and another tribe, the Venda, under the rule of Makhato. There was bound to be clashes between these various groups. But, João thought, I am only interested in ivory, white gold.

With his well-manicured hands, João held the looking glass steady so that he could focus on the squatter camp way down below the elephant path. He saw them, the foreigners, that is. So, it was true then - they had come to stay.

This vast expanse of *Terra incognita,* no-man's land, was a place where anybody could trade and hunt elephants without jurisdiction. Opportunities like these had made him rich. He needed no interference.

On the map that his friend Karl Trichardt had shown him, the coastal ports of Quelimane, Beira, Sofala, Inhambane, Xi-Xi, and Delagoa Bay were clearly marked but the vast interior to the west of the east coast of Africa remained a blank space.

The document was signed:

Statement

In the country of the Xhosa
District: Oudshoorn

Daniel Pfeffer

Profession: Teacher to the *Voorste Trekkers,* Louis Trichardt and followers.

Without question, he knew he had already filled in a considerable part of that blank space. He would have to wait and see. It could be advantageous, and not only to him, but the possibilities were endless. He just needed to convince the authorities in Lisbon.

Imbeciles, he thought.

In the scramble for Africa, Portugal had pleasant dreams of a *mapa-cor-de- rosa* (rose coloured map) linking East to West. João thought this would be his opportunity to serve King Luiz. Frankly, he didn't care what colour was used. Pink wasn't his favourite but as long as they just damn well got in there and put down roots!

No demarcation of the land was stipulated. He had made a start by buying land from Chief Magashula. It was his first dot on the blank canvas. He had plans to make many more and, in time, connect the dots. The first time he had heard about Magashula was when N'wamanungu told João that he would take him to a chief's *kraal* that was considered to be the central gathering place for travellers and traders taking the inland route to the North.

On the outskirts of the *kraal* (village), João was taken to an *Isivivane,* a traveller's cairn. As many travellers before him had done, he had to pick up a stone with his foot, spit on it and place it on the cairn. It meant good luck.

The effort João had taken with the stone was well worth it because Magashula, the chief who had come to see what all the mirth was about, liked João's theatrical efforts and, later on, was only too willing to sell João this piece of land for 22 oxen. Magashula was not a prominent chief in the area but well known to be peace loving. He immediately bargained for

João's protection and an arrangement was reached. João gave instructions for the cultivation of the land, the planting of wheat and having water races dug to run from the river to the property.

The land was a gem. Situated on the banks of the Sabi River, there was an abundance of game, including elephants aplenty, fertile land and enough space for his own followers and Magashula's people to make a living in peaceful coexistence. It also suited João well as a halfway house for trade from anywhere in the region.

A new passport, stamped 10 September 1836, was tucked away in the breast pocket of his captain's uniform. It read:

Surname: Albasini.
First name: João.
Nationality: Portugal.
Place of birth: Oporto.
Date of birth: 01 May 1813.

It was easy to fool the authorities. João just had to train his mind to think that his birthday was now 01 May 1813 and not 26 May 1812, as it appeared in the records of the small church in São Lourenco back in Portugal.

He felt good, almost a year younger; not bad for a new start in life. He gave himself a pat on the shoulder for such genius. It was a pity that he did not shave off another year or two. He was thirty-four and on top of his game.

João had taken his bodyguard and young Tom Albach to accompany him on this trip. On purpose, he did not take the route along the Sabi River but chose to approach the settlement from the heights of the Lebombo mountain range. It would give him a good vantage point before he needed to make any decisions.

N'wamanungu stood silently next to João, or Juwawa, as his followers fondly called him. N'wamanungu marvelled at the magic tube in his companion's hands, which had stopped roving from side to side. Juwawa fixed it's focus on something important and deftly adjusted the lenses on the three-draw telescope.

'What is it that you see, my friend?'

N'wamanungu resented being ignored but knew he had to trust the instincts of the man sitting on a white mule. The mule was as well-groomed as its master. The thick mane was neatly trimmed, its hide shone and its tail was plaited into French knots. A rug woven in the colours of Portugal was draped as a saddle. João preferred to ride bareback as it made any getaway much quicker and he experienced a better bonding with the mule. Her big ears twitched, ever vigilant, waiting for the master's command.

N'wamanungu shifted his weight from one foot to the other as he waited patiently. João lowered the telescope. His fingers absently stroked the embossed inscription on the rosewood tube as if to draw courage from the engraving which read:

Antonio Augusto Albasini, Lieutenant Junior Grade.
26th day of August 1772.
Issued Marinha Portuguesa. Bravery.
Saving the captain's wife.

Rumour had it that the young lieutenant, an Italian rogue, seemed to have been irresistible to the captain's wife. Antonio cleverly turned adversity to advantage on the night of a storm when he saved the lady by being in the right place at the right time, namely the lady in question's cabin! The looking glass was a parting gift from his father.

The captain's uniform he now wore also belonged to his father but wasn't gifted. It was a part of his inheritance. João had the uniform altered to fit him since he was a slighter man than his father, a six-feet-two inches, good-looking, charming Italian. João thought that the uniform would give him formality and status if an opportunity should arise.

'Well, I see a church. I see a half-built rampart, ox-wagons and thorn bushes which complete the safe enclosure.' The outspanned oxen grazed freely without their yokes and spirals of light blue smoke coiled into the clear sky. 'I see a graveyard with many graves. The smaller mounds outnumber the larger ones.' It seemed to João that the whitewashed wooden crosses planted on the red earth emitted messages of suffering. 'I have also seen a European woman for the first time in twelve years.' He chuckled but didn't tell N'wamanungu that she seemed a bit young.

The petite figure in a long night dress was a woman, all right. Her fair hair, the colour of sun-ripened corn, floated in the cool, early morning breeze. An angel amongst the unhappiness, he thought.

In the pit of his stomach he endured a strange excitement, a sensation he wasn't quite ready to explore. He knew there and then that he wanted her.

N'wamanungu saw this and lost no time in teasing his friend, '*Eehbo!* A wife is what you came for, not trade!' He sniggered knowingly and was surprised at his friend's total engrossment in the seemingly miraculous object. If he had Juwawa's riches, he could buy many wives. He could not understand the idea of just one wife - impossible!

'I think she is in danger.'

'Who are you talking about?'

'The girl, of course.'

'Ah!' N'wamanungu said. 'Now the woman has become a girl. What did she do? Let me hear!'

João shrugged and couldn't help being amused at N'wamanungu's disappointment when he casually remarked, 'She emptied the chamber pot!' After a considerable silence, João continued, 'I saw a man on a dun-coloured horse secretly watching her.'

***

Gertina, the young girl sitting in front of the *serfeintjie* (pump organ), shuffled the music sheets and checked that all the Psalms she had to play were in the order the minister had instructed her. Her parents had been killed when Lang Hans van Rensburg's trek was massacred. She and her brother Hendrik were saved by a Zulu warrior who had taken pity on them. When Karl Trichardt came into contact with the two children and realised who they were, he brought them to be with Lucas van Rensburg, their uncle.

This moment of solitude gave her a few moments to reflect on her situation. Just thinking of getting married made her cringe. In the community, a few ladies of the *Kappie Brigade* (ladies who gathered from time to time to exchange gossip) had already linked her name to that of Stephanus Schoeman, a well-to-do widower who would be an excellent match. Schoeman was a person of influence and a right-hand man for the settlement's leader, Andries Potgieter. The *Kappie Brigade* discussed her future often as they all took responsibility for taking care of the two orphans who came into their midst and they felt compassion for the quiet girl. The harrowing experience she and her brother had was often regurgitated at their afternoon coffee sessions. They were also quick to whisper that Gertina reminded them of the *Kruitjie-roer-my-nie* bush (the mimosa plant which closes when touched). In other words, she brooked no interference in her private life and was extremely protective of her little brother.

Gertina guessed that there would be about 250 members attending *Nachtmaal* (Communion). She loved the singing and it gave her pleasure to serve the Lord in this way. When she looked up, she saw that Stephanus was already standing next to the pulpit. He had his violin in his right hand and his dark brown eyes stared down at her.

'Good morning, Gertina. I love it when you play the *serfyntjie*. It shows that you're not only a pretty face.'

He meant it to be a compliment but the oiliness of his tone was just too conciliatory to be appreciated. He first praised her but then, with a slightly raised voice, he accused, 'You are not wearing the shawl I brought you from Rustenburg. I assure you it is knitted from the finest wool in Germany.' He elaborated, 'My *tante* (aunt) from the Burenrepublik (*Farmers Republic*) in Schleswig-Holstein sent it to me. I thought that the colour would suit your enchanting blue eyes.' He emphasised the word *Burenrepublik*, making out that it was something holy.

How on earth did he manage to creep up on her without her noticing? Her eyes did not waver when she looked at him and sweetly answered, 'I gave it to *Tante* Sannie. She needs it more than I do.' Her seemingly innocent voice asked, 'Did it belong to wife number one or number two?'

'Mmm, I like a sprightly girl. Perhaps a bonnet next time might soften your heart?'

He lifted the violin and began to play, his eyes still ogling her. The congregation entered the church in dribs and drabs. A revered silence accompanied the sweet music and Gertina had to admit that Stephanus played well. She liked listening to him because he played with emotion emanating from his entire body. His closed eyelids had freckles and she noticed the curly eyelashes matched the twin waterfalls of his moustache. But were those eyes closed? She remembered his scrutinising look and felt trapped.

Stephanus stopped playing and nodded his head as the prompt for the church's leaders to enter from the vestry. Each in a single file, a set of elders walked in from the right and a group of deacons from the left. The sombre-looking men in dark suits sat down on cue. The last man to enter from the vestry was the *dominee* (reverend). He paused at the bottom of the pulpit steps and bowed his head in a moment of individual prayer.

Gertina looked backward to see if there were any late-comers. The doors were about to close and she couldn't believe what she saw.

As the church doors closed, João put his foot in the doorway. He opened the door and, to the dismay of the two young ushers on duty, squeezed past them. He whispered, '*Desculpe,*' (Sorry) and proceeded to walk down the aisle with military precision and proudly wearing his uniform. He knelt on one knee in front of the pulpit, crossed himself, bowed in reverence and closed his eyes in a moment of silent prayer.

When he stood up and turned to look at the congregation, many faces with varied expressions greeted him. Some people gaped, some women turned their heads in open admiration, a few smiled a welcome, and others had pencil-line lips expressing disapproval. There were those who gathered their children closer as if protecting them from possible evil. The men looked stern.

João faced a dilemma. He had nowhere to sit. The decision was made for him when a tall man with fiery ginger hair took him by the elbow and marched him purposefully to the back of the church as if to oust him from the haven. João stopped suddenly. He had come this far and he would not be prevented from attending the sermon, come hell or high water. The condescending way in which the man gripped him made his hackles rise. He extricated his arm and looked up into hostile obsidian eyes.

Surely there would be somebody with compassion in this church. He looked towards the back of the church and saw that a thick-set man with a salt-and-pepper beard draped on his chest had taken a child onto his lap and indicated a vacant seat next to him.

João turned his face to the man attempting to expel him and took great pleasure in innocently pointing to himself with his index finger and then putting both hands together in prayer, indicating that he, João, wished to attend the service. He took the seat next to the good Samaritan. There was a nod of approval from the salt-and-pepper beard, but the ginger-haired man's face remained stern.

The little church was filled to capacity. Small cathedral windows poked like shark teeth into the air allowing only a little light to shine onto the whitewashed walls. There were no images of Mother Maria or any of the saints. The only adornment was a wooden cross that hung behind the pulpit.

The minister, clothed in a black clerical gown, gesticulated with his arms, shook his head and banged on the pulpit to bring home his point.

The man who had gripped his arm was sitting in the second row from the front. He had his arm draped along the pew, not touching the girl sitting next to him, but with an attitude that signalled possessiveness. By contrast, the girl sat straight-backed, looking at a point in front of her. Beneath her bonnet, a sun-ripened, corn-coloured plait divided the neat, prim shoulders in half.

João did not have a clue in the world what the preacher was saying but he didn't mind. It gave him time to reflect and observe this collection of austere-looking people. He smiled, thinking that he was familiar with some Dutch swearwords, but thought it highly improbable that he would hear them in the minister's sermon. He wondered about the girl.

The girl and the man moved forward. She took up position to play the pump organ and the ginger-haired man took his place next to it. The church pews creaked and the ladies' dresses rustled as the congregation stood to sing. João was surprised by the ginger-hair man's exquisite playing of the introduction to the song.

João thought that perhaps he had been too harsh in his judgment. Maybe music could be a common denominator to put things right. He could not get rid of the feeling that he had done something wrong although he did not feel threatened. He couldn't put his finger on the spot but he sensed something was amiss. The congregation sang at the top of their voices, mirroring the minister's oration.

The silver communion cup stood on a long rectangular table decked with a white crocheted tablecloth. The wood-turned plates cradled the sacrificial bread. Two of the younger men who sat at the front of the church stood up and moved along the aisle, inviting each row of people to come forward to participate in the celebration of the sacrament. When it was João's turn, the young man who gave the invitation barred him from going forward and shook his head in denial. Dumbfounded, João sank back onto the bench.

He thought, 'I've been refused participation in the sacrament. Does that make me an unforgivable sinner? I have done nothing wrong.' That was something he would think about later.

Meanwhile, he could sit and admire the girl's face. He was sure she was the morning angel. He memorised every feature, every gesture, imagined her touch and voice, and how fresh she would smell. Tonight, wrapped in his woollen blanket, lying next to the fire, he would look up at the winking stars and pray, 'If this blank space on the canvas was in the process of being inhabited by these grave-looking people, would they please allow me to be a part of the process?' He would think about the girl.

'*Solo Tua,*' (Only yours) he whispered.

Cupid, his bow ready, started his mischievous shuffle-dance over João's heart. Shortly the son of the love-goddess Venus would shoot his arrow.

Intense sadness overwhelmed João. When the congregation stood to sing the last Psalm, which he happened to recognise, João sang with all the emotion pent up within him. The churchgoers were astounded. They had never heard such a moving and emotional interpretation of Psalm 23. João's Italian soul poured out the utter loneliness that had filled his heart. The melodious sounds of the words of the song fell softly on the ears of the parishioners.

João took comfort in the warmth of his father's uniform but that did not take away the fact that he was an orphan. Not only was he robbed of his parents but also civilisation had passed him by like a ghost in the night.

The little boy on the big man's lap pointed at the strange man in a blue uniform with two swords hanging from his belt. The little boy whispered, '*Kyk Pappa, die man huil.*' (Look! Pappa, he is crying.)

He was still trying to come to terms with the emotions that caused him to slip his guard. He blinked back the grieving that had stalled in his eyes and his hand smudged away any traces of a weak moment in his life. As the aftermath of bottled-up emotions still churned in his innermost being, he had to stifle a sob that was gagging him, disabling him from uttering a single word.

Outside, as the people gathered in groups, he stood apart both physically, culturally and spiritually. An unexpected slap on the back made him turn to find the good Samaritan extending a generous hand in greeting.

'*Ek is Lucas, met 'n C*, Janse van Vuuren van Rensburg. *Van waar gehasie?*' (I am Lucas, spelt with a C. Where are you from?')

João surmised that the man was asking about his whereabouts. But before João could do anything, N'wamanungu and Tommy Albach caught up with them. N'wamanungu drew a short spear from his waist and held it threateningly in the air, pointing at the back-slapper.

N'wamanungu turned to Tommy and said, 'Tell this man that if he touches Juwawa again, he will be the next corpse to be lying under a fresh mound of soil in the graveyard.'

Tommy jumped forward and proceeded to explain in Kitchen-Dutch, '*Meneer, Meneer*! (Sir, sir!) Let me introduce ourselves. I'm Tommy, interpreter to Senhor Albasini. He saved my life. I was part of Lang Hans van Rensburg's trek.'

N'wamanungu had not lowered his spear.

Throwing his thumb in the direction of N'wamanungu, Tommy explained, 'Senhor Albasini saved him from slave traders and malaria. He lives as the Senhor's shadow. Nobody gets within an arm's length of the Senhor.'

The muscles on N'wamanungu slim, upright torso rippled like live snakes when he adjusted his stance to an even more threatening position. His eyes focused on who he thought might be the enemy. A sharp exchange of words between João and N'wamanungu followed.

N'wamanungu relaxed, dropped his aggressive attitude, took a step back and smiled. The smile lit up the black, carved face and, if he could ever look embarrassed, it was the nearest he could get, explaining '*Eehbo, eehbo*!!' (I understand, I understand). He retracted his spear but his eyes continued to stare unwaveringly.

'Ah, I'm glad you got that lean, mean barbarian to put his sword down. I got a bit nervous. I only meant to greet this man!' Mr van Rensburg exclaimed. He looked at Tommy's face and saw something like longing in his eyes.

'Tell me, young man,' he had guessed Tommy's age at around fourteen years, 'if you say you belonged to the Lang Hans's trek, how come you escaped? How many were in the *trek-geselskap* (trek-group)? What was Lang Hans's wife's name?'

Tommy was dressed in breeches and a neat cotton shirt. Senhor Albasini was fastidious and liked the people working for him to be neat and tidy in appearance.

He looked at Mr van Rensburg and realised it was a trick question. He promptly answered, '*Meneer*, there were', he stopped to give a show of hands and silently counting, 'about fifty people. That specific evening the Trekkers didn't camp in the laager formation. It was late and they decided that they would camp willy-nilly on the banks of the river. When the attack came, the Trekkers were caught by surprise.

'The savages unharnessed the cattle and all the cattle and sheep were driven away. The savages then started a fire allowing the Trekkers no way of escape. The war cries of triumph couldn't block out the tragic and heart-wrenching shouting of terror and desperation.

'The people were all massacred, except his two children and me. We called his wife, *Mevrou* Sarie. She sent the two children and me into the bushes with some food, hoping that some Trekkers would escape and find us. I heard the screams and the noises of death and was terrified. I jammed the two kids into a hollowed-out ant-heap and ran for shelter high up in a tree where I could see what was happening.

'When the savages who had ambushed Lang Hans had left the scorched scene, I climbed down from the tree to look for the children but they were gone. I looked everywhere but could not find them.'

Tommy shrugged, his face turned sad and he was afraid that they might accuse him of not taking sufficient care of the children.

'*Meneer*, it was terrible. They were there and then they were gone.' His fingers kept pulling his long dark curls. Embarrassed, he groaned, 'I was responsible for looking after *Nonnie* and *Basie*, and they were just gone!

'I don't know how long I stayed near the wagons hoping that somebody had left some food, but they burned everything. None of the corpses were recognisable.'

Tommy had gone pale and tears ran down his cheeks. Mr van Rensburg patted him on the shoulder, touched by the grief of the young man and realised that he was getting an eyewitness account of the tragic circumstances that had wiped out his cousin and the whole of Lang Hans's trek. There would be one more test before he could honestly believe what the boy was telling him.

Tommy continued, 'I stayed near the river, thinking that, as it looked like a trade route, somebody would turn up and take me on as a *touleier* (a boy leading the oxen). Late one evening, sure enough, I heard footsteps and the raucous laughter of people coming down the old trade route to cross the river. I knew we were not far from Inhambane but I thought it best to hide in a tree overlooking the river until I had made up my mind about who would be coming around the bend in the road. They were two travellers and, as they got to the river, I heard them arguing. They spoke a Zulu dialect which I could understand.

'It was Senhor Albasini and N'wamanungu. Senhor Albasini sat down to remove his boots to enable him to wade through the water. But N'wamanungu protested, shouting that no chief of his would get his feet wet. It would be his honour to carry Senhor Albasini across the river. You can see for yourself how strong N'wamanungu is. He swept the Senhor onto his shoulders, then plucked a reed from the bulrushes growing on the banks of the river. He folded the reed into a neat triangle, knotted it securely and cast it onto the water, as is their custom, to ward off any disaster such as sly crocodiles.

'They were about halfway across the river when the Senhor lifted himself onto N'wamanungu's shoulders and balanced himself to have a look around. At that moment, he spotted me sitting in a branch overhanging the river. The Senhor dived into the murky water, swam to the riverbank and walked out onto the dry ground, leaving N'wamanungu uttering words that I cannot repeat in decent company. The Senhor shook off the water, thumped himself on the chest, laughed and said, 'If I cannot fend for myself, I am not worthy of being a chief. And anyway, who said I was a chief? I am a trader.'

N'wamanungu answered solemnly, 'The bones of the wise old men told me that. They are never wrong.' He was furious and said, 'Juwawa! Juwawa, you could have drowned because you have the short legs of a wild pig! *Mampara!'* (Stupid!)

'True,' the Senhor said, 'but I can swim and you can't. Go and look what we've got in that tree to your left.'

Tommy took a break before he continued. 'And that is how they found me, fed me, made me laugh and cared for me to this day.' Tommy concluded with, 'I learned Dutch from the *Trekkers* and my ma was half Zulu and half Portuguese. I am thus the perfect interpreter for Senhor Albasini.'

Van Rensburg had been clutching a voluminous leather-bound Bible under his arm so as to have one hand free to greet the stranger with a good old-fashioned handshake. You could always tell by somebody's handshake if they had strength and character. João took the hand extended to him and squeezed hard and pumped with equal enthusiasm. He then pointed to the Bible under van Rensburg's arm and indicated that he would like to show his benefactor something. Puzzled, van Rensburg relinquished the Bible.

João opened to the first page and glanced at the family register which recorded names, births, and deaths. He saw something he recognised but decided not to say anything. He then turned to the fourth book of the New Testament and pointed to himself saying, 'João *Portuguesa* for', and then pointed at the book of *Johannes* in the Dutch Bible (John in the English Bible) and managed to say hesitantly, '*my naam.*' (My name). He stood back triumphantly and, with satisfaction, accepted Van Rensburg's invitation to what he presumed was a meal or a cup of coffee.

'Bring the boy along so that we can have a meaningful discussion. If you have a name out of the Bible, you must be a Christian.'

'*Ja,*' answered João, '*Catolico.*'

Chapter 2

Connection and Confrontation

João and Lucas walked away from the church with Tommy and N'wamanungu in tow. The mild autumn sun kissed João between his shoulder blades. It gave him outward comfort but, in his imagination, he felt a hundred pairs of eyes tap-dancing on his spine. He shrugged his shoulders to get rid of the uneasy feeling wriggling down his back.

Mr van Rensburg kept asking questions which Tommy politely evaded by cleverly suggesting that he would answer as soon as they arrived at the host's home because it was a long story. Senhor Albasini had instructed him well. He was only to tell what the Senhor wanted him to say.

On the other hand, João observed as much as he could. When van Rensburg indicated that a neatly thatched, mud-daubed house in front of them, one of several similar structures built in the dusty pathway, was his, João sighed with relief.

He spotted an elephant tusk on the veranda which he estimated to weigh between 70 and 80 pounds. Eighty pounds was about the average weight of a tusk brought home by his hunters. He felt a little more comfortable because elephant hunting was familiar territory to him. Above the tusk, long strips of meat and skinny sausages dangled from bamboo rods in u-shaped forms.

Next to the elephant tusk stood a *riempies bank* (a bench with a thronged seat). It was an ornate piece of furniture, well-crafted from yellow wood (which he recognised) and another dark wood which he thought might be stinkwood. A few elementary fold-away chairs spilled over into a neatly swept courtyard.

Peeping from the back, a nipple-like structure built from reeds and mud contained the cooking area. N'wamanungu, João's mule and three-pack mules were directed to the back and they were told to ask for Katrina. She would know what to do. Only when João gave him a nod of affirmation did N'wamanungu obey. He looked back several times before he consoled himself that João would be in good hands.

'Sit, sit, Albasini!' van Rensburg indicated. 'Sorry, my friend, not on that side. That is where my spittoon stands. I am not allowed to chew tobacco inside the house.' As if a snake was about to strike, João stood up while van Rensburg leisurely settled his big frame on the delicate-looking piece of furniture.

'Bring one of those folding chairs nearer, Tommy, and let us find out who, where and what this Albasini is about?'

Before Lucas could start questioning him, João pre-empted Tommy. 'Remember to tell him precisely what we agreed on. Don't make any mention of the wagon ironwork rims which I spotted in the river when we found you. I don't want your imagination to run wild. We want him to know only what I told you to tell him. Remember that I can understand a little bit, therefore I will detect any exaggeration.' João smiled to make the admonishing look softer.

Lucas plugged his cheek with a portion of tobacco and offered some to Senhor Albasini who declined with a polite, '*Nee dankie*'. (No, thank you.)

Lucas squinted as if in deep thought and started with the interrogation.

The first question took João by surprise, 'Do you like the *verdomde* (damned) English?'

João knew he had to consider his answer carefully to win the trust and business of this community. He answered, 'I don't know too much about them, only they have a woman ruling them and they make lousy traders.' As an after-thought he ventured to say, 'Oh, and they abolished slavery about ten years ago.'

'*Ja*, that sums it up,' Lucas growled. He spat the tobacco juice into the spittoon to indicate his attitude towards the English. He resumed his chewing, first rolling it to one side and then the other before shooting his next question. 'Are you married, and how many children do you have?'

João answered the first question with a sad expression on his face. He took his time because responding to the second part was complicated.

'No, *Meneer* van Rensburg, I am not married. Good wives are hard to find in this part of the world. Sicknesses, isolation and savages don't beckon the fairer sex to the dance of a lifelong union, the kind that stays until death do us part.'

Lucas interjected to give Tommy a breather. 'Indeed, indeed!'

Tommy continued. '*Meneer* Lucas, as I have earlier explained, Senhor João Albasini trades goods from Delagoa Bay up to Quelimane, Sofala and Inhambane. Because he is such a well-known trader, he can get nearly anything a person might need. He is known by all the chiefs of the different tribes. They know they get a fair deal from him. He trades as *Albasini and Co.* and hunts mostly elephants. His headquarters are at Magashulaskraal, about a four-day trip by wagon from here, if all goes well. He told me to tell you that he has good news.'

Lucas sighed and his eyes became watery. Just a week before, they had buried a mother and her two children who had succumbed to the dismal bad-air disease. The whole community needed some good news. It was a downhill experience for the *Trekkers* who had given their all to follow Potgieter to this outpost. Everything looked so lush when they first arrived. Water was readily available and game was plentiful to hunt. Several crops of wheat had started to sprout, confirming that it was a fertile area for farming.

Albasini continued with a twinkle in his eyes. It disguised his inner turmoil. Instinctively he knew he could not reveal certain things.

'On the matter of children, I have approximately 4,000 at the moment.'

He saw van Rensburg's eyes widen but Albasini continued, 'Let me explain. After surviving a terrible ordeal, cannibals captured me and kept me a prisoner for six months. N'wamanungu, the Zulu warrior whom you have met....' João stopped and took a breath. 'I apologise for his rude manner but he and two friends heard that I had not perished and came to help me escape.

'The savages captured the governor, Dionysio Antonio Ribeiro, me and twenty-six soldiers at the Forteleza Espirito Santo in Delagoa Bay. All of these poor men were killed at a feast held in honour of Chief Sosangane. I alone managed to survive. My friends found me six months later in a terrible state. I was kept under guard. I was held as a mascot, paraded at feasts and ordered to entertain visitors. The worst was the boredom. I let them believe bad gods possessed me. Therefore, they did not dare to prepare me for the pot. With my friends' help, we managed by some miracle to out-manoeuvre Soshangane's guards and went back to Delagoa Bay.

'The friends who came to rescue me discovered where the Abagaza hunters had buried huge ivory tusks in the ground. We removed them and made post-haste to sell them to Mr Kasimer, the only trader in the Bay. I negotiated to obtain guns which we then used for protection and hunting for food and ivory. Thus, my trading career as a big elephant hunter began. To the east and interior of the Bay, the area was as dry as tinder. Small groups of people were scattered about and saw me as their saviour.'

He lifted his shoulders in a carefree way and stopped talking for a while to give Tommy time to finish translating.

'Simple,' he continued. 'I shot the elephants, they got the meat, they carried the ivory back to the Bay. In other words, they scratched my back and I returned the favour. Gradually the population following me grew to such an extent that I had to consolidate and build a proper shelter.'

Lucas asked, 'Did you steal the tusks?'

João's brows puckered when he answered, 'They did not hide it well enough. It was there for the taking.'

***

He kept quiet about the killing of two lions. The fact that he could kill two lions in close succession was mind-boggling to the *Knopneuse,* a splintered part of the Zulu nation. Ingrained in their belief, a young man had to kill a lion before being considered brave enough to become a warrior. Senhor Albasini killed two in one effort.

He did not tell how awestruck his followers were when he shot a hippopotamus, killing it instantly. Afterwards, out of sheer exuberance, he rushed forward, wrenched open the enormous beast's mouth, and stood his 5 feet 8 inches height inside the hippo's jaws while keeping them apart. This act was a manifestation of his strength and undaunted fearlessness.

He thought it a good idea not to tell about the abuse that he had suffered to his manhood a few days after his birth, which was another matter. Due to his uncle's not so sleight of hand dissection of the foreskin, a haematoma formed and, on healing, left Juwawa with a nodular scar. They also wet his lips with wine to numb the pain, something to which João took an instant liking. He liked the amber liquid so much that drinking it in later years became a habit. His uncle's lack of skill stood him in good stead but not as you might think by increasing or diminishing his virility. No, it saved his life. The night of his capture, the savages forced the 27 men to dance naked on the beach. Soshangane's men noted his irregularity and approached him more cautiously than the others.

A few years later, when splinter groups of hungry, disillusioned men and their families started following him, the mutilation gave him special status in the eyes of his followers. It matched their tradition of circumcising their noses. This practice made them unattractive to the slave traders. The community elders retold the story with delight and stood in awe of a brave man, braver than the bravest who had a knob somewhere other than on his nose. An African legend was born.

At first, João just went with it all, enjoying the adventures and the thrill of living on the edge, until one day he looked at his followers and saw misery in their eyes and their muted questions, 'What if you, Juwawa, are not here to look after us? Who will?' He saw devotion and unsurpassed loyalty.

That day, twenty-year-old João Albasini morphed into manhood, taking responsibility for what he was born to do. He became a man with a different spirit, somebody who knew how to communicate with Africa. He was intelligent, determined and knew that no horizons could limit him.

***

Lucas was dumbfounded. '*Vrou* (Woman), bring us some coffee and come and meet our visitor. That is some story. Do you say you have never heard from your father and brother again? Lost at sea?'

Senhor Albasini nodded his head. 'My mother and sister died before I could see them again. The Jesuit monks at Phalaborwa brought me two trunks my mother had sent to them just before she succumbed to the sickness that befell her and my sister. I am an orphan.'

Lucas looked at Senhor Albasini and liked what he saw. His eyes were bright green, the colour of new grass in spring, of a soul that did not get old. His eyes did not waver, the smile was engaging, and Lucas wondered what the womenfolk would say about the dark, curly hair tied at the back. Long, neatly trimmed sideburns framed João's face. His cheeks were shaven clean and the pointed beard hinted at Lucifer's wickedness. The young man's upper lip was clean-shaven and deep dimples enhanced the handsomeness of his face.

'So, what is the good news?'

'I would like to talk to a *Meneer*, Andries Potgieter. I believe they call him *Ou Bloues*.' (*Kommandant* Potgieter liked wearing blue. Therefore he was given the nickname, *Ou Bloues*, meaning the man who always wears blue.)

Lucas was surprised that this stranger should know the nickname of their leader. 'How do you know we call him *'Ou Bloues*?'

João answered, 'Karl Trichardt.'

That made sense to Lucas as he knew that Potgieter and Louis Trichardt, Karl's father, were cousins, and Karl would have used the intimate description of his uncle when referring to the *Voortrekker*. He also knew that Potgieter had encouraged Louis Trichardt to move as far as possible away from the English scourge who infested their independent community in the Cape of Good Hope. Perhaps Louis Trichardt was better off than those here at Ohrigstad. Stories were told of even better grazing and game further up North.

João continued, 'A Mr Smellerkamp contacted me in the Bay and asked if I could deliver a shipment of Bibles to your community. I have taken the liberty to bring goods such as coffee, cloth, implements, spices and the like to establish myself as a *bondeldraer*, (trader) here in your community. My wagons should be here in two days.'

Lucas threw his hands up in the air and whispered a reverend, 'Praise be to God.' Out loud he said, 'Any medicine? We are in such shortage of everything. Have you any good news on how we can curb the detested malaria?'

'*Ja*,' João replied and continued, 'I planted chinchona trees at my property in the Bay, Quelemaine, and my trading centre at Magashulaskraal.'

'What kind of medicine is that?'

João explained. 'My mother was a Spanish princess and very close to her faith, as was the rest of her family. My uncle, a Jesuit priest, came with my father, my brother and myself when we visited Brazil. He was left there to do his evangelical work but not before he taught me about this tree. If the tree's bark is crushed into a fine powder and put into a tincture, it makes a brew to give the patient a chance of survival.'

Tommy looked at João puzzled and asked how he would explain that funny word.

'Just tell him that I have a magic powder which I mix with good, solid Oporto Port and it helps.'

Tommy explained and wondered vaguely when his task would finish. He could smell the aroma of good cooking emanating from the cookhouse.

'Is it expensive?' Lucas asked. 'We have a great need for such a remedy here. Even in winter we struggle to keep the mosquitoes at bay.'

João thought about the fresh graves he had seen. When he looked up, Lucas sensed a mutual feeling of great compassion.

Lucas was about to explain that the womenfolk would be back from the church when an unholy raucous erupted at the back of the house. João knew he was in trouble and jumped up to go and intervene. Bella's unforgiving braying meant that somebody was invading her space. Lucas and Tommy followed and saw that João's mule was biting and kicking a beautiful dun-coloured horse.

***

When Gertina left the church, she found Schoeman at her side. He tried to hold her hand but she dropped her music sheets and bent down to pick them up, thus avoiding the unwanted contact. Schoeman remained steadfastly at her side accompanying her to the van Rensburg house. Nearing the house they could hear a commotion at the back door and, on further investigation, Gertina saw the uniformed man engaged in breaking up a fight between Schoeman's dun-coloured horse and a white mule

'*Pare! Pare*, Bellahhh, *pare*.' (Calm down.)

The swift hand gestures and commanding note in the uniformed visitor's voice appeased the mule and Gertina realised that her father had invited the man to their home. She was relieved to see that Schoeman had forgotten all about being charming and gallant to her. Instead he rushed forward, yelling at the top of his voice, *'Uitlander*! (Foreigner). What are you doing? How could you allow that half-breed jackass to attack my horse? You're going to pay alright.'

João took command of his mule, caressing her into submission. Reins in hand, he walked up to Stephanus and stretched out his hand in a customary greeting. Stephanus swept his hand away and glared at him, pursed his lips and stabbed his index finger at João's chest. He stood with his feet apart and proceeded to admonish João angrily in Portuguese.

Stephanus has lost it again, the girl thought. She wondered if Stephanus, speaking this strange language, was using the same phrase he usually employed in the Kitchen-Dutch. Everybody knew about Stephanus' temper. His standard expletive was, 'I'll slap you so hard, the snot will fly.' Hence his nickname became *Snotklap*, which meant precisely that.

João willed himself to maintain a neutral expression. Purposely he did not clench his fists. The desire to fight back came naturally but this time he just kept stroking Bella.

'I am truly sorry, Sir. Perhaps we can agree. I am grateful for somebody in this remote settlement who can speak my language. As yet, I am still struggling to master the dialect you speak.'

'And for your information, Senhor, I will inform you that what we speak is not a dialect. As like-minded people, we have a new language in our republic. We call it *Die Taal*.' (The language.)

The man in front of him sounded like a narrator delivering a political speech but João stepped forward and offered his hand once more as he said, 'I am João Albasini. I am pleased to make the acquaintance, although I would have preferred it to have been under more friendly terms. Any damages, I'll compensate. I don't see any bleeding and I think we intervened just in time. You have a magnificent horse and I would love to experience the thrill of taking him for a ride. Is he a thoroughbred? It has been a very long time since I have seen such a beautiful animal.'

Having had the wind taken out of his sails, Stephanus calmed down to see that indeed no damage was done, except to his and the horse's pride.

From the farmhouse, a shrill voice shouted, 'Gertina, get your bonnet on this very moment. You'll ruin your complexation. No man wants a bride with a dried-up, raisin-like face. Quick, quick girl! I need your help preparing for lunch.'

Senhor Albasini looked up to see the young girl looking directly at him. There was an immediate connection between this ethereal being and himself. Was she real? He saw the innocence in her eyes and, he hoped, curiosity as well. He didn't understand what the lady from the house had shouted but tried to remember some words.

The girl turned away swiftly and purposely removed her bonnet which covered spindles of curly hair that had by now escaped from its braid. He heard her speak a few words and wished he knew what they meant. The straight back and defiant little strides made him smile inwardly as she sped away.

'Temper? Temper?'

The blush that crept up into her neck was most becoming. Was she annoyed at what the lady had said or did she blush because of his admiring gaze?

Chapter 3

Plans and Dreams

'Senhor Albasini, shall I bring you your port?' Tommy got no response.

João wore a loincloth for modesty's sake and lay with one hand tucked under his head staring up at the stars. His mother's rosary and a multi-stranded, bolo plaited leather thread lay loosely draped over his chest. Deep in thought, he kept stroking the talisman attached to the cords. He caressed and fingered the claws made up of two lion nails joined in the middle by a gold band. It was as if he stroked it to invoke a magic genie to lighten the frown on his forehead.

He wriggled his toes which had escaped the confinement of his polished boots and reminded himself that, when he placed his next order to Lisbon, he needed to include boots a size larger. He might even order fancy ones embossed around the upper edges. His father's boots should have fit him to perfection but Antonio did not imagine that his son would be roaming the wild African veld in bare feet. White gold, the ivory trade, had been foremost in his father's mind. João's men, the *Knopneuse*, walked, hunted and slept barefoot, and so did he. With everything they did, he had to show his superiority or at least show that he could do it equally well. Boots were for *umlungus* (white men). They were considered lily-livered men.

Tommy threw another log onto the campfire. Sparks flew into the air, hissing messages into the dark highveld sky. It sounded like spitting cobras warning the lion to keep its distance. Tommy took the blanket that had covered Bella and gave it to Senhor Albasini for the night.

'What in heavens name are you doing, Tommy? I'm not an old woman. I need to think.'

Tommy shook his head and went to ask N'wamanungu what had happened to his master. Where was the easy banter they usually had after a day's hunting or riding? Where was the delight they enjoyed over a good meal? The Senhor appeared to be troubled.

N'wamanungu just laughed and said, 'Just leave him alone. He needs a wife. He is thinking of his *engelosi enhele*!' (Beautiful angel.)

'Just shut up, you two. I have many things to think about for our survival. These people will be a threat to us. For instance, did you see the half-built forts? Two! Why would they need two? The forts are in better nick than that ramshackle impression of a fort down at the Bay. Even the church could give protection to marauding tribes. I saw some hidden loopholes for guns in the walls. These people are not stupid, you know.'

'*Eehbo*,' N'wamanungu changed the subject, 'but your angel is ugly! She is so pale she looks like the moon on a winter's night. And skinny! Ahh, give them to me fat and shiny. *Mha*,' he smacked his lips and continued, 'to see the buttocks move like big fat calabashes in a bag warms the heart and the body.' He draped one hand dramatically over his heart and then pointed his finger at Senhor Albasini. 'You know your Mammahela, the girl in...'

But before he could go any further with what he was planning to say, João had jumped up and grabbed him by the scruff of the neck with the one hand and placed his other hand harshly over the astonished N'wamanungu's mouth.

In a low, raw voice, the order came from João, 'Don't mention that name ever again. That goes for you as well, Tommy. That part of me is dead. I repeat, DEAD, and I will be the master who resurrects its existence, when and where I choose to do so.'

After N'wamanungu recovered, he said in a feeble voice, 'I wanted to say, if the girl's buttocks were nicely rounded and the sway in the hips!' He lifted his eyes heavenward and said, '*Eehbo!*'

João continued, 'I am very serious that you swear to secrecy. Our future, and especially mine, depends on it, so this is an order, do you understand?'

A simultaneous *'Bayete Inkosi'*, a salute to the King, followed the outburst.

João went to lie down again. He wrapped himself in Bella's cover. The familiarity of the blanket, as well as its warmth, soothed his feeling of abandonment. He looked at the fire guttering, spitting and glowing red hot in the night. It would be a long night. His brain was very active. It seemed that he was as far removed from these *Voortrekkers* as were the blue sky and the fire burning at his feet.

He had such pleasant thoughts when he looked up at the sky. He believed in angels, one in particular, one with sapphire blue eyes, tiny feet, a peaches and cream complexion and slim ankles. His mother used to say, 'Thin ankles are the hallmark of the aristocracy.'

But when he turned his face towards the fire, 'Snotklap' Schoeman's snake eyes glared at him. The burning coals emanated a relentless pulse of aggression and arrogance.

There was more to 'Snotklap' Schoeman than met the eye and João intended to find out just what it was. He had an intuition: the place to look might be Sofala or the Cape. He pinned a note in the blank canvass of his mind.

He turned his back to the fire and started to plan his meeting with Potgieter. He would not wear his uniform, that would be a mistake. He would send Tommy to ask Mr van Rensburg if he could buy or barter some of the shoes he saw the Boers were wearing. He lay planning his day and hoped to make a good impression on *Kommandant* Potgieter.

He didn't see himself as a divisive person but he had been surprised at the hostility he had experienced at the church. The uniform was an overkill and could have given the wrong impression. 'Ahh,' he sighed, 'hindsight makes you feel such a fool.'

He turned his mind to Gertina. The lady said the name only once but it stuck in his head like nettles in a woollen blanket. He tried her name but found the guttural sound challenging to pronounce. Perhaps if he tried saying it the German way he might get it right. He let it roll from the back of his throat but it sounded too harsh. He tried again in a softer tone but still couldn't master it. In the end, he decided he would ask permission to call her Tineka. Yes, Tineka. The name skimmed delicately past his lips.

Before falling asleep, he did the sums again. There was a problem. He guessed the girl's age to be around sixteen. According to the new passport, he was thirty-three. There was a difference of seventeen years. He remembered the roll of blue taffeta on one of the wagons. It would match her eyes perfectly. Ahh, and the delicate Napa leather shoes in a rich cream could replace the well-trodden, roughly cobbled shoes she wore to church. The Napa shoes would look splendid on her dainty ankles. The mended shawl and the patched lace from her petticoat that he saw when she walked away would also have to be replaced.

Before falling asleep, he shouted at Tommy, 'Hey, Tom, what is the meaning of *kortgat* and *trow*?' Those were the words he picked up when Gertina had turned away to walk into the house.

Still subdued from the verbal lashing he had received, Tommy took his time to do the translation. 'She said it was a pity you were not as tall as her fellow countrymen, and her mother need not worry about her face becoming wrinkled

44

from the sun. There is such a shortage of woman, she would be able to find a rich man anyway.'

'So, *trow* means to marry?' Now that was a word worthy of remembering. As for not being tall, why would she say that?

He fell asleep thinking he would do anything in the world to cherish, protect and hold Tineka to his heart as long as she did not call him *kortgat* (somebody who isn't very tall) or *Papa*.

In the middle of the night, he woke and remembered Schoeman's last words. 'I'll find out who you are, Senhor Albasini.'

The simmering logs blinked at João, conjuring an image of Schoeman staring at him through the ashes. He, João, had nothing to hide. Did he? The grey ash had painted droopy, half-closed lids over the red embers, reminding him of Schoeman's eyes leering at Gertina as she sped away.

The thought was unsettling.

***

Gertina couldn't understand herself. Lately, she had been harbouring feelings of resentment towards her mother. Why was she always taking her to task? Soon she would be presented to the church elders to do her profession of faith after which she would be considered grown up.

The foreigner's arrival has undoubtedly given the three ladies, part of the *Kappie Brigade* sitting around the well-scrubbed kitchen table, something to tittle tattle about other than diseases, diarrhoea and death. She was not going to miss out on that gossip.

Gertina's mother, Ella, had two neatly plaited strands of hair coiled around a smooth doughy face. Her upturned nose gave her the appearance of a piglet and the small, agile blue eyes took note of everything going on about her. They mirrored her restlessness manifested in her tiny hands which kept pleating the rough linen dress when she wasn't busy serving somebody. She sat at the head of the table like a Dresden doll, the coarse dress spread out around her, accentuating her plumpness. She served coffee and offered home-baked ginger cookies to the other two ladies.

'Enjoy. I used my last teaspoon of ginger on these. What will we do? We haven't seen traders since we left the highveld plains to come and settle in this remote place. Sometimes I think this suffering is a punishment from God, but I don't know for which sins. Lucas told me the newcomer was a trader. They usually sell spices.'

'Shame on you,' *Tante* Sannie quipped. 'Do you worry about something as trivial as ginger? We've run out of all our medicine. I thought when we settled here, far away from the Cape, it would be a new beginning. In the last month, we've lost four children, a husband and wife, all the result of the bad air. I told Piet, my husband, we must move to higher ground. It seems we get the fever from the mosquitos breeding near the river. We now have three more orphans to care for and feed. You know what it is like, Ella, don't you?'

Ella sighed dramatically. She tilted her head towards the back door where Gertina had just left, throwing her hands in the air.

'If only she would marry your son, Hester.'

The thin, scrawly woman sitting furthest away spoke up with an all-knowing statement. 'Don't worry, my friend, Stephanus knows how to win a maiden's hand. Especially one as stubborn as Gertina. He likes the chase.' She nodded her head in affirmation and took one of the ginger biscuits, bit into it, closed her eyes to savour the taste and said, 'Ella, I don't think I've got this recipe.'

'*Ja*, the texture is slightly different as I had very little flour and mixed it with some of the maize'.

'Mmmm, lovely!'

Stephanus' mother lent forward, drawing the others into a conspiring circle.

***

Gertina, after smirking at the comment her mother made, *'children should be seen and not heard'*, had closed the door behind her and crept to sit in the dust beneath the kitchen window to eavesdrop shamelessly.

The uniformed man? So many questions, so few answers. Her thoughts ran wild, like meercats scattering away from the swooping eagle. Fear? Yes, she was afraid. Apprehension? Yes, because there were many questions she couldn't answer. Did she have hope? She shrugged her shoulders and thought, perhaps?

A smile lit her face when she recalled the moment their eyes had met. It was as if a star was falling from heaven. She just had to catch it. The trick was how? She kept thinking about those eyes which were surprisingly green. The stare was direct. She was captivated and embraced the pleasant thoughts of those tender moments, marvelling at the cognisance of a particular moment in her life.

The late afternoon sun warmed her as she leaned against the wall. Hugging her knees to her breast, she suddenly thought about the number of buttons on his immaculate uniform and wondered, if she married him, it would be her task to buff them to such shininess. Now where did she get that thought from? The buttons had drawn her eyes upward to look at the visitor.

His direct stare had changed to amusement when he realised that he had caught her off guard. Even though Stephanus towered over the stranger, the man carried himself with an assurance which showed who the victor was.

She remembered details such as seeing the well-manicured hands stroking the mule. She had thoughts about those hands, and marriage, and could not reconcile those thoughts with her faith. Was it immoral to think that the stranger could caress her with those hands, or was it natural to have such thoughts?

When their eyes locked and she felt the blood rushing into her face, she realised she had to break contact with those laughing eyes. She turned around and fled but not before she saw a dimpled smile with perfect white teeth and mirth dancing in those vigilant eyes.

She heard Stephanus' mother say, 'They say he is married to a heathen woman!'

'Can't be,' Ella replied. 'He is far too good looking to be married to a woman of one of the tribes. Imagine!' She rolled her eyes upwards. 'He looks educated to me. No educated man will marry one of these savages. We know about the Buys family in the North's hinterland, but that Coenraad de Buys is a real villain and a good for nothing.

'The young boy who translates for the *Porra* (Portuguese man) is one of Lang Hans' group who survived the horrendous attacks. What did you say his name was? Tommy? Well, one can see he is a ginger biscuit. Evidently, he is the child of a servant. Shocking, I tell you, shocking to have a relationship like that. But, no. This stranger is not one of those. You can see he has some breeding behind his back. Polite. He even kissed my hand when Lucas introduced us.'

Hester interjected, her lips drawn into a firm line, 'Ella, you can be swept off your feet by the looks of a young man, but Stephanus told me in confidence that this Senhor Albasini is a slave trader. I tell you, that is how he made his money.'

Ella was getting more and more uncomfortable, 'Well, if he told you in confidence, why are you telling us? Does your Stephanus, who knows everything, have evidence? It is not a light accusation to make. I know we left the Cape to keep our slaves, but they are part of the family and we have the *inboek stelsel* (apprentice system). When they are eighteen they are free to go. Every evening they join us in the kitchen when we do our Bible reading. I cannot imagine selling off another human being or children to make you rich. I think you should check your facts.'

'Ella, Ella!' Hester continued. 'If you are siding with this Senhor, it seems my Stephanus would not be good enough for your Gertina who, strictly speaking, isn't yours. Sometimes I think you and Lucas took Gertina and Hendrikie under your roof like sort-of slaves and that is why you want to marry her off to some rich man in the hope they will look after you.'

Tante Sannie, who had contributed nothing to the conversation, came to the rescue. 'Dear friends, let us not hurt each other by words. Calm down. I am sure time will show who the real Senhor Albasini is.'

'Hi Hester, I did not mean to offend you. I apologise.'

'Never mind, Ella. But I can only say that he looks sinister, something from the devil. Did you see the ridiculous tuft of hair that is supposed to be a beard? A real goat's beard and, as we all know, a goat is a *bliksem* (swearword). It seems as if you've got a soft spot for him, but don't say I did not warn you.'

Gertina heard the scrape of chairs on the dung floor. The rustling of skirts indicated that the ladies were preparing to leave. She hurried away to gather wood. She thought, Womaniser? Slave trader? Married, and married to a woman of some tribe? But she did not see any wedding ring. What she did see was a very elaborate ring on his pinkie. It looked like a ruby set intricately in gold.

Her mind had to absorb the accusations but her body felt warm. The image of the mesmerising man's caressing hands kept popping into her head. She wanted to discard it as if it were dishwater thrown out the back door, but those vigilant eyes kept returning to her thoughts and doused the evil gossip that had surfaced at the kitchen table that afternoon.

***

Schoeman felt quite pleased with himself. He took off his heavy welding gloves and put them on the table.

'*Oom* Jannie, I think we have done a good job. The arch is a bit plain but, considering the time we had, I think it will look smart. The only thing remaining is to attach it to the trunks. I think *Kommandant* Potgieter will be pleasantly surprised. This arch will symbolise the founding of our new colony. I will leave you to do the finishing touches while I have a coffee with my ma. Expect some lunch in a while, then we can attach the flag and wait for the *Kommandant* to arrive. Thank you. I will reward you for your effort.'

51

'No, no, no. You don't have to pay me for my work, only for the materials. It is my pride and joy to make this small contribution.'

'*Oom* (uncle) Jannie, you know what? It is unselfish, God-fearing people like you that we need to build this great nation.'

'Thank you, thank you.'

He went up to *oom* Jannie and spontaneously shook his hand in addition to the verbal praise.

It was amazing what a bit of physical exercise could do. Hitting the hot iron with a four pound blacksmith's hammer took some of the anger away. He was angry at the intruder and did not quite know why. Perhaps it was because he saw how Gertina had blushed when she walked away from them yesterday.

He smiled absently. Ah, Gertina, my beauty. You need somebody strong like me. There will have to be some bending to do. When we are married, I don't want a rebellious filly to distract my attention from becoming President. I am the head of the household and what I say is the law. He pursed his lips and pointed his finger at an imaginary Gertina in front of him.

'Ma, is the coffee ready?' He had already inhaled the aroma of coffee brewing, but he liked to put his mother on edge.

'In a moment, son. What did the devil cough up on your grave this morning that you should be so impatient?'

Stephanus walked into the kitchen and saw her sewing at the table. 'Haven't you finished yet? And did I not tell you, you have to treat this flag reverently? I don't like you working where it smells of oil and stew. The *Voorhuis* (lounge) is a much better place to work on something holy, ma.'

Hester shook her head, calmly removing the cloth and embroidery yarn from the kitchen table. Still holding it in her hands she said, 'Let's have our coffee in the lounge. I made us some nice *vetkoek* (bread dough submerged in hot lard) and fine ground meat as a morning snack. You can take some back to *oom* Jannie. I am sure he will enjoy a bit of extra lunch. He is such a hard worker.'

Hester looked at her son. The mid-morning light shining through the front door made his red, coir-like hair shimmer, radiating the image of an angel. She thought to herself, he was born to lead. He will be our guiding angel in the future.

'You will be pleased to know that I have just finished. Let me show you. Take this end and then we can spread it out wide so that you will be able to see better.'

'*Ag Moedertjie!*' (Mother.) He loved his mother dearly. She was such a frail lady but possessed an indomitable spirit. He was sorry that he had snapped at her. He took her arthritic hands in his and gently stroked the knobs on her fingers.

'Thank you. I knew you would do a good job. Sorry, I was not in a good mood, but this is excellent. It lifts my spirit. *Moedertjie,* sit down and I will bring us the coffee.'

Walking back to the kitchen he thought of the up-coming meeting. The flag would look splendid when he and Gertina unfurled it. He had asked Gertina if she would help him at the opening of the meeting which *Kommandant* Potgieter would conduct shortly.

He liked the simplicity of the flag. The clear royal blue for the background and a blood-red diagonal St Andrew's cross made a strong impression on the eye. *Die Kruisvlag*, he whispered in reverence to himself. About four inches into the blue on the bottom half, his mother had meticulously embroidered *1836* in white cotton.

He looked at his mother and said, '*Ja*, 1836, the beginning of the *Groot* Trek. (Big Trek) Away from the *verdomde* English!'

He finished his coffee, grabbed *oom* Jannie's *vetkoek*, and charged out of the house to complete the triumphal arch.

Chapter 4

A well laid plan

It was decided that the best place to meet the *Kommandant* would be at the Potgieter half-built fort. Schoeman was a bit nervous. He had to set up everything. One of the finished walls formed the backdrop for the meeting. He brought his family heirloom, a long pearwood table, to serve as a desk. There were three chairs, one for the *Kommandant*, one for himself and one for the secretary to take notes.

On the table he placed paper, two ink wells and several sharpened porcupine quills. A few tables draped in blue and red checked tablecloths stood to the left waiting for the much talked about refreshments his mother and *Tante* Ella had prepared.

Schoeman managed to obtain a few bottles of *Jenewer* (gin), which added to the display. He was a genius. The *Jenewer* came with compliments of the Schoeman family. If the *Kommandant* couldn't persuade this bunch of people to reject the idea of a universal Parliament joining all the districts together, Schoeman was sure that he could put forward a few ideas of his own. It would be far better to have their own governing body and be separate from Rustenburg and the other states that had mushroomed. He did not trust Burghers after hearing rumours that he was ready to bury the hatchet with the English. Over my dead body, Schoeman thought, as bitterness welled up in the back of his throat. I will ask *ou*

Bloues if I, Stephanus, might say a word or two. By that time, the *Jenewer* should have put the settlers in a good mood.

The festivities planned to take place after the meeting would give him the opportunity to shine. A bonfire was stacked and ready to spit roast the two buffalos which had been killed. His participation in the wood chopping and target shooting contests would show his strength and skills. He would show that Albasini a thing or two! To his chagrin, he heard that van Rensburg had invited the newcomer to the meeting.

He stood behind the table, cleared his throat and spread his hands like ducks' feet at right angles onto the table. He swayed a little bit and thought, I will wait for everybody to be quiet before I reveal the flag. (It had been placed, neatly folded away, in a purposely made wooden box on the table.)

'*Uit respecte,*' he said as he practised his opening to the meeting. He listened to his voice carrying through the half-built fortress and thought that he could put a little bit more feeling into those two words. Perhaps he could look up to the heavens and say it a little slower. He tried again. At that point, he would invite Gertina to come forward to help him unfold the *Voortrekker Flag. Die Kruisvlag.*

Gertina's presence would give it a soft touch and project the image of the Nation's Mother, a worthy mother for the next generation. That would set the tone for his speech.

He walked out of the enclosure, repeating, '*Uit respecte*'. He smiled and thought the tone and emphasis were just right.

***

'Hold still!'

Senhor Albasini admonished Tommy who was holding a mirror for João to shave.

'But Senhor, can't you hear the bell ringing? It must be something important happening in the village. I got a fright.'

Senhor Albasini didn't miss a beat. With a steady hand, he continued to shave.

'Keep still. How will you be able to keep your cool if a lion should storm you? Most probably, *Kommandant* Potgieter's arrival is imminent. Be vigilant, Tom. Always. Don't let your guard down.'

João, after considering how the other young men in the church had dressed, decided to get rid of his soul patch and moustache. He left the dark stubble to match up with the rest of the goatee to start a chinstrap beard as he had seen worn by the young men. He pulled his face first to the left and then to the right, fingering the neatly trimmed goatee as if he was making one of the most significant decisions of his life.

'Give me the scissors, Tommy.' João rounded the pointed beard deftly. The mirror smiled back, showing off the handsome face of an Italian-Boer mix. 'Hey, Tommy, you've got to integrate, man, integrate'. The two-day stubble enabled Tommy to create the chinstrap beard look as requested by the Senhor.

'I am a good-looking devil, what do you think?'

Tommy just grinned and started to pack away the shaving gear.

While waiting for his coffee and breakfast, João opened his journal and noted down what he thought the settlement needed most. In his neat copperplate writing, he listed:

Medicine/Cinchona Bark (quinine)
Spices
Cloth
Stationary
Sugar
Coffee
Flour

He would gauge the quantities at a later stage. He turned to the back of the journal where he had started his Kitchen Dutch dictionary.

'Hey, Tommy, how do you spell *trow*?'

'I do not know, Senhor. I have never learned how to write or read.'

João made a mental note to remedy the flaw.

***

Back at the village there was a bevy of activity. Women scurried about finishing chores and everybody seemed to rush towards the triumphal arch at the entrance of the fort.

Men on horseback flanked both sides of the entrance. Their guns were slung over their shoulders and their veldt hats roosted jauntily on their heads. The guard of honour was supplemented by men without horses, the women and their children.

Senhor Albasini was dressed in breeches and his newly acquired *velskoene* (shoes made out of hide). He had to admit, the soft leather fitted comfortably. He wore a maroon waistcoat over a clean, white-bleached calico shirt. The waistcoat was embroidered on the lapels with a sprig of white flowers. To complete the look, he knotted a dark blue silk scarf around his neck. He was eager to meet *Kommandant* Potgieter with a new face, new shoes and toned-down dress code. He was glad he remembered that the honourable member liked blue.

Chapter 5

Trade and Tension

Senhor Albasini's men knew the drill. They outspanned the animals, gave them water to drink and haltered them in a nearby paddock. The trading party consisted of two wagons and a gig. The wagons stood at right angles and the gig stood in the shade of a Marula tree to the side of one of the wagons. It was as if the colourful wagons and gig painted a picture of hope and that, in itself, was a worthy cause to celebrate.

The licks of gold paint on the black letters was a display of wealth. *A. A. Albasini & Co.* The triple-A symbolised the striving toward excellence instigated by his father, Antonio Augusto Albasini.

Senhor Albasini had rushed from the official talks to meet his men and greeted Mario with a hug and welcoming, 'M-L, *Filho da puta*!' (Son of a bitch.)

M-L stood for Mario-Luis de Sousa, an orphan who was under the care of Father Alfonso, the Jesuit Priest living at the Phalaborwa Mission station. Father Alfonso told João about the talented young boy and, based upon that recommendation, Senhor Albasini took Mario under his care and, in addition, bought Mario a slave by the name of Alcant.

Under Portuguese law, João and Mario were orphans and qualified to obtain free land. Senhor Albasini sought out a strategically placed parcel along the foreshore which gave him the monopoly of trading directly with the incoming ships.

While João travelled further inland to set up half-way houses at Magashulaskraal and further afield, the young and very capable Mario-Luis managed the trade conducted from the warehouses at *Albasini Strand* (beach) as it became known.

'Am I glad to see you! You made the journey in good time. It is a bit earlier than I had expected but never mind. They call the village Ohrigstad. It is going to be a trading hotspot. We will have Tommy do the interpreting as much as possible. Otherwise, we can have a show and talk business.'

Senhor Albasini had concerns about how the trading would fare. These people were Europeans and were not interested in blue beads, Indian cloths, mirrors and the like. He considered himself fortunate that a consignment of goods had been mistakenly sent to him. Opening the crate, he did not know initially what to do with the fine lace ladies' undergarments and fopperies. Ohrigstad and their *Kappie Brigade* presented an excellent occasion for the ladies to indulge themselves in buying silk, lace and beautiful things.

Help came unexpectedly from a petite little girl. He guessed her age to be about nine years. A dark auburn halo of curls set her apart from any of the other children and young adults who started flocking to the strange melange set up in the middle of their town. She was pretty with wide-set blue eyes, an impish upturned nose and an infectious smile. She had small, pearl-like teeth set slightly apart and a gap between the two front teeth gave her speech a soft lisp.

She approached the outspanned wagons with the various goods on sale and, to M-L's consternation, put her hand in his and guided him along to look at things to which she had taken a fancy. She did not let go until she got to the table with children's toys and various porcelain dolls. She promptly annexed three and put them to one side. She grabbed a small folding chair and sat next to the table laden with bottles full of candy and newspaper squares ready for business. She beckoned Tommy to come to her and, when he arrived, told him she would help sell their goods.

In her soft lisp and with a slightly hesitant stutter she said, 'Tell that man, the good-looking man with the soft, sad eyes, tell him I am going to marry him.'

Tom was dumbfounded and hastily told Mario what the girl had said. Surprised, Mario looked towards this self-assured little girl sitting at the table ready for business. She looked back unphased, confident and with a bearing which said that she would brook no nonsense. Unbeknown to Mario, she took a moment to appreciate the tidiness of his apparel, his small sloping shoulders, high forehead and elegant, slightly hooked nose. She would make that generous mouth smile.

M-L allowed himself a stiff smile and proceeded to ring the bell, after which Tom started his sales pitch.

'Jy kan koop die jas und die tas und die enige ding wat jy wil, jy kan koop.' (You can buy a bag, a coat or anything you like, anything that might take your fancy.)

Trui, pronounced 'Troy', smiled back at Mario, wriggled her little bottom on the chair in satisfaction and started to sell the candy. 'Get a free scoop for an invitation to dinner for Mario and Senhor Albasini.'

***

'Senhor Albasini?'

João turned to find a man whom he thought might be *Kommandant* Potgieter commanding his attention. He had piercing blue eyes and wore a light blue shirt with a blue necktie and mole skin pants cut short at the ankles. In his most elementary Kitchen-Dutch, João conveyed his desire to have a private word with the man.

The *Kommandant* took in the excitement of people buying ammunition, medicine, spices, coffee, rice, sugar and many other commodities. He was surprised to see his wife putting on a blue veldt bonnet decorated with small roses and a velvet ribbon. It suddenly struck him that the womenfolk had missed out on such niceties. Some ladies giggled at the sight of delicate underwear and opted to have it put onto their husband's accounts.

Tommy realised the importance of *Kommandant* Potgieter's appearance and appeared from nowhere to make the translations.

'I am *Kommandant* Potgieter. Albasini, you are the *bondeldraer* (pedlar), I assume? We have a coin scarcity here.

You will have to be satisfied with bartering,' the *Kommandant* said.

The obligatory handshake took place with the two men accessing each other's strength by the force of the greeting.

'That will not be a problem. Ivory, good, good! I come to visit often.'

João took cards out from his hip pocket and showed them to Potgieter, his name stamped on the back and IOU on the front.

'Well done, Senhor Albasini, I see you are familiar with the *Goedvoors*. (Good fors.) I'll see you in the morning then. We can discuss trade opportunities and a safe route to the coast.'

Potgieter turned to Tommy and asked, 'Why do these bizarre donkeys pull the wagons and not oxen?'

Tommy laughed and said, '*Meneer*, we call them Zonkeys. It is the donkey and the zebra came together.' With his hands, he imitated a coupling. 'In this area, it is the best draught animal you can get. The way Senhor Albasini trains them, they are very reliable. He has already put some on a boat to England. The Senhor made sure the *verdomde Engelse* (blasted English) paid handsomely but you can negotiate a good price with him if you are interested. He is very fair.' Then he added, 'We have never lost a consignment due to the sleeping sickness the oxen get because these are immune to the bite of the tsetse fly.'

The *Kommandant* nodded his head in thanks. He picked up the pretty bonnet and asked, 'How much?'

Senhor Albasini, always quick to notice a possible sale, waved his hands in a manner to indicate to *Ou Bloues* that it was free.

The *Kommandant* looked intently at João and said, 'Instead of tomorrow morning, make it supper.'

Albasini nodded in agreement.

***

Trading was going well. The young boy who brought the news that the wagons had arrived, obliterating Schoeman's speech, approached João and indicated that he should follow him.

'What is this about?' He asked.

Tommy said, 'There is a *Meneer* who wants to see you.'

Senhor Albasini called Tommy, grabbed a box of cigars and left Mario to finish up. As a parting comment, Senhor Albasini told Mario, 'Remember the roll of blue taffeta and cream Napa leather ladies' boots are not for sale.'

The boy led him to meet with another leader, Burghers. It was then that João realised that two factions had beset Ohrigstad. The quarrels were bitter and seemingly unreconcilable. They had two common goals, however: to be as far removed from the English as possible, and to find a safe route to the ocean. Albasini realised that he had to tread carefully so as not to upset either party and so enable him to build a successful trading relationship with them both.

***

Schoeman stormed into Potgieter's *voorhuis* (lounge). 'How could you allow such an upstart to infiltrate our community? This *Porra* (Portuguese) is like a rotten apple. All shiny on the outside but when you cut it open it is rotten to the core. *Moeder* (Mother) tells me you gave him an *Erf* (a block of land) here, here in our town? Do you know he has been in Ohrigstad for only three days and the people with their ugly noses are already building a shop? Did you stop to think, *Kommandant?* I'll call them *Knopneuse* (knob noses). The *Knopneuse* carry guns! It is impossible to think that you did not consider that you are putting all of us at risk.'

'Calm down, our *Stormvogel* (storm bird).'

'What about my men?' Schoeman interjected. 'They went down to Lorenço Marques to see if we could find a suitable route that is tsetse fly free. They got no compensation whatsoever!'

Potgieter replied in a calm voice, 'Burghers and his Volksraad gave him an *erf* as well. What could I do? Albasini is a fast mover. He will soon start to build a bakery next to the general store on that *erf* too. We can all do with some decent bread and flour. At his depot, Magashulaskraal, he planted vast amount of wheat.'

Schoeman, not yet pacified, continued in a high-pitched, agitated voice, 'I am telling you the *Porra* is a two-faced *bliksem!* He promised 100 pounds of gunpowder and 400 pounds of lead in the event of an expedition to be led to Delagoa Bay by Burgher's men. As a bribe, he threw in fifty Bibles'.

'Now, my son, I can understand your disapproval, but Portugal is a neutral country, as the Senhor explained to me. He, Albasini, only wishes to trade and not take sides. What is of more importance, he told me about Zoutpanzberg and the Makatese tribe living at Beja. Albasini has a farm of sizable proportion there that he has bartered from the Beja inhabitants.'

Potgieter stopped and tears welled up into his eyes. From a drawer in the table he pulled out something wrapped in an oil canvas cloth.

'What is that?' Schoeman asked.

'Senhor Albasini gave me this. It was given to him on Louis Trichardt's death bed with the promise that he would place it directly into my hands. It is Louis Trichardt's *dagboek* (diary). Do you realise the significance of this book? And then, look at this!'

Kommandant Potgieter reverently placed the larger of two books on the table and handed a small, leather-bound psalm-halter to Schoeman.

Surprised, Schoeman fingered the well-used, faded red pages. He read the message written on the inside of the cover:

The carrier of this book, Senhor Albasini, can be trusted with your life. He tried everything to save me from the fever, but I know I will be with my Lord and Saviour. Please see that my dearest wife and family come into possession of this book as a last token of my everlasting love.

Willem Pretorius.

Potgieter sniffed the tears away and, in a broken voice, said, 'Albasini told me he nursed this stranger and had to bury him near a hill top where his trusted induna Josekhulu tended cattle. He is willing to show me the grave if I wish to go and see it.'

'My suggestion to you is, look before you leap.'

'I have already commissioned Pieter Combrink and Lucas van Rensburg to take two wagons of goods such as ivory, hides, dried meat and so on down to the Bay. Albasini has given me a guarantee to get the wagons there and back safely. He reckons it would be safe to travel early in May when the tsetse fly is not so active. I sold him Rustplaas. Albasini will be of immense value to us. I warn you, keep that temper in check, or you may find yourself back on your farm in Rustenburg.'

Schoeman shrugged the reprimand off with a laugh and asked, 'Who, may I ask, oversaw the transactions of Rustplaas? How valid is the transaction? I wanted to buy that farm myself because of its proximity to the river.'

Potgieter answered, 'Albasini. He showed me his credentials. He is a lawyer and so has the necessary authority to draw up documents. He came well prepared with documents already translated by Smellerkamp and signed by the Governor of Delagoa Bay. Stephanus, my son, I had no choice. Have you got 700 Riksdalers to pay? You know our treasury coffers are non-existent. How could I refuse such a large sum of money? Did I tell you? I had fifty Bibles delivered to my front door this morning to distribute to those I think need it most. The Bibles arrived with a note saying, 'No charge', signed João Albasini, 'God's blessings.'

Chapter 6

Courage and Guile

'Kill him! Kill him!'

João heard himself shouting, 'No, no, no! Don't kill him. He is the Captain. He will give you what you want. He is the leader.'

'Ah, look, one of the pink pigs can speak our language. Take off your clothes, pig, and tell the others to do the same. Tell them they must line up and then we will let you all dance.'

Senhor Albasini awoke from the bad dream. Sweat dripped from his body. N'wamanungu had shaken Juwawa awake and offered him some port to calm him down.

'It is the dream again, Juwawa. Spit it out, empty your mind of the poison. Then it will go away.'

Senhor Albasini gripped and ungripped the pewter goblet, wiped the sweat from his forehead with the back of his hand and shuddered.

'You know, N'wamanungu, I have never told anybody about my capture that evening. You are my brother. I will tell you and never speak of it again. You understand?'

'*Ehbo*, Juwawa.'

Albasini began his story. 'On the 22nd of October 1833, a group of warriors of the Gaza tribe appeared before the fort on the Espirito Santo. They had no weapons other than short-handed stabbing assegais and so could not force an entry. During the night of 27th, the fort's captain, Dionysio Antonio Ribeiro, saw an opportunity to escape and evacuated the Forteleza de Lourenço Marques with his 26 men and me. We fled to the island of Shefina which lay close to the coast. The following day, the Abagaza destroyed the fort and pursued us to the island and we were all captured. We were brought back to the ruined fort as prisoners. I remember it clearly and will never forget it. I can still hear the ring of their leader's raspy voice giving us the command to undress.'

N'wamanungu said, 'Were these Soshangane's men?'

'Yes, I had to do something to make me look different. From hearsay, I knew that Soshangane's tribe didn't eat mad people or kill them. I decided to act crazy. As soon as they spoke to me, I went into a handstand and talked to them from an upside-down position. I would then fall back onto my haunches, come forward and walk on all fours, growling like a jackal. They laughed at me and threw pieces of raw meat at me to eat. I wagged my behind as if it were a tail because that's what a jackal would do, right? I grabbed the pieces of raw meat with my hands and tore them apart with my teeth. In my mind, I ate my mother's cooked food.'

João shuddered, 'Never give me raw meat to eat, ever. When they tried to take my meal away, I gnarled and snapped at them furiously, holding on to a bone for dear life. At first, they joked and prodded me with their spears. They laughed and had lots of fun but they got worried when they saw that I was eating the raw meat. One man pointed to my manhood and saw the nob that I had on that delicate part of my anatomy, and I think that is when they felt a disgruntled forefather had nestled himself in my body. They spared my life and decided that I would have to fight a mad dog the next day. If I killed the dog, it would be proof of my madness.'

Albasini downed the rest of the port in one gulp to suppress the bile that had risen in the back of his throat. N'wamanungu had never seen Juwawa like this before. His friend sat doubled up with grief.

When João looked up into N'wamanungu's eyes he said, 'They took the others away to prepare them for the pot. They cordoned off Captain Ribeiro. I thought that I might have saved his life when I explained to them that he was the captain. But that was not the case. His fate was equally as bad as that of the other soldiers because the next day, as they led me past the burnt-down fort's ruins, I saw the captain who was still only a young man.

'His half-charred body dangled from the branch of the fig tree at the entrance of the fort. They had used the silk shirt that I wore the night before as a noose. How can I look at a silk shirt again and not remember? It was at that moment that I realised the Lord had other plans for me.'

Albasini drifted into a state of semi-consciousness as he recounted in his mind the awful events that followed.

The hut spoke of neglect and barrenness. Its darkness welcomed João to a prison with a macabre host waiting, grimacing at yet another victim to harbour.

He sat down on the damp floor, stretched his legs and lay down to sleep. He had some consolation: the overwhelming smell of rat ensured him he wouldn't die alone.

The energy had leaked out of his life's vessel. All he wanted to do was cry but no tears would come. He didn't even question his existence. He merely accepted life's circumstances. He was a foreigner, a Portuguese entrepreneur who could speak a smattering of several African languages. Neither his noble blood nor the sweet love of his princess-mother, neither *cum laude* law degree nor his dog could help him in this state of hopelessness.

His head throbbed. He wasn't even sure if he was conscious. Irrelevant images flitted alternately between his mother and the Abagaza king, Soshangane, a Zulu chief.

First, his mother would fidget with the diamond tiara in her coifed hair. Her hand was busy, desperately straightening a garland of human incisors hanging at a strange angle from her well-formed bosom.

The image then switched to Soshangane and manifested an angelical halo of beeswax plaited into his hair. There was no delicate, jewelled hand fidgeting with his headgear. Instead, his puffy fingers caressed his mother's pearls hanging over his bulbous belly. He fingered them, one by one, as if they were a rosary.

The Albasini trade venture had gone wrong. The gash over his brow had stopped bleeding. He was sure he suffered from concussion and he feared nothing, but an unholy fear numbed his thinking and suppressed his optimism.

He lay there wide-eyed, listening to his nocturnal companions churning, chaffing and snivelling while doing their business. Sometimes they ran over him in a flurry of excitement. Others sniffed at his boots. At least the rats had a purpose, to procreate as quickly as possible. A pest to be feared, a problem to be eradicated. Perhaps Soshangane thought the same of him. João was a rodent bent on infesting his habitat. A colonist.

He curved his back, bent his head and drew his legs up to his chest in a foetal position. Resigned to his fate, he went to sleep thinking, 'I want my Mamma!'

He was running. He was the hunter in his mother's bed-time story. Hounded by hunger, dogs were yelping in his wake. He saw the eternal flames spewing from their mouths but couldn't breathe or move. His brain was waking but his body felt stiff, sore and unresponsive. He tried to whistle like a hunter but his parched lips would not obey his desire. In his state of semi-consciousness he smelt food but it was not the Basque myth's baker offering him bread. The aroma filtering through to him was the maize cooking in big black pots that he had come to know in his short stay in this dark continent, this No-man's Land. A land of fear, a land of sickness, a land of the survival of only the fittest. He was fully awake and the tears that trickled down the sides of his nose were evidence of the feeling of being far, far away.

Sadness cloaked him. He licked his dry lips, tasted the saltiness of his tears and fell into a state of pensiveness. He realised that the yelping dog was Letitia and no flames spewed from her mouth. She had killed a rat and wagged her tail in recognition of her master's awareness of the surroundings.

A woman opened the door and, with casual indifference, put a plate of maize and a calabash of water down on the floor. Then she closed the door firmly. He heard the chain rattle and took it as an ominous, sharp welcome to the grave.

He took the calabash of water and forced himself to sip slowly, quenching his thirst. He ate the stiff lukewarm *pap* and gave some to Letitia. He wasn't going to let her die without a treat.

The Latin phrase *Memento vivere,* 'remember to live', sprung to mind. He sat up straight and started to pray for the first time since he had set foot on this continent, this piece of dirt that consisted of a complex layering of cultures, beliefs and barbarism.

He remembered his mother's words, 'Keep to the faith, my son.'

He prayed, 'Dear Lord and Heavenly Father, today I choose to live. I need your Divine intervention in my unfortunate case. I believe in your son Jesus Christ. I believe in the forgiveness of sins. Therefore, dear Lord, if it is your will for me to survive this ordeal where human flesh is considered cheap, choose to let me live. Strengthen my soul, and I will not shrink from my responsibilities. Help me to accept the life awaiting me. Amen.'

Through the crack in the door he could see that his enemies were slowly waking from their feast of beer and dance of the previous night. They were preparing the area where the fight between a wild dog and a jackal would take place.

He saw that they built a circle of thick thorn bushes to form the fighting ring. Through the crack in the door he heard the hum of excitement filling the air. It sounded like distant thunder announcing a storm. João willed his stiff limbs to stand before he stretched and walked about as much as he could. With the prayer paramount in his thoughts, he conditioned his mind to win. After all, it was only a dog he was going to fight, not an army. There was hope.

Late in afternoon the ululating began. The drums' palpitating beat invited the dancers to create their circling dance, binding them to the earth and strengthening their supernatural belief. Their body parts were extended by feathers and rattles, and adornments of all sorts waved in the air. The foot-stomping and aggressive rhythmic communication between dancers and drummers carried on for some time, sweeping them into a trance. The drums stopped and João saw two men approach the hut to bring him forth.

The door opened and the face that morphed carried a vile smirk and exhibited sharply filed teeth through which he hissed, 'Get up, you pig!' A sharp assegai nudged him in the back on his way to the fighting pit. With his shoulders squared he inspected the scene. There was no dog in sight. Trying to put himself into his enemy's mind, he wondered at their strategy. He already had them doubting his authenticity and so, if he were to be the enemy, he would try to spring a surprise. That might be the reason there was no wild dog in sight.

He expected a trap. The thorn-bush pen was roughly three metres in diameter which would not give him much room for movement. Stealth and speed could save his skin. One of his guards opened the enclosure and they pushed him forward, closing the pen behind him.

The drums started to beat again, louder and louder. Two men carried an ornate looking chair into the onlookers' arena. The late afternoon sun caught glimpses of the chair's elongated legs and gilded red and green floral upholstery.

Instead of looking like a chair for royalty, it bordered on the comical. João thought, 'Concentrate! This is no time for silly observations.' It became eerily quiet when a booming voice brought a sudden hush over the crowd.

Soshangane's tall figure entered in full regalia. He wore a headring of twisted hide, crested with several long tail feathers from a blue crane. A leopard skin kilted his loins and tufts of oxtail adorned the arms. Copper bands shimmered around his wrists and ankles and, in a guttural voice, he gave an order.

João adopted a bold stance, folded his arms and made unwavering eye contact. He sent a clear message to this bees-waxed, haloed demon that he, Albasini, was intent to fight and win! The contact was brief but intense. João displayed no fear and the two men accepted an intangible challenge of mutual mental strength which sizzled in the air.

João shouted in Zulu, 'Bring it on, murderer! Let the fun begin. You will see no fear from me.'

In a whimsical moment of despair, he was glad he did not see his mother's pearls adorning the muscled torso of the tyrant in contrast to what he had visualised in his state of semi-consciousness.

Too late he realised that the entrance of Soshangane was the decoy for the surprise attack. Warned by his innate sixth sense, he turned away from the captivating stare to look behind him. His opponent stood on the ready, stiff-legged and foul-breathed.

The wild dog's head, marked by narrow lines of dark hair splitting the face in two, pushed forward, its torso sunk into a crouching position, ready to attack. The hair bristled on the back of its dappled coat and the thin line of the dog's small mouth displayed a straight line of fearsome teeth ready to break the bones of the creature in front of him. The large bat-like rounded ears stood erect while the small penetrating, unwavering eyes narrowed to scrutinise his enemy.

João was terrified. His throat constricted and the dryness of his mouth made it difficult for him to swallow. His heart palpitated wildly as an unbearable feeling of impossibility swept over him. He shook his head to let the beads of sweat which oozed from his forehead and temples fall in the dirt.

The dog hesitated because it was used to fighting as part of a pack. João was quick to observe the hesitation and prepared himself. He saw the dog's white, bushy tail rising in preparation for the leap. The thin smile changed to an open wide snarl, ready to strike.

João waited. As the dog leaped at him, João aimed his kick at the torso hoping to strike the dog in the ribs. The dog was hurtled into the air. An agonised wail escaped the animal and bloodied froth leeched from the straight-toothed grimace. The dog landed with his back to him. Joao's well-aimed kick had broken several ribs, puncturing the animal's lungs. With its thin legs buckled, the opportunity was provided for João to jump on the dog's back and grip the animal around the neck with his arm, strangling it with all his might. An offensive odour emanating from the wild animal penetrated João's nostrils while, in the background, yells of encouragement or disbelief inspired him to impose supernatural strength to continue to strangle the struggling dog.

Dust particles frolicked in the air, dancing over the grunting man and flailing beast. The muscular dog managed to turn João on his side. In the scramble that followed, its nails inflicted a wound on João's free arm. He ignored the pain and kept tightening his grip. At last he saw the long legs becoming limp. The dog's ears flopped and there was no tail raised in combat. The grimace lapsed and the dog's soul made preparations to enter the realm of non-existence.

Panting from exhaustion, João lay on the dog, not trusting that he had indeed killed it. After a few moments, he struggled to his feet and, with newfound energy, he stomped his left foot as hard as he could on the animal. Its mouth snapped open and blood-stained froth spewed in the air from the throat, caking the dust as it fell to the ground. The dog lay dead with a sullen expression on its face.

Standing victorious, João felt like collapsing but his spirit soared. He looked at the silent, stunned crowd. With a triumphant sigh, João knew he could now forget the death knell of the rattling door chain which he had heard when he was brought to face this ordeal. He gave a quick salute to embrace the adventure he was born to live.

Soshangane rose to his feet and gave the order. 'Let no person touch this man. He has a devil living in him. Eat his liver and you will howl at night when the moon is full and the thirst will never leave you. Don't let him escape, I can make good use of him. At night, lock his door. Place two sentries to guard the hut.'

A subdued silence followed as the men and women began to slink away. A few quarrels arose about who would feed this powerful creature. It was the medicine woman who settled the matter when she offered to take over this task.

Chapter 7

Closer encounters

Senhor Albasini heard the laughter of Tommy and wondered what the merriment was all about. He saw Tommy striding towards him, shaking his head and then bursting out in a new bout of laughter.

'Tell me the joke. There certainly isn't much to laugh about in this little place.'

Tommy placed his hat back on his head and tried to be serious when he said, 'It's Mario, Senhor, he wants you to come and help.'

When João approached the newly built shop he felt immense pride. Once again, his *Knopneuse* had risen to the occasion. A neatly thatched roof topped the daubed mud structure. Steps took you to the entrance of the shop and a tin sign hung out the front proudly displaying the tell-tale ***A. A. Albasini & Co.***

He noticed that Mario had added some extra squiggles of gold and black paint because, underneath the sign, he had written ***Winkel***, meaning shop. 'A good addition, Mario,' he thought. Mario had put out some chairs and a table together with a spittoon and a jug of water on the veranda. Farm implements lined one side of the wall next to the door and a few ivory tusks stood along the other. To the surprise of all present and Senhor Albasini, Trui was putting up the fight of her life. Albasini saw the little girl, her eyes swollen from crying and her mouth wide open in a silent struggle. As she let out a huge sob, she ran to Senhor Albasini.

She pointed her little finger at João and said, 'You, Senhor, you are the boss. You tell him,' she pointed towards Mario. 'He cannot go away with you. I may never see him again, and I promised to marry him.'

Mario was embarrassed but, since the day Trui made that first emphatic statement, she was his shadow. She helped him unpack spices, haberdashery, toys and did what her hand could find to do. If somebody might unlawfully put something in his pocket, Trui would tell Mario. From time to time, she would fill the water jug. Mature beyond her age, she had a firm understanding of what people needed and an uncanny sense for business. Mario realised he had a good helper and started to teach her Portuguese. He also noted that Trui had an exceptional memory. She also told him that they should give free coffee and that all footwear, old or new, should sell for one pound. The footwear idea brought in a sizeable profit.

She ran back to Mario and clung to him. Her mother tried to free her, but Trui latched onto Mario like a baby baboon to her mother.

Senhor Albasini looked at this extraordinary scene. He went to sit on the veranda steps and called Trui in a soft and gentle voice.

'*Kom*, come.' He indicated she should sit on his lap.

An unwilling Trui untangled herself and went to see what Senhor Albasini was going to offer.

'What?' she asked.

The Senhor arched his eyebrows, took out a pristine looking handkerchief from a pocket inside his waistcoat and dried Trui's tears.

'*Mario kan bly*.' (Mario can stay.)

He saw the consternation on Mario's face and, with a twinkle in the eye, said in Portuguese, 'You will cope. You have always done so.'

The problem solved, he took Trui's hand in his and led her back to Mario. The embarrassed Mario took her into the shop to make coffee.

***

They loaded the Combrink and van Rensburg wagons with ivory, giraffe skins, hippo teeth, dried fruit, honey and butter. The two trekkers were eager to start the journey but Senhor Albasini advised them to travel only at the full moon. He knew the habits of the tsetse fly which were active only at dawn and dusk. If the trekkers followed the old trade route along the river, which was far less overgrown with bush than the interior, they would avoid the deadly pest.

A gathering of well-wishers lit the barbeque fires. A jolly mood prevailed, especially after they imbibed the port Senhor Albasini provided. The company would depart near midnight to give them a reasonably safe passage.

This journey was an experiment because it would show that if these wagons could reach the Bay, then Ohrigstad had hopes of survival. A route to the sea would mean they did not have to trade with the English in Port Natal. Delagoa Bay was also much closer than Inhambane which was much further north along Mozambique's east coast.

Senhor Albasini commandeered some of his troops to walk beside the wagons as an extra precaution to ward off attacks from plundering tribes. He sighed with relief when he knew they were in safe territory and ordered that the oxen be outspanned. They all needed a rest before starting the three-day journey that remained to reach Magashulaskraal.

While some kept vigil, others made themselves comfortable to sleep under the wagons. They didn't light any fires to avoid attracting unwanted company. Everybody worked as quietly as possible.

***

The African sun had just started her early morning blush and the bush whispered a faint 'good morning' to the day when João had the uneasy feeling that somebody was watching him.

He feigned sleep, the stiletto strapped to his chest in a leather sheath always at the ready.

As unobtrusively as possible, he peeped through his eyelids and, to his surprise, saw delicate thin ankles. The second surprise was the greeting in the Zulu dialect he spoke to his *Knopneuse*.

'*Sawubona* (good morning), Senhor Albasini.'

'What on earth are you doing here? I could have killed you, and how come you speak the *Knopneus* dialect?'

Gertina answered, 'Yes, I learnt to speak the dialect at a young age and think we may be able to have a better conversation than your attempted use of *Die Taal*.'

She paused, handed the Senhor a mug of coffee and a rusk, and then continued, 'My Ma is a forceful lady. When my father thought he was safe and sound, she popped up from under the hippo skins where we were hiding.'

Senhor Albasini was suddenly wide awake. Having two ladies in the company made it much more difficult. He also took the opportunity to observe her from close up and realised that her appearance was stunning. She was so close to him that he could see a sprinkling of freckles on her nose. He felt his hands becoming sweaty. For once, caught out by this sudden change of circumstances, he could not be the charmer.

'Why?'

The answer came straight as an arrow, 'My Ma told my father that she wanted to find out for herself if you are married, sell slaves, and if you are rich.'

Disappointed at the answer, the Senhor looked at the stony ground, saw the ants busy at work, dipped his rusk slowly into the coffee and put it in his mouth. He drank and ate at leisure before looking up at Gertina, his eyes blank and his reply cold.

'Is that what they say behind my back? Your mother has a three-day ride to find out.' He saluted her with the mug. In a stubborn tone he replied in his best kitchen Dutch, *'Dankie vir café.'*

He reverted to Zulu and said, 'If you are a lady, you will go back to your inquisitive Ma. Nature is calling.' He couldn't get the harshness out of the remark.

Gertina looked at him pensively and said impishly, 'What if I don't want to move?'

For a second time that morning, Senhor Albasini did not know what to say or think. He made it as if he would throw his blanket off whereupon Gertina giggled and scampered back to her father's wagon.

***

The wagon leader called the oxen by their names, '*Witlies!*
Botterbek! Witsmoel! Vat voor my liefies!' (Encouragement.)
He cajoled them continuously to give their best performance.

From time to time, Lucas swished his hippo-hide sjambok to
urge the oxen forward. The whip-cracking and urgent calls to
the oxen woke Gertina and she realised that they were starting
to climb a hill.

A vista of craggy mountains and jagged cliffs which towered
above the wintery, yellowed grasses saluted her. Autumn
colours in rich, penny-like gold and rusty, ochre leaves of the
Mopani trees whispered sweet-nothings in the late afternoon
breeze and left her feeling content.

A short distance further along they reached a wagon road
paved with cobblestones which brought them to a stone-
walled rampart. An arched entrance displayed bold letters
reading **Cologne de San Luiz** and, on a sign swinging in the
breeze, **Villa Albasini**.

Two sentries who were dressed in loincloths that wrapped
around their bodies, arrows nestled in quivers on their backs,
rolled open the wooden doors. Their shields of zebra skin
tricked the eye, confusing the viewer to question whether they
were warriors or zebras. They stood immovable until
everybody was inside before they rolled back the gates and
bolted them firmly. When Gertina looked back, she saw that
the sentries had already climbed the rampart walls to take up
their duty as guards for the night.

Lucas and his party walked across a rectangular, paved courtyard to the front door. Verandas with red-tiled roofs and thick whitewashed pillars hemmed the yard. In the middle of the rectangle stood a big chair which was carved out of wood and draped with a leopard skin. Terracotta pots decorated in the native style stood randomly on the verandas overflowing with colourful bougainvillea.

Senhor Albasini, who had gone ahead, stood at the front door waiting for them to enter. He looked fresh, clean and smart. He had chosen a dark-green velvet waistcoat with breeches fastened just below the knees and matching velvet ties, emphasising his muscular legs. The black boots were as shiny as the first day Gertina had seen them.

Tommy and N'wamanungu stood respectfully behind Senhor Albasini, dressed in black, wide-legged trousers and short sleeved jackets trimmed at the edges with decorative, ornate gold braid.

Senhor Albasini pointed to the beautiful tiles on the threshold which were inscribed. Tommy translated, *'Welcome to Portugal.'*

Gertina entered the large room and stopped in her tracks. An abundance of colour dazzled her. A big rectangular table with carved legs stood in the middle of the room and deep, salmon-coloured upholstered chairs tucked their seats under the table. The walls were mirrors decorated with small cherubim which smiled down in gilded amusement at the guests. The table featured a crazy patchwork runner in glorious colours of cerise pink, ice blue and red. The colourful embroidery and gold thread was a statement of luxury. A miniature succulent with bright orange flowers planted in a copper container stood boldly in the table's centre.

Rugs with intricate patterns and deep rich and blue colours covered the clay tiles on the floor. Gertina saw the fire crackling in the hearth, the only thing that reminded her of her own home.

As if they were in a dreamworld, Tommy took the guests to their rooms, delivering Gertina to her room after three flights of narrow stairs.

Tommy said, 'It looks good, doesn't it? Wait till you see dinner. You will hear a gong. Take time to refresh yourself and rest a little. We will see you downstairs soon.'

Instinctively Gertina wished she had included her church clothes but, of course, this was something out of the ordinary which she had not expected. They had packed the bare essentials and had just managed to squeeze into the hiding place her mother had devised.

She made the best of the situation. She brushed her hair and, on a whim, decided to leave it hanging loose over her shoulders and tumbling down her back. She would make her entrance look as regal as possible, keeping her head high and her back straight.

Two candelabra sprayed soft candlelight in a rosy hew over a white linen tablecloth. The dazzling silverware reminded her of the *Nachtmaal* cup used every quarter when the farmers gathered to celebrate The Lord's Supper.

Silver bowls filled with floating flowers stood amongst a setting of knives, forks and crystal glasses. It all shimmered in the dim light adding to the vibrancy of the room. She counted the place settings: her parents, her brother Hendrik, *Meneer* Combrink, herself and Senhor Albasini, which added up to six. She noticed a seventh place had been set and she wondered if it could be for the Senhor's wife.

When she came down the stairs, Gertina noticed Tommy and N'wamanungu standing by the entrance to what she presumed was the kitchen. She could smell fish and freshly baked bread. Her stomach ached because she was hungry.

***

Albasini positioned himself so that he could see Gertina when she came down the stairs. When she appeared at the landing he thought she looked regal. He fingered the ruby ring on his pinkie and involuntarily wondered if there might be a possibility for him to end his lonely life. Would she be worthy of the family heirloom? Would she understand why his father had fled from Tyrol to Lisbon? How would Gertina react to the fact that he was a *bondeldraer* (a mere pedlar). A *Catolico*? He remembered that his friend Karl Trichardt had said that the farmers would rather accept a Jew than a Catholic. Perhaps that was the reason for his cold reception

90

when he first entered the church and was not allowed to partake in the sharing of the sacraments.

There were just too many questions to answer so he would think about it all tomorrow. Tonight he would enjoy the company of his guests and pluck up the courage to ask if he might call her 'Tineka'. He stood up from his chair and indicated that dinner was ready to be served.

Lucas beckoned to Tommy, 'What must I to do with these? I only need a spoon. Take these away.'

Lucas gathered the extra cutlery and handed it to Tommy. Ella was quick to intervene. 'You don't think you are embarrassing us?'

'*Vrou*, (woman), let me be. If you had not come along I am sure we would have slept in the veldt and barbequed our meat on a stick! This man is a good fellow and will understand that we live the simple life.'

Tommy removed the unnecessary cutlery. In that moment, Albasini knew that he had overplayed his hand yet again. How could he have not read the signs? These people focused on humility and hard work. If it had not been for *Mevrou* van Rensburg's inquisitiveness about how rich he was, he would not have succumbed to the temptation to show off his mother's fine tableware. He knew about hard work. Tomorrow he would show them he was not shy to do just that. Perhaps that would dampen the extravagance he exhibited this day and make them realise that he had attributes other than worldly goods. In his line of work he had to make a show of things, especially to the big game hunters from overseas, the merchants from the East and the Arab traders.

He stood and raised his goblet. 'To the joint venture of Ohrigstad and Portugal.' N'wamanungu had come forward on cue and filled the crystal glasses to the brim with Oporto port. 'Today is my birthday, 1st May. I thought it appropriate to share it with you. My cook from Portugal has prepared a feast. Please enjoy the meal.'

Tommy translated as fast as he could.

'*Smaak soos Nachtmaalwyn* (It tastes like communion wine),' Hendrik said. He was a quiet boy who hardly said anything. Lucas wondered how much Marula-brew, which was offered to the men before dinner, Hendrik had had to drink.

Ella put down her goblet, went up to the Senhor and gave him a spontaneous motherly hug. '*Mag jy geseënd wees.* (May God bless you.)'

The men followed with slaps on the back and pumping handshakes. '*Hoor! Hoor!*' (Hear, hear!)

And then it was Gertina's turn. As soon as she moved, Tommy was behind her. He helped her to move her chair so she could go to congratulate Senhor Albasini. It would be her first time in close proximity to him and her heart raced. How should she approach this man? He was undoubtedly the best-looking man she had ever seen in her life. The sharp green eyes she had noticed previously looked at her mockingly. On closer inspection, she noticed a scar on his left eyebrow where the hair had not regrown and she wondered in what kind of a fight he had acquired it. She had a strong urge to touch his smooth skin and wipe away the sadness in his eyes. One day I'll ask him about the scar, she decided.

Senhor Albasini must have realised her predicament and took the initiative. When she stood in front of him, he took her hand and brought it up to his lips without actually touching it. The expressive mouth, too well moulded for a man and yet not feminine, smiled and, in a soft voice, he said in Shangaan, the Zulu dialect they both spoke, 'You are beautiful. Call me by my chieftain name if you wish. Juwawa. You may find saying João too difficult. I find G...' He struggled with the guttural sound and eventually managed a garbled-sounding 'Gertina'. The other diners laughed at his dilemma.

'May I call you Tineka?' he asked in a quiet voice.

She looked into his wonderfully expressive eyes and answered, 'I'll think about it, *Oom.*' Uncle! She was teasing him deliberately.

He let go of her hand but not before his eyes lost their playfulness. The corners of his mouth turned down, leaving Gertina with an uneasy feeling that she had hurt him rather than teased.

Not long after, everybody retired to bed. Gertina's room was at the top of a stone-built tower. Earlier in the evening she had a view over the valley. Now, when she looked out over the moonlit courtyard, she saw the lonely figure of Senhor

Albasini sitting in the carved chair she had noticed on their arrival. He sat motionless, the leopard skin kaross draped over his shoulders. Was he looking up at her window? The lace-trimmed inner curtains danced in the evening breeze and she leaned forward to close the window. Senhor Albasini answered her question when he acknowledged her by blowing her a kiss.

Chapter 8

A new friend

Gertina woke refreshed. The featherbed she had slept in was a first-time experience. The comfort was luxurious. She swung her legs out of the bed and walked over to open the window. A smile hovered on her lips, thinking about the kiss that Senhor Albasini had so impudently blown her way. What should she call him? Juwawa, João, or Senhor Albasini?

She couldn't quite analyse her feelings. Was it the feather bed or was it the warm feeling she went to bed with after the good night kiss? A feeling of calm crept over her which countered her habit of living in fear of the marauding and hostile tribes. She felt safe. She dressed quickly and went down the stairs silently.

The soothing smell of freshly baked bread flooded the freshness of the winter morning. Gertina's step was light as she walked into the kitchen. She loved cooking and thought she might glean some tips from the cooks who had prepared the tasty meal the previous evening.

The kitchen was large. The glow of two wood-fired ovens chased away the morning bite. In Shangaan she asked the Portuguese-looking cook, the one to whom Senhor Albasini had spoken about the previous evening, 'Where is Senhor Albasini?'

The cook stared at her with a blank expression, lifted his shoulders, smiled and nodded his head. A very tall, strongly-build man came to her rescue. He promptly sat down on his haunches and enveloped her small hand between his in the customary greeting of the *Knopneuse*.

'*Avuxeni*, Sehorita. My name is Josekhulu. My name means 'the Big One'. I am one of Juwawa's *indunas* (generals). You can trust me.'

Somewhat taken by surprise, she acknowledged his greeting. He did not rise but said in the softest voice, 'Senhor Albasini has already left with the other men to go to the Bay. He has left me in charge to take you safely back to Ohrigstad as soon as you and your mother have had breakfast.'

She felt disappointed on hearing the news of João's early departure. She was looking forward to seeing him again having decided that she would call him Juwawa. The thought that she might have lost something made her feel unsettled.

In the few months in which she had observed Senhor Albasini, she could vouch that he was born with an inbuilt magnetism. Nobody could resist his attraction. He charmed her friends and all the *tantes* (older ladies) with whom he came in contact and yet he was strangely aloof with her. He was a genius in the art of attracting the opposite sex. Young and old had fallen over their feet to invite him to dinner. She wasn't quite sure who were his most ardent admirers, the young eligible girls or the girls' mothers. He was also learning to speak *Die Taal* at an alarming speed. She had warned her mother to be very careful of what she said in front of him. He might just be able to understand.

Senhor Albasini could be a dangerous man. The menacing look she had seen when he looked at Schoeman made her realise that he was a man to be reckoned with behind the engaging smile. Senhor Albasini was much older than she was, but that was not going to put her off.

Outside the front door, Josekhulu waited for the women to emerge from the building. He stood upright and proud, honoured to have this task. Three of the best mules stood ready for departure.

Ella came out first, squinted into the bright light and said in her bossy way, 'Gertina, ask this man if he expects me to ride back home on a mule? Mules are stubborn creatures. I have not ridden anything since I was your age. My bones won't survive!'

Patiently, Gertina explained to Josekhulu that they might have a problem. An expression of concern crossed the big man's face and, in a flash, he barked some orders to some of the men next to him. They hurried away and came back with a bier.

'This will make our journey a bit cumbersome and we will not be able to go as quickly as I would like. Please ask your mother if she will be comfortable if we transport her this way.'

Ella waved her hands in the air, pulled up her skirts, plopped into the bier and said, 'Let's start.'

'Is my mule fast? I don't like slow coaches. Will I have a gun?' Gertina asked.

Josekhulu smiled at her and said that the mule was not the fastest but was very reliable. Senhor Albasini himself had handpicked that particular one for her.

'I take it that you will ride it?' Josekhulu asked.

'Do you think I can't ride? It's a pity you did not saddle the black stallion I saw roaming in the paddock.'

'No, no Senhorita, that devil takes after his master. Fearless, dangerous and brave. Only Juwawa understands him.'

'You think I am not up to the challenge?'

Josekhulu gave her a questioning look, smiled, chuckled and said, 'Who? The master or the stallion? Let's get moving.'

***

The small group travelled quietly and as unobserved as possible. When they reached safer territory, Josekhulu and the six men accompanying them sang, harmonising and encouraging each other to perform better and end the journey in record time. They sang of their Juwawa.

Yo ya yo ya amaqada
hanci ya Juwawa-
Tata nga vu yi
Hita day mapa
Wa mpapa wa xi lungu
Kigigi

When Gertina asked what it meant because she did not understand all of it, Josekhulu explained. 'It translates as,

We are riding on horseback.
The horses of Juwawa.
Father is not coming back.
We shall eat bread.
The bread of the Portuguese man.
Kikigi

'You see, Senhorita, we call him FATHER because we are all his orphans. We are like his children. We are never hungry, we sleep with our bellies full. He is just, he listens to our problems and asks the elders for advice. He is very wise in making decisions. We will do anything for him.'

He had taken off his hat. Juwawa had given him orders to dress in a rough linen shirt and pants. Josekhulu had agreed to everything and admitted that, if he were to look after the Senhorita, the people would accept him better if he was to dress their way. Still, when it came to shoes, they had agreed that it was a bad idea. Juwawa said it was because he could not get shoes to fit Josekhulu's big feet; Josekhulu protested that he would not be able to run fast if he was wearing shoes.

Josekhulu pointed to the beeswax ring in his hair and said to Gertina. 'It crowns me as one of Juwawa's generals. If I should disappoint him, he has the power to wrench it from my head. If that ever happens, I will die from the bleeding. That is our way of living. Don't look so disgusted, I don't want to die. Be assured, I don't wish to disappoint Juwawa.'

He then proceeded to point to his left ear lobe. 'You see this? It is the mark of a thief. If you steal something and they catch you, they cut off your ear lobe.'

Gertina said, 'I don't believe you!'

'Juwawa, he saved me. The traders from Sofala caught me stealing. They were going to kill me when Juwawa came upon the party. He knew the men very well and asked what I had stolen. The men answered that I had stolen food. Juwawa then asked me if I was hungry when I stole the food. I answered that I was not hungry at the time because I had stolen the food for my mother who was sick and old. Juwawa then told the traders he did not think the offence was so great but suggested they cut off my ear, which is the custom to show that I was a thief. Juwawa said he would take care of me and see that I would never steal anything again. They didn't need to kill me. Juwawa took care of my sick mother and me. Therefore, I can never disappoint him.

'I also have the honour of wearing this headband of leopard skin. Only very few of his men get this honour but Juwawa said that, to show everybody how special I am, I am to wear it like this.' Josekhulu showed with his finger circling his head, "No, not like that. Juwawa said I am to wear it low down at the back coming forward covering the scar. This way, nobody would know my shame. Juwawa and N'wamanungu keep my secret, and so do you Senhorita, hey?'

Gertina saw the honesty and trust in this big man's face and knew there was an invisible bond between herself and this gentle giant.

'*Ehbo*, I see a loyal servant.'

***

'Josekhulu?' Gertina paused before she continued, I wonder about those lion claws he wears around his neck.'

'*Ehbo*, Senhorita, it is one of the bravest moments I have ever seen in my life. I will gladly tell you because we will relate this story of bravery to our children and grandchildren.

'It was late one afternoon and we were looking for a place to set up camp. Suddenly we heard the roar of a lion so close that we all scrambled into the bushes looking for the highest tree to climb but no, not the Senhor. He did not run into a panic like us but stood his ground and shot the lion which had appeared from behind a big antheap.

'N'wamanungu, who managed to scale the nearest upside-down tree (the Boab tree), told us how Juwawa had side-stepped the beast because the lion was in full flight when he shot him. He said Juwawa was about to walk towards the dead cat and pat him on the head when a lioness appeared on the other side of the antheap. Juwawa did not wait for the lioness to attack. He rushed forward and plucked that thin knife he always wears in a pocket next to his ribs and threw it with deadly accuracy into the lioness's neck. She vaulted in the air and fell at Juwawa's feet, dead as a rock, not moving.

'Juwawa just laughed, patted both lions on the head and told N'wamanungu and me to cut out two toenails. He kept them for himself and later had it made into the talisman you saw hanging from his neck.'

'I don't believe you, Josekhulu,' Gertina said.

'True, Senhorita, I swear by all my fathers and grandfathers and my mother's womb it is true. Something else happened as well. The tree that N'wamanungu had climbed held a big surprise. A mulatto girl was crying of fear in the hollow of the tree, skeletal from not eating for days.'

'A mulatto girl, what does that mean?' Gertina asked in utter bewilderment.

'Yes, N'wamanungu recognised her as the daughter of one of Magashula's wives. Her mother was a Portuguese Mazungu (educated children of mixed relationships) and could read. Mamahila's grandfather was a Portuguese soldier who married a chieftain's daughter, giving him the rights to own a *Pizarro*.' (Land given to the Portuguese if they married a chieftain's daughter.)

Juwawa felt so sorry for her because she had wounds still fresh from shackles on her ankles. She fainted when N'wamanungu brought her to Juwawa because she thought he was a slave trader who would want to sell her to the ships that lay anchored in the bay. Juwawa's order was sharp, I remember well.

'Get yourselves moving, you G-string wearers, and stop staring. Get a cask of brandy ready on that tree stump and let's celebrate. I killed two lions today!' As a final thought he added, 'N'wamanungu, look after this girl.'

'The next day we all had the head that ached and it felt as if the big river's water would never be enough. We were about three days of travelling away from Magashulaskraal and decided to take the girl back to him.'

'You mean you were all drunk?' Gertina asked incredulously.

'Yes, Senhorita, drunk as the baboons when they eat the fruit of the Marula tree.'

'Juwawa as well?'

He looked at her, uncertain of how to answer, and decided that honesty would be the best policy. 'Yes, Senhorita. When we got to Magashulaskraal, we told Magashula about the Senhor's bravery and compassion towards the young girl. The leaders of the different groups of people following Juwawa got together and decided to make him a chief because he was so brave to have killed two lions. That is when we all started to call him Juwawa. We called ourselves the *Mashangaan*.

'Juwawa says that my task now in Ohrigstad will be to bake bread. I said that is a woman's work, but he just told me to find somebody to help me.'

What Josekhulu did not add was that while he worked under the guise of overseeing the bakery, he would also be able to keep a close eye on Gertina. He hoped that she would realise that it was she, Gertina, that he would like to help him in baking bread.

The journey back home passed without incident. When the travellers returned to their homes, they shared their stories over many cups of coffee, a multitude of questions and numerous oohs and aahs with the *Kappie Brigade.* Ella warned Gertina not to disclose the extent of Senhor Albasini's wealth because the people of humble means residing at Ohrigstad would not comprehend such affluence. They agreed to say the minimum until Lucas and her brother Hendrik came back.

After six weeks, Senhor Albasini and the rest of the party returned successfully without having lost any of their trek oxen. There was a short-term effervescence of optimism that the settlement of Ohrigstad could become a new independent republic but, alas, infighting between the Buhrgers and Potgieter factions nearly ended in war. Malaria infested the area and there was scepticism about a safe route to Delagoa Bay. Senhor Albasini realised that Ohrigstad might have to be abandoned.

He became well known and much loved among the Trekkers, but he was still not allowed to partake in the sacraments when he attended church. He did realise, however, that these staunch, upright people had the same restlessness as himself and a call to adventure always beckoned from places to be explored and developed.

Chapter 9

Competing plans

It came as no surprise that in 1847 'Zoutpanzberg' was the most exciting topic for the settlers in Ohrigstad. The trekkers walked around with starstruck eyes as they considered the possibility of a new settlement to be a case of Divine intervention.

As a *Volk* (nation), it was their destiny to move North. 'To lead by day with a pillar of cloud, and by night a pillar of fire to give them light on the way they were to take.' Just like the Israelites, they were a chosen *Volk*.

The trekkers saw their movement away from English oppression as the exodus of a new nation. Their leader *Old Bloues*, Andries Potgieter, propagated the idea. Stephanus Schoeman, an accessory, cracked his whip to mobilise the people's thoughts into packing up their belongings and leaving the infested swamp of Ohrigstad.

His booming voice could be heard everywhere, starting with '*Uit respecte!*', and then moving on to a well-constructed argument comparing the positives of the move to the North with the negatives of staying.

Never had the small community been swept up by such enthusiasm. A barbeque and a day of *Boersport* (gymkhana) was organised to welcome the young men who had scouted the new horizons. Schoeman, who excelled at organising, took the lead. There would be horse racing and various sports like three-legged racing, egg and spoon races, and the likes. The woodchopping competition was popular because the widows of the community benefitted from the money raised.

There would be dancing, of course. Schoeman looked forward to the opportunity to dance with Gertina. She was now seventeen and the promises of a budding beauty at sixteen had come to fruition. She carried her beauty with humility and dignity. She was always ready to serve. She was smart. She helped Josekhulu run the *Bakhuis*, Albasini's bakery. Schoeman was not quite sure how it all happened but Potgieter was correct in his assumption. Albasini was a fast mover. He had eliminated all other possible traders and charmed the community to become the settlers' sole trader.

The men of the scout patrol returned to town the week before with glowing reports of good grazing, elephant hunting and the relative absence of hostile tribes in the district of Zoutpanzberg. It would be the land of milk and honey, and so remote that an autonomous republic would flourish. The possibility of an export harbour at Inhambane would give them total independence.

***

Trui was now twelve years old and had established herself at the side of Mario. She refused to call him M-L, preferring 'Mario'. Mario was intrigued by the girl but soon realised that she meant what she had said - she would marry him one day.

Trui and Gertina's mothers were cousins and very fond of each other. The situation worked quite well. Trui worked in the shop next to the bakery where Gertina helped Josekhulu bake the bread for Mario and Trui to sell.

***

Gertina's friendship with Josekhulu was something exceptional. He found ingenious means of pampering her in any way he possibly could. When it was *num-num* time, Josekhulu presented her with a bucket full of berries every morning. She decided whether to eat them or make them into jam. He ensured that she had enough sugar if she chose to make jam. He never allowed her to carry water or heavy articles. Gertina thought that she still had to gather wood but, when she arrived home, a pile of chopped wood and small branches stood neatly packed at the back door.

The people of Ohrigstad often called on Gertina to look after sick people. It was Josekhulu who saw her distress and offered to dig the graves for those who died under her loving care.

They called the Senhor's workforce 'Albasini *Volk*', Albasini workers. They lived on a farm referred to as *Klipkraal* which he had bought on the outskirts of Ohrigstad.

'Josekhulu, don't your people get sick of the deadly mosquitoes?'

He just smiled. The next day he brought her a small clay jar filled with an emulsion of soft goat's fat and something else which smelt vaguely familiar.

'What is this?' she asked.

'We make it from the marula tree roots. Rub it on before you go to sleep or walk outside in the evening. The mosquitos don't like the smell.'

One cold winter's morning Josekhulu looked very pleased with himself and kept on humming the *Kidigi Kidiki* song.

'What is making you happy this morning, Josekhulu?'

'Mh, mh,' Josekhulu hummed. 'I've got a present for you, Senhorita. Go and look in the basket near the oven.'

Gertina went into the room where the bread was baking and spotted a woven hamper with its lid closed. She knelt on the floor to open the cover. Inside a pitch-black puppy slept, blissfully unaware of the emotions it evoked in the onlooker.

'Josekhulu, it must be a she. Oh, she is adorable. I will pay you.'

'No, no Senhorita. The puppy does not come from me. It is from Senhor Albasini.'

***

'I've come to see Senhor Albasini.'

The only sign that Senhor Albasini was in the shop was the hessian curtain flapping at the rear exit. He had disappeared through the doorway as soon as he noticed Schoeman approaching.

Mario, who had quickly stowed away the half-consumed glasses of sherry, smiled and answered calmly, 'The Senhor is not in at the moment. If you like, I can take a message. Is there anything else I can help you with today?'

'I thought I saw him come in not long ago?'

Schoeman gave Mario a threatening look, lifted the counter flap and rushed forward to peek behind the hessian curtain.

'Albasini! Where are you?'

He pulled the curtain away and poked his head through the opening but there was no sign of the Senhor. The only thing that greeted Schoeman was the smell of spices, sulphur and mothballs.

'*Verdomp*!' he exclaimed as a large ginger cat jumped on him from nowhere, fell to the ground and rushed between his legs to go and sit on the front steps.

Mario kept his composure, shrugged his shoulders and waited patiently. Schoeman came back to the front of the counter and tried to display an air of disinterest.

'De Sousa, it grieves me to ask.' His voice was secretive. 'As there is nowhere else, I would like to buy a present for a certain young lady. What would you suggest?'

'Ah, *Meneer* Schoeman, it depends. How old is the lady?'

'Oh, it will be her seventeenth birthday this coming Saturday.'

'Is that the same day as the gymkhana that you are busy arranging? If you don't mind,' Mario said, 'I can give you a better option if I were to know a little bit more about the lady. Is she a relative?'

'No.'

'What colour are her hair and her eyes?'

'Fair, rosy-cheeked and cornflower blue eyes.'

'Has she any hobbies?'

'Oh, she loves music and takes care of the sick.'

'Thank you, *Meneer* Schoeman. One last question and then I can make a few suggestions. Do you have any intentions of a future with this girl?'

'That is very personal, but I can say I will ask her to marry me after the dance on Saturday night.'

'Interesting, interesting. What are your chances, do you think?'

'No problem. Everybody around here knows that I am an excellent candidate for marriage. You see, I'm going to be the President of our republic one of these days. I have two farms in the Rustenburg district and plan to buy more as soon as we set foot in the Zoutpanzberg.'

Mario nodded and remarked. 'You are holding the celebrations for the young men who came riding into Ohrigstad the other day? Telling us of the land that can be prosperous'

'*Jaa*, I would like to shake the dust off my boots from this hell-hole.'

'Thank you, *Meneer*. I could look for an embroidered hanky with the girl's initials. They come from Madeira, are beautifully made and are embroidered.'

'*Jaa,* we might look at that later. It's Gertina. Highly unlikely that you will find that name under the Portuguese. No, I was looking for something more permanent, something that she can remember me by.'

'Meneer, may I present you with some jewellery that has come into Senhor Albasini's possession. It is the newest fashion in Europe but a bit useless to the Senhor. He cannot peddle it to the tribes in the interior or Delagoa Bay. The women there like beads and copper bangles as gifts. I am sure I can give it to you at a reasonable price. We only have two. Perhaps one of them would suit you very well.'

'Show, show!'

Mario took a key from his pocket and unlocked a drawer in front of him. He pulled out a sturdy wooden box and opened the lid. There were a few pieces of jewellery on the blue velvet inlay, three rings, a strand of pearls and, one could not miss them, two odd-looking pieces of jewellery.

Mario explained, 'They call them a lover's eye.' Mario took out one of the brooches and said, 'I thought this one would be most appropriate. The eye has been painted a black brown, just like your eyes. Unfortunately, the lashes are black, but I think this is near enough.'

The garnet in the dip of the heart-shaped brooch was kept in place by filigree gold fronds. Mario and Senhor Albasini thought the eye had an evilness about it and they might never be able to sell the piece. Schoeman presented an ideal opportunity to get rid of it.

Mario continued, 'If, as you say, the girl in question, her name is Gertina? Is that correct? If she has blue eyes, this one would be the perfect gift for her to give to you.' He took out the other brooch for Schoeman to hold. 'I mean to say, if the feelings were to be mutual. You are supposed to hide it under your lapel. Senhor Albasini had in mind to give one to a girl he likes but the eyes on the broaches did not match his green ones. So, I think you are in luck, *Meneer*. What do you think, will Gertina come and buy the blue lover's eye? She is young, isn't she?'

Schoeman was taken off balance but answered, 'You've got to take the girls young and train them your way, not so De Sousa? We will have to wait and see.'

Schoeman bought the brooch.

'It comes with a small box. I will throw in the hanky for free. I have had a look and I don't have one with a G embroidered on it. This one has a P. They are so pretty. Any girl would treasure it.'

'The P will do. Gertina's second name is Pitronella.'

Schoeman pocketed the packet and asked casually, 'Who would be the girl that Senhor Albasini is interested in?'

'Oh, I don't know, *meneer*. All I can say is that the girls are interested in him. They bat their eyelashes when they see him and sales increase when he is in the shop. Anything else you might need? We have just received a consignment of *Jinewer* (gin). Could I interest you in a bottle?'

'*Ja*, I'll take one.'

Schoeman paid and left the shop, shaking his head and fiddling with his lapel.

***

Having listened to the conversation, João realised there was no time to waste. He smiled and silently thanked Mario for extracting so much information from Schoeman. João knew Tineka was to be his wife and so the sooner he set about it the better. João was glad the lover's eye was a hideous piece of jewellery. Tineka could rest assured that he would never give her such a monstrosity. What he had in mind was to provide her with a life so wonderful that she would never be in doubt as to how much he treasured her.

He left his hiding place behind the sacks of maize where the ginger cat had been sleeping. He hurried but made sure that he got to the home of *Meneer* Lucas van Rensburg and his wife without drawing any attention to himself.

Lucas was sitting in his favourite spot on the veranda.

'Ah, Johannes, I can call you that?' Lucas said.

'You certainly can, *Meneer*, as I am to become your son-in-law.'

'What?' exclaimed Lucas.

'Now, *Meneer* Van Rensburg, before we go any further, may we discuss this inside the house with *Tante* Ella also in attendance so that I can explain?'

Lucas was quick to notice the subtle difference in addressing his wife. The *Porra* must have softened up his wife's attitude to go from the formal *Mevrou* to the informal *Tante*.

Lucas lifted his heavy frame from the *riempies bank* slowly and called, 'Ella, Senhor Albasini, *jou witbroodjie*, (teacher's pet) has come to discuss serious matters. Make some coffee and let us meet in the *voorkamer* lounge.'

When they were all seated, Senhor Albasini knew he would have to be very careful with his words. He started by asking, 'I have to know the answer to my question before I can continue. Whatever your answer is, I can assure you it will only be between us, on my word of honour. Gertina and Hendrik, are they your children, or have you adopted them?'

Lucas and Ella looked at each other. Lucas sighed. He looked worried and asked, 'Why, Johannes?'

'When I took your Bible on the first day of our acquaintance to show you that João is the Portuguese for Johannes, I saw there was a late entry of two names, those of Gertina and Hendrik.'

Ella's hand clasped her husband's. The two older people looked at each other and, because there was no harm in telling Senhor Albasini, they both nodded their heads. Lucas said in a gruff voice, 'Yes, they are adopted, but they are like our own. We could never have any children. Lang Hans was my nephew. They were God-sent when Karl brought them to us.'

João continued, 'You see, the entry started me thinking. When I put the dates together, the puzzle fell into place. After the massacre of the Lang Hans van Rensburg trek, it happened that one of my very trusted warriors saw two children hidden in an antheap. He knew what was happening and so he grabbed the children and brought them to me. He thought I would know what to do with them.

'My friend Karl Trichardt and I were just at the point where he was going inland and I had business to complete in Sofala. I suggested that Josekhulu, my warrior, take them to Chief Magashula at Villa Albasini where they would be safe. Karl would then take them from there to his people who, he said, had plans to move to this side of the mountains. I agreed. When I saw Karl again, he told me that Lang Hans van Rensburg's children lived with their uncle, Lang Hans's cousin. I never gave it another thought until I saw the inscription on opening your Bible.

'The dates written on the first page of the Bible made me think that Gertina and Hendrik might be the very same children that Josekhulu brought to me.'

'*Vrou*, 'Lucas interrupted, 'I think we need something stronger than coffee. Bring some *Jinewer* and glasses. I am interested to hear what Johannes wants to talk about.'

Lucas poured the gin into small glasses and took his straight. Lucas refilled his glass, took a sip and said to Senhor Albasini, 'Please continue.'

'*Meneer en Mevrou*, I come in humility to ask for Gertina's hand in marriage.'

Lucas started to protest but João said, 'I have given it careful consideration. I know there are about eighteen years of difference in our ages but that does not have to be wrong. An older husband can give his wife guidance and care for her. I have ample means to care for her as you might have gathered when you visited Villa Albasini. I am not only rich, I am very rich. Hard work and perseverance got me there.'

Before Lucas could say anything João continued, 'Yes, yes, I am *Catolico*, but I can assure you I will not interfere with Gertina's beliefs. She can raise our children in her mother tongue and your Protestant faith. We all believe in God. I will come back in one year's time and I will be able to speak *Die Taal* fluently. Gertina will then be eighteen and have had a

116

year to contemplate what it would be like to become Senhora Albasini.

'I will also take care of you and your wife in your old age. If you should fall away before Hendrik reaches maturity, I will take up his guardianship. You will never have any hardships if I can help it.

'I have also heard that you might uplift to go and settle in the Zoutpanzberg. I am willing to do the same as I already have many trade posts and a farm in that area.'

João was not nervous and felt that he had done his best.

Ella asked, 'Johannes, does Gertina know about your intentions?'

João was relieved. Ella had called him by *Die Taal's* name, a change from Albasini or Senhor Albasini.

At that very moment, N'wamanungu was calling from outside, 'Juwawa, I have brought what you told me to bring.'

Senhor Albasini excused himself and came back into the room carrying what looked like a rifle wrapped in an oilcloth.

'I would like to present Hendrik with this. I think it belonged to his father. I had it restored in the Bay.'

He unwrapped the parcel and the front loader looked as if new. Engraved in inlaid ivory in the butt-end of the rifle was the inscription **J.J. (Lang Hans) Janse van Rensburg.**

'I think Hendrik will be pleased. I found parts of it under a tree trunk at the scene where the massacre took place.'

'*Mevrou.*' A smile hovered on João's lips. He cocked his head to one side and said with confidence, 'To come back to your question, does Gertina know? On that, I am willing to take a calculated risk.'

***

'Well, that took some convincing.' Senhor Albasini breathed a sigh of relief. He had left the Van Rensburg's home in good spirits. He had their approval and a promise that they would not reveal to Gertina that it was he who had saved her and Hendrik's lives, albeit indirectly. He also had a dinner invitation. He would declare his intention to marry Tineka and hope to get an affirmative response.

Walking back to his shop, he contemplated how he would approach Tineka. He noticed two people walking towards the shop. He waited for his short-sightedness to bring them into focus.

A fit of uncontrollable jealousy took hold of him and, if he could have had a wish, it would have been for a lightning bolt to obliterate the tall figure of Schoeman holding Tineka's hand. The man's arrogance was beyond good manners. João detested him and could not think why Schoeman would go out of his way to annoy him.

The answer came as clear as a bell. Tineka was the common denominator. Schoeman might not know of Senhor Albasini's feelings for Gertina. Still, he might anticipate it and therefore try to thwart any plans Albasini might harbour.

An overwhelming fear gripped him. To make it worse, the devil's angel sat on his shoulder, echoing the gossip that circled among the afternoon tea sessions of the babbling *Kappie Brigade*.

'That Senhor? Let me tell you, he is a foreigner. He is a *Bondeldraer*. Traders collude with all sorts, you know.' Another would add, 'He is a Catholic.' Another might interject, 'An English spy?'

Senhor Albasini was all too aware of the rumours doing the rounds behind his back. What if Tineka rejected him tonight?

For the first time in his life his plans were vague. He was moving into uncharted territory. The only advantage he had over Schoeman was that he had heard the conversation taking place with Mario in the shop. He was glad that he had such a sincere and fruitful discussion with Lucas and *Tante* Ella. He also hoped that Tineka realised his honest intentions. His fears increased when he thought that he might have waited too long. Was it an error of judgement to think of her as being too young to take such a far-reaching step?

There was nothing he could do.

His thoughts continued. 'Well, I did say I was taking a calculated risk. Did not Josekhulu tell you that Tineka mentioned that nobody had ever been so kind to her on receiving the puppy he had sent her? Josekhulu even reported that she kissed the puppy and said that if the Senhor were there, she would have hugged him.'

N'wamanungu also gave the advice, 'Take what belongs to you.'

'How would you know?' He had asked N'wamanungu, who just lifted his eyes upwards and indicated to the stars and said, 'She carries herself like a queen. She looks at you when you walk away.'

Slim chances. All these arguments flitted through João's mind but, when the couple eventually came into his clear vision, Schoeman was still holding Tineka's hand.

***

Senhor Albasini hastened his pace and cleared his throat to draw attention to the fact that he was just behind them. Schoeman turned around and as soon as he saw Albasini, he sneered.

'I would like to have a word with you. I have a feeling you have been avoiding me, Senhor Albasini?'

Schoeman lifted his eyebrows and stroked the side of his nose in his customary manner.

'I have two issues.'

He wagged his finger at Senhor Albasini and a sly smile inched its way across his thin lips.

'Number one.' Schoeman let go of Gertina's hand and proceeded to pull the Portuguese flag out of the sheath in front of the shop. 'You, Juwawa, king of the Albasini *Volk,* you have no right to plant a Portuguese flag here. You cannot claim this land as Portuguese territory. Secondly, I have come to inform you that you have breached the laws of this settlement. You will have to pay a hefty fine. You have blatantly defied the laws of Ohrigstad and brought in seven of your *Volk*, armed to the hilt. Have you any idea what danger you have put us into?'

On saying that, he pulled Gertina protectively nearer to himself.

Senhor Albasini looked at Schoeman. His outer expression gave nothing away but, inside him, a red-hot fury was threatening to overturn his outward appearance of calm. The kindling wood feeding the fire was the green-eyed monster and the degradation in front of the girl.

'How much is the fine?'

'250 Riksdalers, to be paid immediately. I'll take the money to *Kommandant* Potgieter.'

Senhor Albasini unclipped a leather pouch from his belt, threw it at Schoeman's feet and proceeded to pick up the flag.

'Keep the change, *Kommandant's* toy-dog. As yet, I can't see any other flag wagging its tail over the sacred ground.

Imagine? Five hundred miserable souls divided in opinion like obstinate mules. Can't even decide on which side of the river to build the town.'

He threw his hand up in the air and pointed two fingers, emphasising each statement he was making. 'Two fortresses for protection, two leaders, two flags, no coordination. No unity! That will be the undoing of these humble and honourable people that I have come to know.'

João snorted, 'While you make up your minds, I will take the opportunity to show you how neutral Portugal is. We believe in *assimilato*, strong leadership and common sense. I am a trader, not a colonist! Do you know what *assimilato* means? It means give everybody a chance in the sun. Live and let live!'

With an exaggerated sweep of the flag, Senhor Albasini placed the flag back into position. He was so cross that he stomped up the stairs, turning his back on Tineka and Schoeman. His only compensation was to see that Tineka's body language was as stiff as the Spanish reeds he had planted at Villa Albasini.

Chapter 10

A proposal

'Let go, let go of me!'

Gertina yelled and tried to stamp her foot but Stephanus had lifted her from the ground leaving her more or less defenceless. His warm tobacco wheeze exploded like a cloud in her face. The sneer on his face made the usually handsome visage change into the grimace of a hellion. She knew instinctively he was going to kiss her.

'Say please!' he whispered threateningly.

No man had ever held her that close. She felt nauseated but did not quite know if it was fear or disgust. Stephanus had her in a steely grip. Terror sharpened her brain. She remembered that antelope would fake death in the claws of a predator only to jump up and run away when released. She went limp.

'That's better, my *kruitjie roer, my nie.*' (A plant which, if touched, closes.)

The odour of his maleness swallowed her. When he forced his lips onto her mouth, she bit with all the ferocity her anger could muster. Stephanus roared and let her go, clasping his lips.

She rushed from the stables as fast as she could, using her skirt to wipe the salty taste of blood from her mouth and spat in the dust. She felt like tearing her clothes from her body. She would do anything to eradicate the experience from her mind.

She was nearing her house and slowed down so as not to draw suspicion. She was calmer now except for Stephanus' last words which tattooed many unanswered question marks in her mind.

'Watch out for Hendrikie, my *kruikie roer my nie.*'

***

A storm was brewing. Dark clouds had dimmed the African sun and the roaring of angry gods fighting in the air anticipated the heavy raindrops that were about to fall. Chickens squawked their way to shelter and women brought in their washing quickly.

Gertina felt relief when Ella didn't even look her way. 'Gertina, I ordered Josekhulu to bring you some hot water. You must wash and tidy yourself. I have put out your best dress.'

'What's the fuss, *Moeder*?'

Ella was wearing her white, impractical muslin apron which was embroidered on the bib and featured a double layer of frills around the bottom. Her mom only wore this special apron when the *dominee* came to visit. She saw the baked milk tart sitting on the sideboard and the aroma of venison cooked with bacon infused in the air.

'Never mind, my child, you will know soon.'

Gertina looked at the table set for six. Her parents, Hendrikie, herself, and who else?

'Are the *Kommandant* and his …,' she nearly said, 'Toy Dog', Senhor Albasini's apt name for Schoeman, but changed it to, 'his wife, coming to dinner?'

'No, Gertina, stop asking. I am keeping it a surprise.'

'Milk tart in the middle of the week? Surely this must be an exceptional guest?'

She could relax. Stephanus would not dare to come and ask for her hand without his mother in tow. She anticipated a proposal but nothing had prepared her for the unpleasant experience she had had that afternoon. It did not matter how evasive she tried to be, he somehow managed to invade her space.

Her mom looked up from polishing the wine goblets and gasped in surprise, 'Gertina, what on earth happened to you? There is blood on your skirt!'

'Nothing to worry about, Mother, I stumbled and fell in the dust.'

A loud clap of thunder reminded her of the apostle Peter hearing the rooster crow but she kept her face blank and continued through the door to her room to wash and get dressed.

A little while later Ella walked into her room holding a small rectangular velvet box. 'This is for your birthday. It belonged to my mother but I want to give it to you today.'

Ella opened the box and took out a short string of pearls. 'I'm glad you have put your hair up.' Ella lifted the curls on Gertina's neck and clasped the necklace into place. Ella took out her hanky and daubed at her eyes. 'You look beautiful and all grown up.'

They looked into the mirror and Ella, who looked at Gertina every day, saw that she had become a woman of remarkable beauty. Against all the odds, she knew that they had made the right choice for this humble but strong-willed niece of Lucas.

'Our visitor has arrived. He is waiting on the front veranda with your father.'

The storm had passed as suddenly as it had come. The rain's aftermath left a freshness in the air with scattered clouds and an African sun to flood the sky with soft pink, lime yellow and purple hues. The faint powdery smell of the honeysuckle creeper, which had wound its way up one of the veranda poles, spilled its perfume like a love elixir over the silhouette of the man casually leaning against the prop.

He had tied his jet-black hair with a piece of leather curling in at the nape of his neck. The smile he gave Gertina was lazy but appreciative. She knew she had made an impression. Likewise, she could not take her eyes off this dazzling man who held her gaze.

She was so pleased it was not Schoeman because she secretly feared her parents had already agreed to an arranged marriage to him. She shuddered at the thought.

Senhor Albasini seemed to have noticed the change in her bearing. His teasing eyes became concerned. He uncrossed his legs and put down the goblet of wine he was holding. He came forward and took Gertina's hand in his. He turned her palm upwards and this time his lips touched her skin as he left a feather-light kiss in the palm of her hand. The man was beyond belief! No other man would be so audacious as to take such a risk. Does he charm all the ladies like this, she wondered?

'Good evening Tineka, I see you have quite grown up.'

She lifted her eyes coquettishly and, with a bravado she did not know she possessed, said, 'Well, treat me like that then.'

Senhor Albasini looked on in total surprise as she turned on her heel and quipped, 'Food is on the table. *Moeder* has taken extra care and we don't want to spoil it.'

The food was delicious and the conversation was somewhat halting because Senhor Albasini was not yet fluent in *Die Taal* but sufficient to thank the hosts. The ladies cleared the dishes while Lucas took the Bible and opened it at a place which he had marked in advance.

'Johannes, I'll be reading from Genesis 2:21,21.'

It was when he began reading the familiar passage of how God took Adam's rib to make a woman that Gertina realised the purpose for Senhor Albasini's visit. She looked to see what his reaction was only to receive a steady gaze of confidence.

So that is how we are going to play the game, she thought. Gertina lifted her chin, looked him directly in the eyes and decided that Senhor Albasini would have to work hard to get her consent.

***

'Gertina,' Lucas said, 'Johannes would like a word with you in private. We will leave and go to bed. *Kom Vrou.*' He took the lamp and left Gertina, Senhor Albasini and the *opsit kers* (a candle which was burned to determine the length of a suiter or sweetheart's visit).

Gertina and Albasini sat opposite each other. The dim light of the candle's flame painted figurines of two people dancing the waltz of love on the walls, teasing and flirting with each other, mimicking each other's fears and uncertainties, unsure of the other person's feelings. It was an unfamiliar emotion and she yearned to sit nearer to Juwawa. If only she could just put her hand against his cheek and tell him how attracted she was to him. But there was doubt.

Senhor Albasini said, 'You are beautiful.' He took the ruby ring she had noticed on the first day of their acquaintance from his pinkie, looked at it, kissed it and gently nudged it in her direction across the table. In perfect *Taal*, he said simply, 'Will you marry me?'

She was quiet for a while before she pushed the ring back and said firmly, 'No.'

Even in the dim candlelight she could see a flush creep up into Juwawa's face. He took the ring back and rolled it towards her again. 'Perhaps you have not understood me clearly, Tineka.' He asked again, 'Will you marry me?'

'No,' she replied with a tremble in her voice and her eyes nearly closed. The diamonds and ruby sparked in the weak light as she rolled it back to him a second time.

He stood up from his chair, picked up the ring, walked over to her and gently gathered her to him. 'Give me your right hand, Tineka. He cradled her hand with incredible gentleness and pushed the centuries-old heirloom into place. He contemplated what he had done before pulling her even closer into the circle of his arm.

She fitted neatly into his form and a warmth engulfed her. He was so right for her but she had so many doubts. How can someone be so rich? Was it only from selling ivory? She heard gossip of the possible slave trade. How many women were there in his life? He belonged to another faith. A small consolation was the fact that it did not bother her parents. Her mind kept spinning with all these questions. Will he become a *Voortrekker*? Will he accept my faith? He was from another nationality and the Bible says, '*Do not be unevenly yoked.*'

All her misgivings evaporated when Senhor Albasini placed a soft kiss on her neck, turned her around and said, 'Believe it or not, my destiny is to die in your arms. The *dolosse* (the witchdoctor's bones) predicted it.'

There was a firmness in his voice when he changed the wording of the question to a statement. 'You will marry me.' He lowered his head and kissed her with a tenderness beyond belief. He whispered in her ear the Italian, '*Sei mio.*' (You are mine.)

***

Suddenly she had no misgivings. Juwawa's touch was not forceful, like Schoeman's. Albasini guided and caressed at the same time. She knew for a certainty that he would take care of her.

Gertina stood on tiptoe and reached for the scar on his eyebrow. She gave in to the temptation of wanting to be near him and, with feather-light fingers, touched the spot. She moulded herself even closer to him. She wanted to feel his body, the pulse beneath the soft shirt and wished to feel his heart beating in time with hers.

Still touching the scar, she said: 'If only I could have been there, I would have nursed it for you. Will you tell me what happened?'

The flaw made the handsome face even more attractive and excitement welled up in her. It will be dangerous to be married to this man, she thought, but the pull was too strong for her to resist. She dropped her hands to feel the dark stubble on his skin as she cupped his face and returned his kiss with passion.

'Yes, Juwawa, King of the *Knopneuse*,' she paused, 'my king. I will marry you.'

Senhor Albasini groaned and held her even closer.

'Before I can kiss you again, I need to tell you about the rings. The ring I gave you belonged to my mother. It comes from my father's family who fled from Tyrol in Italy. The last time I saw my father he told me how his family crossed the borders herding their flocks of sheep and hiding the family jewels in hollowed-out staffs.'

He unbuttoned his cotton shirt and Gertina saw his muscled torso draped by a string of beads and a leather rope on which a brooch was clasped together with a ring similar to the one she was now wearing. She saw that the rings came as a pair and João proceeded to explain the inscription. 'This is how I would like our marriage to be.'

He took his ring and showed her the inscription, '*Manus un Manu*, which means 'hand in hand', and yours *Pari Passu*, which means 'with an equal step for all'.'

He put his ring on his finger and kissed her with intent.

'Let's go and tell your parents and Hendrik the excellent news. I have to take care of urgent business. I'll be away from you but I promise I'll be back one year from now. I will have mastered *Die Taal* and you do not have to change your faith. We can bring up our children as Protestants, but I will remain *Catolico.*'

***

While her spirit was still flying high, she knitted the memories of the beautiful three days she had spent getting to know Juwawa as a friend, a lover and a fiancé firmly in her mind. There was much laughter, teasing and kissing.

Early on the morning of her seventeenth birthday, she met Juwawa before he left on his journey. He stood next to his white mule ready to go. As soon as he spotted her, he ran, picked her up and smothered her with kisses. The moment was too precious to say anything. The delicate embrace embodied mutual feeling.

Juwawa bent down and smoothed her tears away. 'Don't cry, my Tineka. I will love you until my last breath. I'll be back. God saved me to do greater things than hunt. Together we will reach the heights designed for us in this universe.'

Josekhulu handed him a small posy of dried veld flowers tied with a piece of lace. Attached to flowers was a small leather pouch. 'It is time to go, Juwawa. I will take care of her.'

'Take this, the love of my life. There is enough gold in there to help in time of need. Use it at your discretion. One year, take or leave a few months, and I'll be back.'

Chapter 11

A disaster avoided

That same afternoon, with the gymkhana already in full swing, Schoeman approached her. He had a foul expression on his face as took her by the elbow and led her to a secluded spot.

'I believe you have engaged yourself to that scumbag of a *Porra*! I thought of you as being noble and righteous but how the mighty have fallen.' The familiar sneer streaked his face. 'The swine has the cheek to come and steal you away. How much did he pay you? Perhaps enough to honour your stepfather's debts? I'm warning you, watch out for Hendrikie. The *Kappie Brigade* told me you have to wait one year. I will also wait this one year and then, if the *verdomde* foreigner does not turn up, you, your brother, your father and I will have to have a little chat and I will not take 'No' for an answer.'

Gertina, mortified, asked, 'What do you mean about my father's debts, and what is it about Hendrikie? You are hurting me, Stephanus, let me go immediately.' She felt her cheeks becoming hot and she held back the tears she felt coming to her eyes. She would not give him the satisfaction to see how much he had upset her. 'We never had an agreement and never will.'

Josekhulu appeared with a dish full of kebabs. 'Senhorita, where would you like me to put these?'

Gertina marvelled at the ability of Josekhulu to always appear when she needed him most. She had an escape but only after Schoeman warned ominously, 'Gertina! I can promise you, one year from now I will marry you.' Schoeman endorsed his intent by holding her chin between his thumb and forefinger, adding,' You can rest assured I will make sure of that, come hell or high water.'

***

From that day onwards the harassment started. Whenever he saw her walking in the street, at music practices for the church or on any other occasion when he had an opportunity, Schoeman would show how many months were left. Then it became weeks and, finally, days.

Today Schoeman had walked past her, removed his hat, laughed in her face and, without saying a word, pointed his finger in the air to indicate just one day remaining.

'How much money is owing?' she asked on impulse.

'Money is not the object, my dear, you are.'

He emphasised the 'you' by emphatically pulling her nearer to him. 'Refuse,' he smirked, 'and I will tell the church elders of the 'For Yous' that mysteriously disappeared. We might as well have our commandments being read out in church.'

Josekhulu was ready to strike if anything happened to Gertina but Juwawa had warned him to think before he acted. Instead, he shadowed her to the bakery.

***

The day couldn't have begun more miserably. It was now three months after her birthday and Juwawa had not yet returned. The veld was tinder dry and the wind swept down the gravel street blowing dust into small puffs of red powder to swirl in the air. The spiky remnants of knee-high grass standing on the median strip looked like hostile broken-down soldiers snarling at the wagons as they left the God-forsaken, ill-fated Ohrigstad. The potholes were so big that little children would hide in them, scaring the drivers of odd wagons which passed.

Ohrigstad was giving its death rattle. Some families had already departed to begin a new life in Lydenburg's new town, mostly followers of Burghers, while others, swept up by Schoeman's propaganda stories of immense wealth, trade in ivory and the indomitable spirit of adventure were either preparing to or had already left for the Zoutpanzberg district.

On Lucas' arm and with Ella trailing behind her, they plodded to the church. It was her wedding day. She had taken Juwawa's ring off and hung it on a piece of string around her neck under her clothes. He had said she was his and, in her heart, she knew he was hers.

Circumstances made Gertina believe that João had exchanged the present for the everlasting. Schoeman's use of blackmail had forced her into a situation she could not ignore. She now had other responsibilities.

Schoeman had given her an engagement ring. It was a vulgar looking atrocity. The decorations were elaborate and she knew he had bought it to show off his wealth but Gertina refused to wear it.

'If I am to be your wife, sell this eyesore and give the money to the widows and their children who cannot escape the dreariness of this place. That is what a true leader would do,' she said.

Schoeman harrumphed and said grudgingly, surprising Gertina, 'I'll do just that and show them what a dedicated people's choice you will be.' He had cleverly taken her defiance and turned it around to use it as a stepping stone to his ultimate goal, to become President of the republic.

Her bottom lip trembled and she kept fumbling with her hanky. Ella said, 'I have raised you as my own and I love you and Hendrikie more than I would have done my own because your lives have not been easy. You know, my dear Gertina, it is not too late. You can still wait for Johannes.'

'It is no good, *Moeder*. It is now more than a month since Josekhulu left to look for him or find out what has happened and they have not returned. Mario also does not know. The only thing Senhor Albasini told him was to count their losses here and start a new shop in Lydenburg.' She hugged her mother and whispered in her ear, 'Just believe me, I have to marry Schoeman,' putting the emphasis on the word 'have'.

***

They entered the church and the proceedings commenced. The *dominee* who had come from Potchefstroom to marry them reached the point where he said, "if anyone can show just cause why this couple cannot lawfully be joined together in matrimony, let them speak now or forever hold their peace."

At that moment, there was an almighty noise as the church doors were thrown open and a bloodied Senhor Albasini, waving papers in his hand, was carried to the altar by N'wamanungu,. He looked to be in a state of delirium, his green eyes burning with fever. He choked out a weak, 'Yes. Yes. I have.'

He could barely stand. He crossed himself before stating his case in halting sentences. 'I cannot hold my peace. It will be so wrong for *Meneer* Schoeman to marry the young girl, Gertina Maria Pitronella Janse van Rensburg.'

The few people attending the ceremony gasped and were confused by the arrival of this 'stranger'. They recognised Senhor Albasini, but a very different one from the man they had known previously. His clothes were dirty and torn, and

138

his hair, usually immaculately coifed, looked grimy and caked with blood.

Gertina closed her eyes and thought she was going to faint. 'Dear Lord,' she prayed, 'I believe in miracles. Please let my Juwawa understand that I had no choice and, please Lord, let the causes he is about to lay before the *dominee* and church leaders be valid.'

The attendants were shocked into silence and, after the *dominee* had discussions with the leaders and Lucas, said, 'I believe you are Senhor Albasini, previously betrothed to this young woman. You may proceed with your objections.'

The look on João's face was grim. He started, 'I have here in my midst several documents. First, *Meneer* Schoeman is still legally married to Christina Helena du Preez. She was placed in an asylum by *Meneer* Schoeman, hoping that it would not be discovered. Sadly, he never applied to be divorced from her.'

He took a pause and shifted his stance, wincing from the pain. 'Secondly, if a marriage should go ahead, it would be against the law, but not only that, the children will bear the sins of their forefathers up to the fifth generation. Miss Gertina Maria Pitronella Janse van Rensburg and Stephanus Schoeman are first cousins. Their mothers are sisters. Unfortunately, I have to give you the following information that very few people know. Gertina and her brother were saved from the van Rensburg massacre and are Lucas and Ella van Rensburg's adopted children.

'Thirdly, I have evidence that Gertina offered to pay her father's and her brother's debts but Schoeman refused her offer, thus resorting to blackmail to force Gertina to marry him.'

The *dominee's* face contracted in disbelief. The guests sitting in the pews choked with surprise, eagerly awaiting the outcome.

'Is that all?' the *dominee* asked.

Before anybody could do anything, Stephanus dropped to his knees and grabbed Gertina by the waist. 'No, no. Please listen to me.' It was an agonising, nearly hysterical cry from Schoeman. 'My Gertina, please forgive me. I did not know that Chrissie was still alive and there was no communication between us. Therefore, I had no means to know. I love you more than anything in the world. Being first cousins, I can do nothing about that. We cannot marry. Lastly, I would have taken good care of your family.'

Gertina did not know what to feel, elated by fleeing the trap, utter joy at seeing Juwawa, or to rant and grab Juwawa by his scruffy hair and ask him, 'What took you so long, Chief of the *Knopneuse*?'

The proceedings adjourned and the *Kappie Brigade* had much fuel for their discussions. This extraordinary event was definitely a tale to be told to the grandchildren.

Senhor Albasini collapsed. When he revived, Gertina was busy bathing his wounds. 'How soon can we be married?' she asked.

Senhor Albasini was surprised at her haste. She cast her head down, not looking him in the eyes.

Chapter 12

A wedding

It so happened that when a *landdrost*, a Boer magistrate from Rustenburg, visited Lydenburg João took the opportunity to respect Gertina's wishes to get married as soon as possible and so a civil marriage took place without any fuss.

Senhor Albasini was puzzled by Gertina's aloofness but thought to give her time to adjust to married life.

'Gertina, I would like to see you in my study at ten o'clock sharp. We have some business to discuss.'

Gertina looked up from where she was busy mending some clothes.

Senhor Albasini could hardly bear to look at his wife. He loved her so much and yet he had the feeling something was amiss. When she spoke to him she cast her eyes down most of the time. He heard her laughing when she talked to Mario and Trui but her sentences were stilted when she spoke to him. She stood stiff in his embraces and João sensed that something must be wrong. He had some idea of what it could be and was determined to get to the bottom of the problem.

The mail from Potchefstroom fuelled his anger. He recognised the handwriting on an elaborately decorated envelope smelling of lavender immediately. The scrawl was that of 'Snotklap' Schoeman.

João was ready to murder. He hated himself for calling her Gertina and hoped he would never have to do that again. The sound grated his ears and the fact that Gertina still had contact with Schoeman was unacceptable to him. He felt physically sick and ordered Mario to close the shop and not allow anybody to enter. Everyone had to leave the moment after Gertina arrived.

He sat down at his desk and poured himself a large glass of port. He banged the glass down on the desk to vent his frustration. How could she? Did love so blind him that he could not see through her deceit? Well, he was about to show her exactly who she had married.

'De Sousa, bring me that roll of taffeta that I told you not to sell, and the shoes.'

His friend and mentor never calls him De Sousa. One would think that he, Mario, had committed the worst crime ever. But hearing Senhor Albasini's request, he knew he had some delicate negotiation to undertake.

'Ah, Juwawa, what worm has crawled into your fruit this morning? I'm afraid I sold the taffeta.'

'And the shoes?' João asked.

' Yes, they've gone as well.'

'You did what? '

'Yes, I did. We thought you were never going to return and I had to make the transport of goods to Lydenburg as smooth and cost effective as possible.'

Senhor Albasini's eyebrows lifted a fraction, still questioning the sale of the cornflower blue material. 'In that case, see that Gertina gets whatever she needs to make a beautiful wedding dress. No flower girls or bridesmaids. There must be no uncertainty; I tell you there must be no uncertainty whatsoever as to who she had married in front of the *Landdrost* in Lydenburg. The church wedding will take place early in the New Year. There will be celebrations like no one has ever seen before. The old *Kappie Brigade* will wag their tongues till doomsday. Start organising. Get the church at Potchefstroom booked for the wedding. I want it to coincide with the first *Nachtmaal* in the year, 6th of March. My wagons should be ready to take on the move to the Great North by then.'

Mario tried to appease João. He had never seen him so upset. 'Can I pour you another glass of port?'

'Get the hell out of here and leave me alone!'

Mario hesitated but the Senhor waved him away impatiently. 'What's the matter, have you got lead in your feet? Get a move on planning a wedding for one thousand people or more. Make sure you invite Domingos, the Governor. Have the best port and cigars delivered to his accommodation. Let his party stay in Mario's *dorphuis*. Then there is the architect von Marnecke, Carl Mauch the scientist and explorer.

'Don't forget the President of the Transvaal, whoever is the flavour of the month at that time. It seems the election of a President changes at a whim. Ask *Dominee* de Clerq if he will marry us, and I want the elders Nel and Fourie to be witnesses. My wagons will be ready in three months to move to Zoutpanzberg. I have never been in favour of a civil marriage ceremony but these people are in for a surprise. Everybody will witness a proper church wedding with bells and whistles.

'Get N'wamanungu, Josekhulu and Monene to organise a feast for my followers. They will be waiting on the outskirts of Potchefstroom. It is time I introduce them to my wife! Understood?'

Senhor Albasini ignored Mario when he left the room quietly closing the door behind him. João refilled his glass and gazed at the label as he put the bottle down - the warm liquid running down his throat scorched instead of soothing him.

He was about to put the glass down when the anger burning inside got the better of him. He hurled the glass against the wall and, for good measure, he let the bottle go the same way. 'There goes my best bottle of Taylor & Fladgate port.'

***

Gertina stood in the doorway. Her blue eyes looked at João accusingly. Senhor Albasini felt embarrassed and shy. Gertina had caught him in an uncontrollable act of childish foolishness, something very foreign to him. He prided himself on always being in control of his emotions unless it suited him to do otherwise.

He moved towards his desk and opened the drawer noisily. The offensive, lavender-smelling letter sat there like an adder ready to strike. 'Explain, young lady.' He flipped the letter towards her. 'It seems that a civil marriage is not enough to have your loyalty. Do you want more? What more can I give you? Explain why you wanted to marry me so hastily.'

He waited before continuing, 'Perhaps you don't even have to do that. Lya reported to N'wamanungu that your monthly rags were exceptionally more soiled than customary. Tell me,' Senhor Albasini's voice was icy, 'did that serpent, Schoeman, manage to put you in a delicate condition after all? Answer me!'

'Juwawa!' She paused to let her words sink in. Her face was ashen and the corners of her mouth turned down. Her shoulders lifted ever so slightly showing how awkward she felt. 'You were away for one year, nine weeks and two days. Not so? We had an agreement for one year!'

Her voice rose a little and the blue eyes kept asking questions. 'Let me put it this way. What do soiled rags indicate?'

He did not answer but went on the counterattack, 'Yes, we did agree on one year, give or take. Thank N'wamanungu for carrying me for more than five miles, saving you from marrying that bombastic son of a bitch,' he added

146

sarcastically, not even attempting to hide the use of swear words in front of a lady.

Gertina stood her ground. 'You have had too much to drink. You should thank me. Did I not nurse you to life again?'

Senhor Albasini ignored her and said, 'Read the letter.'

Gertina looked at the jagged edge of the opened envelope. 'It seems that since you saw me emptying my chamber pot, you take it upon yourself to spy on my every move. Since the letter is open, why don't you tell me what you read? That might explain your unreasonable anger.

'I don't stoop to snakehead tactics.'

Senhor Albasini was confused and could not rationalise his feelings. The only thing he wanted to do was to kiss this beautiful girl. He walked around the desk and did just that.

Outside Mario heard the door jambs rattle as the door shut with a bang.

***

Guests packed the church to capacity. They opened the windows wide so that the overflow of guests who sat on makeshift benches and chairs flanking both sides of the church could participate in the service.

The well-cut, dark blue woollen tailcoat tailored to perfection showed João's superb physique of broad shoulders and narrow hips. Pin-striped pants complemented the tailcoat. The pride in his stance was there for all to see as well as the increased heels of his shoes to make him look taller than his 5 feet 8 inches.

Tommy, who had grown into a lean, broad-shouldered and handsome young man, stood on his left-hand side while the modest Mario, who held the rings, stood to the right. The wedding bands sparkled on a dark blue, gold-festooned cushion, embroidered with the motto, *Manus un Manus* and *Pari Passu*. The gold trimmings paled at the magnificence of the two ruby rings which glinted mischievously in the morning sun welcoming a new chapter of two souls becoming one.

Mario whispered, 'Take your hands out of your pockets. It is bad manners. Don't look back until the music starts playing, you know that is bad luck.' And finally, 'If you fiddle with that bunch of flowers on your lapel again, they might just fall off.'

From the pocket of the cream coloured silk waistcoat, João took out his 18-carat gold fob watch, flipped it open and groaned quietly, 'She's late by twelve minutes and twenty-two seconds.'

Tom and Mario both shrugged their shoulders and Mario quipped, 'You made her wait a whole year, what do a few minutes matter?'

'It damned well matters a lot. I've waited all my life for this moment.'

João put his hands behind his back to keep them still and concentrated on the hand-carved wooden pulpit in front of him. The two violinists standing at the front of the church took up their instruments and started to play Psalm 123.

The beautiful words spoke to João's heart.

'May the blessings of God be yours,
All the days of your life;
May the peace and the love of God
always live in your heart.'

He was so sure of his love for Tineka but did she feel the same for him? Had he been too forceful? Their cultures were so different. He was an extrovert, she an introvert. He would indeed need the blessings of God.

Well, he thought, I love a challenge. He had waited for Tineka's spontaneous response but the marriage bed was still cold. Perhaps he did not have to wait that much longer. A church marriage would undoubtedly cement the union.

When the music stopped he turned around slowly and there she stood in the doorway, Lucas holding her by the arm gently. She moved forward slowly, her gaze fixed solely on him. His heart leaped and he stood mesmerised.

She did not waver in her slow, determined steps towards the pulpit. She was breathtakingly beautiful. Tineka had piled her corn-coloured hair up into a bunch of curls held in place by tiny veld daisies. She wore his mother's tiara that he had sent her and, with renewed respect for his friend Mario, he realised Tineka's dress flaunted the blue taffeta in which he had initially envisaged her. The skirt was high-waisted and plain, shorter at the front to show her small feet encased in cream coloured, flat Napa leather shoes. They were the shoes that he had forbidden Mario to sell because he hoped to give them to her one day. The cape trailed behind her in a short train, sewn in the same cream silk as his waistcoat. Mario, with his attention to detail, had added yet another touch of class. The simplicity of her outfit enhanced her beauty.

A feeling of utter joy engulfed João. He knew this was the happiest moment in his life. No wealth, no status in life, nothing could bring him more excitement, knowing he would never be alone again. He had somebody to treasure, somebody to spoil and, above all, somebody to love. He was excited.

When Lucas handed her to him, João bent down and whispered in the language made for love, *'Ti amero finche ho vita.'* (I will love you while I still have life.)

Dominee de Clerq, at the request of João, took the passage about Naomi and Ruth, declaring that *Jonge heer* (young man) Johannes had taken the same viewpoint as Ruth,

'Where you go, I will go, and where you stay, I will stay. Your people will be my people and your God my God. Where you die, I will die, and there I will be buried.'

When João kissed the bride, there were spontaneous cries of *Die Taal's* '*Hoor, hoor*' and some Portuguese '*Ouca ouca*'. (Hear, hear.)

A shout came from the distant *Knopneuse* camp and the magic message reverberated in the beating of the drums. A cry of reverence, '*Bayete Inkoshi*' (Be greeted, our King and Chief) drifted to the ears of the surprised guests at what would be the most distinguished wedding of the year.

Chapter 13

Blessings and curses

'You are in a good mood, Juwawa?'

Juwawa lifted her from the gig into his arms and kept whispering words she could not understand. She guessed it must be Italian.

'Mmm, *ja, ja.* How else, my dream has come true. We are now together till death do us part.'

He started to sing while carrying her to a tent pitched under an acacia tree. Cradled in his arms, she was surprised at how easily she had allowed one hand to unbutton his waistcoat. The silkiness of the beautiful material was sensuous to her palm. She let her hand slip inside the waistcoat and felt his rhythmic heartbeat throbbing against the inside of her wrist, generating a tickling of excitement that glowed in her stomach.

A state of frenzy overwhelmed her when his hand trailed down her back as he lowered her to the ground. She did not want to part and so she lingered, afraid of what her body told her she desired. She needed this bonding, this feeling of belonging. The ambience of Juwawa's total protection soothed her uncertainties. He would lead and she would follow. She left Juwawa's embrace reluctantly, not wanting to separate from the pleasant aroma of her husband's scent, cigar smoke, good port wine and male arousal. He led her to a table set for two under the tree.

With sure, deft hands, Juwawa took the champagne bottle and eased out the cork. The sparkle continued as he poured the wine into the crystal glasses. When some drops fell onto the linen tablecloth, Juwawa smoothed it away and lifted his glass in salute.

'To our future.'

After having a tentative sip, she stood up and walked to Juwawa's side of the table. She cupped his face and placed a soft kiss on his lips, tasting the sweetness of the evaporated bubbles.

'Thank you for choosing me.'

Juwawa pulled away and flushed profoundly as he crossed his arms. He gave a nervous laugh and said, 'First things first. As soon as we have had our meal, you are to enter the tent. My tent, which will eventually become our tent for the trek's duration, is pitched about five hundred metres away from yours. Lya is waiting inside your tent to prepare you for how my *Knopneuse* want me to receive you as my wife. It is nothing you should worry about. It's just a tradition they want me to follow. How do you feel about that?'

'Juwawa, did you not say where I go you will follow? So, the same goes for me. Where you go, I will follow.'

Gertina was surprised at Juwawa's embarrassment. He seemed so confident in the company of other women, always joking and flirting. She could not fathom why he was so uncomfortable with her and yet, when he kissed her, the magic started. I will have to remedy that, she thought, I like the magic.

After the meal, Juwawa stood up and came to take her in his arms, giving her a long and lingering kiss.

'Let the *Knopneuse's* tradition work its wonders.'

He opened the tent flaps and indicated she should enter. Gertina was surprised. A mattress lumped by straw lay to one side, but she could hardly move because wedding presents filled the tent. It had already turned dark and Lya waited, arms folded, sitting on the trousseau chest. Ella had worked endlessly to fill the trunk with sheets, blankets, soap and various other items.

***

Lya was a young Xhosa girl who fled with her father to seek refuge under João's protection. Her father succumbed to the wounds inflicted on him soon after their arrival. João took pity on the sprightly little girl and gave instructions that she have her own room in Villa Albasini and help with the cooking. When he married Gertina he brought Lya to Ohrigstad to be a companion and help to Gertina.

'I see you, Senhora Albasini,' Lya said before proceeding to offer some advice: 'You must be clever. Come back to sleep here tonight, even if you desire to please your husband. That must wait until tomorrow night.'

Some of the Portuguese wedding guests had called her Senhora but this was the first time anyone among Juwawa's followers had called her Senhora. She felt elevated and important.

'Do you mean me and the Senhor will not sleep here tonight?'

'Listen carefully. The Indunas will give a sign and then you must go and collect your wedding presents from your husband. As soon as the full moon gives good light, you will see that the Senhor had put a present down every few yards for you to open. If you like it, you keep it. You can just leave it there and I will collect it for you, but if you don't like it, you must turn back to the tent and let the Senhor try to lure you to his tent again.'

'But honestly, I do not understand. Why have we got a mattress in the tent? Will Juwawa not join me here tonight?'

'If you are a fool, yes, he can join you, but these presents, according to custom, will be yours for life to do with as you please. It is... How can I put it? It is your insurance. If he should suddenly die or he beats you and you want to return to your family, he cannot take anything back. So, make sure he gives you enough to last you a lifetime.'

Gertina had never heard of this custom before in her life and slowly started to smile. 'I wonder what Senhor Albasini can still give me. He has already been very good to my family and me.'

'Oh, and another thing, you must pick a fight with him tomorrow to see if he loves you. Then tomorrow evening, eh, the same thing happens again. If you are satisfied, you then go into Juwawa's tent and the *Knopneuse* can look forward to a stone in your belly.'

***

Gertina undressed and put on a simple, lightweight cotton nightdress and observed the chilly evening night. When the moon's face was shining bright and on Lya's command, she left her tent and, to her surprise, a few yards from the tent stood a wagon a little smaller than the ones the settlers used.

It was impossible, she couldn't believe it! Juwawa could not possibly give her a wagon - that was too big a present to accept.

'Do you like it?' Lya asked. 'The Indunas chopped off acacia branches to hide the wagon but N'wamanungu said he hoped you will have eyes only for Juwawa and won't see anything else.'

Gertina was dumbfounded and walked around the wagon. In the bright moonlight she saw the Albasini logo, except it did not have the triple A but instead **Senhora G.P.M. Albasini** painted in gold and black. Before she could answer, Lya urged, 'Come, come Senhora, there are many more.'

The moment was too overwhelming for her to absorb it all. She almost walked into a stick planted in the rough path. On closer examination she saw something tied to the stake. It was a key that she presumed would be used to unlock a pretty casket standing on a table a few metres away. The gold casket adorned with rows of pearls zig-zagging across the lid invited her to unlock its treasures.

She unlocked the case. On top of magnificent strings of pearls, rings and earrings lay a card in Juwawa's copperplate handwriting which simply stated,

Belonged to the only other woman I ever loved, my mother, now belonging to the only woman I will ever love.

She closed the lid in amazement and stepped towards the other gifts which were set out at intervals along the path. They included two beautiful patchwork coverlets, blankets, a butter churner and other household goods.

She could see Juwawa's silhouette dancing against the walls of his tent and wondered how far she still had to go before she had to turn back. She had no intention to do so because she was so grateful for everything given to her. The next present was a hessian bag and, when she inspected it, she realised that it was a bag of coffee beans sufficient to brew coffee for a whole year! She sank down onto the bag, let out a contented sigh and was about to get up when ten indunas led by Josekhulu knelt by her feet.

N'wamanungu came forward looking majestic in his traditional war garb. 'This is for you, Senhora, to hold close to your heart. The leopard skin will show that you belong to our father, Juwawa, King of the *Knopneuse*.'

Josekhulu came next and gave her a necklace of intricately woven beadwork. The bright colours made Gertina smile.

'The wives of the indunas designed it with a lot of blue and yellow. The blue colour says you will be royal and the yellow beads show how rich you are. They also say that if you interpret yellow wrongly, you can land yourself in trouble. The yellow gives you a warning not to be jealous. You must trust implicitly. Jealousy is powerful, it can destroy love. You will sleep well, little one. Juwawa still has to give you more. He paid no *Labola* (a ransom for the bride) so he cannot have it that easy.'

Gertina chuckled. Her smile was welcoming as each induna brought a present to lay at her feet. The last to give her a gift was Monene, a jovial character who made everyone laugh as he dumped a goat, feet tied, in front of Gertina. The goat bleated and Gertina jumped up in surprise. She did not quite know what to do but acknowledged their presents and well wishes.

'I am also an orphan saved by Juwawa, and I will serve him and you.'

***

The shadows across the canvass of the tent shimmied in the light of the early morning sun, reminding Gertina of how her thoughts were scuttling here, there and nowhere.

I'm married and yet not married. The strange events of the previous night and the idea of picking a fight with Juwawa when she had no desire to do so made her gloomy. She just wished to lie in his arms.

She sat bolt upright in her bed and thought of the letter she had received. It had the same lavender smell and the same scrawly handwriting as the previous one. Unlike the other envelope that she received in Lydenburg, which made Senhor Albasini act so strangely, this letter was sealed. One of the elders of the church had handed it to her discreetly. She tucked it away in the pocket of her gown and now looked to retrieve it.

The contents of the letter were disturbing. Gertina thought it was now or never but she had to find out the truth from Juwawa as soon as she could. After drinking a mug of coffee and refusing the lavish breakfast, she asked, 'Lya, where can I find the Senhor this morning? You said I am to pick a fight with him.'

'You can wait for him in the tent that he uses to write all his letters. You will see it is the smaller of the two tents.'

With every step in her haste to see Juwawa, Gertina was sure there would be an explanation to all the accusations made in the letter. She caught sight of a bright red wagon parked in the shadows of some acacia trees. The wagon looked like a house on wheels and even had a chimney. It was so different from the jaw-shaped simplistic *Voortrekker* wagons drawn by oxen. The marigold yellow door stood ajar and on the steps were two women dressed in luxurious, multi-coloured flowing dresses. She could see golden armbands shimmering in the sun as the woman nearest to the door flung her arms around Juwawa's neck and pulled him inside the inviting grotto. Gertina's first and only thought was, that is my husband and only mine! She had never before encountered whores in her life but, from what she knew from her Bible, she was sure that was precisely what those two women were.

Even if it took her all day, she would wait for Juwawa in his tent.

***

She heard his firm footsteps walking in rhythm to the tune he was whistling as he neared the tent. The flap opened and Senhor Albasini entered, striking in all his handsomeness in front of her. It was unfair that a man could be so good-looking. His welcoming smile and readiness to embrace her nearly made her lose her resolve to sort things out. She had to draw a line in the sand.

'What a charming surprise, my Tineka. What makes you visit me so early in the morning? I thought we could wait until this evening.'

Senhor Albasini's voice was seductively tantalising as he spoke *Die Taal* with his foreign accent.

'I have here evidence of you buying and selling slaves. What does that mean? Have I married a slave trader?'

Senhor Albasini stopped in his tracks and a deep frown creased the smooth forehead. Gertina saw him struggle to find words.

He drawled, 'What? What, may I ask, gives you the idea that I am a slave trader, and may I kindly see the evidence?'

She pulled out the invoice and offered it to Senhor Albasini. 'Is that how you make your endless money to give such an extravagant wedding and lavish me with unheard of riches?'

She wasn't sure if it was her hand or his that was trembling. The noisy paper and the sound of tense breathing made her feel as if she was walking over a river coming down in flood but not quite sure when it would rage in full force.

The voice was honey sweet when he asked, 'Anything else?'

Mortified, Gertina pushed forward. Her finger came down on a document that she had removed from the drawer in his neatly arranged desk. 'This?'

In bold letters at the top of the page stood ***Casa Prostituta*** Punda Maria. It was a contract and she had seen Juwawa's signature at the bottom.

'Explain, if you please. Were you having a good time this morning with the two women in that crab-looking wagon? I saw you entering the wagon with a woman snaking her arm around your neck. How can you explain that?'

A deathly silence was disturbed by Senhor Albasini's controlled whisper. She saw him inhaling before he said, 'I recognise snakeskin Schoeman's scrawl. It smells like the pissed ink of the hyena. Typically, a fighter with no backbone. He has to crawl in the lion's dung to feed himself. His poison has oozed through your soul, taking away reason and killing your charming nature. What must I do to eradicate this disease from your pretty head? Look at me, Gertina!'

He grabbed her by the wrists and pulled her close. She could hardly bear to be so near to him but she would get an answer, of that she was sure. 'Do you see this mark on my eyebrow? The one that you so fondly caressed and gave me hope that I may love you.'

He took her hand and made her feel the scar on his eyebrow. 'Feel for yourself, dear woman. Let me tell you about it. Shoshangane's men bashed my head against a wooden door until it opened. The rusted nail in the door chose to give me a Cain's mark. They kept me for six months as a slave and a glorified jester in chains. Shackled, bored to death, and in fear that they may discover I had deceived them by acting like a mad man.

'They don't suffer a fool; they anoint you with hippo fat for the pot or spike you on a stake for later use. They cut out the molars and use them in necklaces to boast about their achievements. They did this to my friends. Imagine looking at some of the men and recognising your friend Filipe's gold-filled tooth hanging around the neck of one of the savages. Come on, think for yourself.'

He let go of her momentarily and then said, 'Look at these.' He pulled up one sleeve to show her the indelible marks of iron shackles on his wrist. 'N'wamanungu saved me and gave me life again. Do you for a moment think…,' he stopped to breathe. 'Would I stoop so low as to enslave these creatures who are war-fatigued, constantly living in fear and who look upon me as a saviour? Do you think I would sell them for one pound ten shillings apiece or to the highest bidder? Do you? When I have been a slave myself?'

He let go of her as if he were holding a hot iron. He clasped his hands over his face in despair. He continued, 'Who gave you the right to come snooping in my private matters? Trust is a building block of a good marriage. It would have given me great pleasure to share my business ventures with you. I even appreciate your cunning business mind. Did you marry me for riches, or was it to escape the shame of pre-nuptial dangling, or did you marry just for the thrill of it?'

Gertina pointed at the piece of paper on his desk. 'And this? What kind of contracts do you sign with a house for prostitution?'

'You need to do some growing up, my girl. Maria is a good friend of mine and, yes, she owns the Casa Prostituta near Zoutpanzberg. I signed the contract. I will open a shop next to her as most of my business will be concentrated in the north near Sofala, Qualimane and Inhambane. You may go. I will keep my side of the promise I made at the altar in front of your people, but you are welcome to stay.'

Gertina did not know what to think. She felt embarrassed and sad. This is not how it should be between man and wife. She ran out of the tent leaving the fuming Senhor Albasini still spluttering explanations. When she came near to her tent, it was comforting to see Lya waiting for her. At least she would have somebody to talk to and ask for advice. She would let Lya call Josekulu and instinctively knew that these two friends would be able to explain any misgivings she had about Senhor Albasini.

Chapter 14

Conflict and reconciliation

The next morning, the dark clouds boxed themselves into a clapping frenzy of lightning strikes and with them came the rain. Gertina sat on her make-shift knobbly mattress regretting her impulsiveness. Like the welcoming rain, she wished with all her heart that she could retract the accusations and bring relief to the tension between herself and Juwawa. Her heart was heavy, she felt miserable and she just wanted to hide but there was nowhere to go. Most of all she thought that she had been unfair to Juwawa.

Her puffy, swollen eyes were evidence of deep inward thought. She had jumped to conclusions, believing the clever, convincing Stephanus. She was wrong and hadn't even allowed Juwawa to defend himself. There was only one thing to do and that was to seek him out immediately and ask for his forgiveness and a second chance.

After the storm passed, João rolled open the tent door and was busy securing the ties when he saw Gertina picking her way carefully through the puddles left by the heavy rain. He knew he could never love anyone else. He dreamed of having a son, a son to carry Portugal's flag and plant it in the rich soils of Magashulaskraal, a *Cologne* for King Luiz and Portugal. He set his heart on having a bambino Antonio who could take over the reins and be the next leader of his tribal followers. He still cringed from Gertina's verbal assault which implied that he was a slave trader and adulterer.

Caressing her and bringing her to the full ripeness of her body was not to be. He was surprised at her return and wondered if she was going to rub salt into his wounds and hurl more abuse at him.

After she had left, he ordered Tommy to bring his shaving gear and, for the first time in more than twenty years, he intended to use the present his mother had given him on leaving Lisbon. His hand lovingly brushed the box before he loosened the clip to reveal the Wade and Butcher set of seven razors and the tell-tale coin. The tortoiseshell scales, marked in the Portuguese way with gold inlays of the numbers 1 to 7, nestled next to each other in lush cream casings awaiting the master's hand.

Albasini superstition meant that he had to return the coin to his mother. If this was not done, he would sever the friendship. He flipped it in the air. If it came up 'heads' he would shave off the ridiculous chinstrap; if it came up 'tails' he would return to Portugal and bury the coin next to her grave, plant an olive tree and finish his Law studies. Returning to Portugal was not an option because the head of King Luiz on the coin made the decision. He started lathering his face, sharpened razor six and meticulously removed his beard. He felt a twinge of guilt, thinking of how he had swapped his mother's choice for him to finish his studies in Law for answering the call to adventure. The fever had snaffled Maria de Purifiçacao, once a renowned beauty of Spain's Royal House, and his sister to a premature grave.

The unpleasantness of the morning had left him fatigued. A strange sense of fear gripped him. Claw-like fingers squeezed his heart. Between strokes of shaving, he fortified himself with a tumbler of neat gin to dull the effect of the thick blanket of depression.

He outwitted and survived the wild dog with brute force and an indomitable spirit but what weapons can you use when an impregnable barrier faces you? His bloodshot eyes and the sneer on the face that stared back at him from the mirror twinned the image of a stranger. The gin-halved bottle and his soul were both at an ebb. Razor number six shaved away the ridiculous chinstrap beard. He towelled his face and, when he looked up, Gertina entered the tent. He looked beyond her, avoiding her eyes.

In a slow, alcohol-slurred speech he said, 'I could say it gives me great pleasure to show you my office, but seeing as you had already snooped around, spied and found me out, there is no reason to show you how I became rich and, for your information, very rich. O, but I've already told you previously that I am very rich.'

She ignored him and asked, 'Why did you shave off your beard?'

He took his time to steady himself as he half-turned his back to her and folded his arms across his chest. When he eventually turned to face her, he looked her up and down. His desire for her had dulled to an ache deep down in his inner core but he wasn't going to allow that to make him live in futile hope. If there was any glimmer of hope, he might have tried again but this morning was the last straw.

'I shaved my beard as a sign that I have nothing to hide. Are you satisfied? Or do you still have the gall to come in here and tell me what I am doing is wrong? Let me tell you, these people,' he gestured towards his followers outside, 'chose me.'

'I didn't choose them. It is hard to find a compromise between right and wrong. Judgement is easy to pass but you did not live with them for twelve years. They elevated me, a foreigner, to the highest honour, to become their leader. I listen to their problems, judge the guilty, respect their customs and have a fondness for using my talents and expertise to help them live peacefully. They call me 'father' which is a far more noble honour than wearing the imperial *karos*. Neither you nor anybody else will take this duty away from me. I will continue to protect them from warmongers and judgemental people who believe they are the chosen race like the Israelites. A pillar of cloud during the day and a pillar of light during the night will protect them. Anything outside their intimate circle the Devil created with his hairy hand.

'No, my dear Gertina, as I said, N'wamanungu can take you back to your family. I will grant you a divorce, on which grounds I do not know, because I have not dabbled in adultery which your church believes is the only reason for divorce. Still, for me, my promise that I had sworn before God the Almighty I will uphold. According to my Catholic faith, you will be my lawful wife till death do us part.

'You will be looked after financially and I will give your future husband a written letter that it wasn't me that soiled the precious virgin. We never consummated our marriage. You tested my hopes, my patience, my virtue. Go, my dear, get packing, don't waste time with your husband. Or, as you so eloquently put it, 'Murderer of innocent people, slave trader, a stupefied drunkard and husband who whores and practices polygamy'. Before I have to undergo another humiliating tirade of an uncaring, ungrateful, spoilt, pretty little girl, please go.'

He took his time. He turned away again and folded his arms across his chest. When he turned to face her, he looked her up and down. He sensed a change. It put him on his guard.

Slowly, as if floating, she walked towards him. She reached up to him. His body stiffened. Her soft body brushed his and he realised once again she wasn't as tall as he had imagined. For an instant, her body moulded perfectly into his. With the back of her hand, she gently stroked his freshly shaven cheek with a feather-like touch. Her fingers explored and lingered and, to his utter surprise, lovingly caressed his lips. Shyly, she removed her hand, reached up to him and brushed his lips softly with an exquisitely tender kiss.

Was the impossible, the incomprehensible happening, he thought, confused by the germination of hope that snapped in his gin-befuddled mind. Would he ever be free from this beautiful, wonderful creature who had swept him away?

'Dear Juwawa, I just had to feel what it would be like to kiss this stranger before I go. I'd better start packing.'

She turned away swiftly, picked up her skirts and ran like an antelope back to her tent. As she smiled and thought, 'Clever, smart Juwawa, King of the *Knobnoses*, let's see how you can handle a determined woman who has changed her mind. We have not lived as man and wife.'

As Gertina ran from him, Albasini called after her, 'I will order N'wamanungu to take your wagon, your belongings, your gifts and you,' he emphasised the *you*, 'back to where you belong. There is no future for us together. Get out, Gertina!'

***

João was in a quandary. He had already started cutting ties with his associates in the Delagoa Bay and Lydenburg regions. Ohrigstad was a dead horse. He decided to go north to follow his bride and her people but he wasn't quite sure what to do about this turn of events with Gertina.

Ivory was abundant up north and the farm he had set out for his followers was starting to bear fruit. The coffee plantation had yielded its first crop and he had already delivered citrus as far as Qualimane. Should he give all of that up and stay safe and secure at Magashulaskraal and do business only locally? He had never been indecisive in his life but Gertina's cat and mouse tactics were different from his everyday wheeling and dealing. The featherlight lips that brushed his so briefly that morning trapped him like a quivering mouse with Gertina the pouncing cat.

The fact that she mistrusted him was a foreign concept. People always trusted him. On the other hand, did he trust her fully? She still had not told him what the lavender smelling letter with Schoeman's scratching contained. The letter she had received in Lydenburg was mistakenly opened but not read.

He afforded himself the luxury of brushing his fingers against his lips. His thoughts lingered on the pleasantness of the sensation. He ached for Tineka's nearness. His despair at the thought of losing her numbed the thoughts churning in his head.

The fast and furious ride he had taken into the bush had somewhat calmed him but, coming back to the camp, he was surprised to see that his followers had packed up everything and were waiting patiently for further orders from him.

Once again he was amazed at the insight of his *indunas* who must have known that something was amiss between him and Gertina. The three chief indunas, N'wamanungu, Josekhulu and Monene stood with their arms folded in front of the crowd of about three thousand. They were ready to move.

'What's happening?

N'wamanungu, who was finding it difficult to contain his glee, said, 'They were the orders from the Senhora. She is impatient to get to start her new life with us. She is waiting in her wagon for you.'

He noticed the deep flush which crept up his *Inkosi's* face. The silence of the crowd willed him to leap into action. He opened the flap of the wagon and entered. The African sun had not yet said, 'Good night'. Inside the wagon, the sweet aroma of a burning beeswax candle mingled with cinnamon and the spiciness of cloves greeted João. The soft spitting of the melting candlewax hissed at irregular intervals begging for the silence to continue at this perfect moment.

Tineka, dressed in a white, lace-trimmed nightgown, sat on the bed with her head bowed. She looked up at him, a smile hovering on her lips, her eyes sparkling.

Her beauty overwhelmed him. The cornflower blue eyes were dark, perhaps with fear or desire. Juwawa hoped the latter. Her hair had been brushed and fell into soft curls spilling over her shoulders, making his desire to touch it insufferable. Youth painted her with innocence. The stiff shoulders spelled fear but, as soon as she straightened up, there was a braveness that welcomed him.

The pertness of her youth peeped from the unbuttoned nightdress as João sighed deeply and thought, 'This is a child-woman, but more child than woman.' He could forgive. He could forget.

Gertina spoke, 'The letter I received in Lydenburg was a wedding invitation from Stephanus. Of course I refused. The sun has set, the chickens have roosted. It's time for you to come to bed. We have an early start tomorrow.'

Chapter 15

Love grows but troubles loom

During the following three months, Gertina realised the magnitude of Juwawa's intellect, force, diplomacy, organisational skills and tenderness. He seemed to be in total control of every situation, always getting the best place to camp, ensuring that there was enough water, enough shade and enough game to feed the hundreds of *Knopneuse* who followed the seven wagons.

Every day started early and, by mid-morning, they outspanned the oxen to allow them to graze and rest. They inspected the animals' hooves and took care of any possible bites from the dreaded tsetse flies or scratches acquired during the rough trek.

'Juwawa, how many people are following us to Zoutpanzberg?' Gertina asked one day.

'Oh, it is hard to say, but my safari groups usually consist of 500 men. I have about twenty gunbearers walking in a square or rectangular formation to protect the cooks and porters in the middle. When they have made their trades, the porters then carry the valuable ivory in the middle of the group to take it back to Lorenço Marques. A double layer of gunbearers gives more protection. I trained my troops to fight the European way which is very foreign and different from vagabonds' attack of trade safaris. The square formation is very effective. As yet, I have not lost anything from the safaris that I have sent into the hinterland.

174

'I also make sure I know what the chiefs would like most and then I send some of the spies to give them gifts. I am well known as a fair trader and have made many friends.

'To get back to your question, I have four units to protect us on this trip. As you can see, they have come with their families and their belongings. I have left two teams at Magashulaskraal to keep trade going there as a backup in case things don't work out up north.

'A year ago, I dispersed two units and their families up to Beja. The Beja tribe has permitted me to settle north of the mountains and allowed me to take water races out to where my people are living. They bartered for my protection rather than goods. I have never really counted how many are following me but that should give you a rough idea.'

As always, Lya set a small round table and Gertina and João enjoyed Filipe's good Portuguese cooking. The weather was balmy and Juwawa sat feeding Gertina *numnoems*, wild berries, that he had picked for them that morning.

'Open your mouth wide, my darling,' he said as he playfully dropped one of the sweet sticky berries into her mouth.

'I have another question to ask, Juwawa.'

'Ah, and I have a question to ask you, too.'

'You go first then, I am a bit shy.'

Juwawa saw her blushing and wondered what it might be.

'Oh no, you were first.'

'What does it mean to be placed in a *delicate position*?'

João started to chuckle but soon realised how serious she was about her question. He saw her brow pucker. If she honestly did not know, he felt ashamed at the accusations he had made.

To gain time he said, 'In all fairness, you told me the contents of the letter in the fancy envelope. I have a confession to make as well.'

Gertina's eyebrows shot up, as if asking a question. She waited patiently.

'When N'wamanungu carried me into the church just before you were to marry Schoeman, I was in the wrong to say that Schoeman was still married. I took the risk that he did not know that his wife had died. The news had reached me the previous day and I was confident that he was not aware of this fact. In other words, technically speaking, he could have married you if you had so wished.' He asked as an afterthought, still not sure of her true feelings, 'Did you?'

She looked at him in mock surprise, 'So, you mean to say you lied? I could have been *Mevrou* Schoeman?' Not looking him in the eyes and evading the question, she proceeded to ask, 'Tell me then, the meaning of being placed in a *delicate position*!'

Juwawa was very embarrassed. He looked down at his feet and then replied. 'I am so sorry, my dear, but it is an unflattering way to say that somebody is pregnant. Why?' he asked.

Gertina's face lit up into a smile and she replied, 'I think I have been in a *delicate position* for...' she paused and held up three fingers in the air, '...months'.

***

N'wamanungu, who had moved towards them silently and sat on his haunches waiting to speak to Juwawa, not wishing to disrupt this poignant moment.

'Juwawa, I need to speak to you alone. There is a great danger.'

When they had outspanned that morning, call it his sixth sense again, Senhor Albasini had that uneasy feeling about the place. They were about four days travel from Zoutpanzberg. A small mountain range flanked them to the left with a river flowing through a gorge at its base. This was the shortest and most obvious path to take but uneasiness pricked his sensitivities. He paid keen attention to this sixth sense. He had seen vultures circling and wondered at their numbers. There were more than might be expected if it was only the debris left by lions that attracted them. Rather, it must have been a sizeable killing. The hair on his forearms bristled.

'You are as white as a *Bakhuha*, my friend. If there is any danger involved, the Senhora must learn the best way to cope with it. They have spies, so if we scuttle away like fearful old women or chickens after noticing the vultures, we give them the advantage, letting them know we are afraid. No, N'wamanungu, stay calm. Tell us what the spies have told you.'

N'wamanungu shifted from one foot to the other showing his uneasiness. Standing behind Gertina's back, he proceeded to demonstrate the gruesomeness of the situation in such a way that Juwawa would understand.

'It is Makapaan. He is the grandson of Mugwambane, a great general of Chaka's, and therefore from the same house and totem as Isoshanaan, great-grandfather of N'wamanungu. The surname Dengeza carries magic. Makapaan's people will realise this Shangaan is untouchable without their chief's personal command. He hates the pale skin *Bakhua*. Let me go and speak to him.'

When everybody was fed and had visited the water holes, they took a siesta. Even the lions and other predators gave everybody a time of hiatus. But they needed to remain vigilant which that was what João decided to do. He held Gertina's hand as he felt the sweat trickling down his back. He had to think fast and maintain a high degree of vigilance.

Juwawa said to N'wamanungu, 'Take a woollen blanket, a hunting knife and some beads. Make sure there are many blue beads in the mix. Travel light, bewitch him, and save our future King.' He pointed towards Gertina's abdomen. 'You are very brave. My affection for you goes beyond the word. God speed you, my friend.'

Gertina looked across at Juwawa and saw that he had turned pale and was deep in thought.

***

N'wamanungu encountered Ndebele warriors soon after leaving the wagons and asked to be taken to Makapaan to present a message from Juwawa.

On arrival at the village, N'wamanungu found Makapaan in an exuberant mood. His impis had just that day annihilated a strong force of *Bakhuha* at the river crossing and had come back with cattle and guns. The might of Chaka was still in the body of his grandchild. The *Bakhuha* were doomed in this country. Makapaan was the Lion and the Elephant, and nobody could stand against his power and might.

N'wamanungu listened to the speeches and flattering songs in silence, not even partaking of the beer he loved. After a while, Makapaan noticed his reticence and called him to the throne.

'Son of my fathers and child of the elephant, you don't seem to appreciate the fact that I have this day dealt the white man a death stroke. I am told that you have forsaken your ancestors' ways and now follow one of the hated *Bakhuha.* Is it true?'

'True, my father, but with a difference of interpretation. The man who is now my accepted Lord and Master is King amongst Kings. He is a wizard and a soldier such as even our

Father Chaka never was. He is the bravest of the brave and even strikes back at the lightning. He can throttle a lion with his bare hands and kill a bull elephant with his eyes. The ones you attacked and killed were only farmers and not wise in the way of war.'

Makapaan said, 'Do you scorn my soldiers and medicine? Are my warriors less than your so-called King? Speak, oh son of Soshangaan, or depart here in shame.'

'I speak, oh Lord Makapaan. I foretell that the white men will become lords and masters of your country soon. They are like locusts and as vicious as a she-leopard whose young have been taken from her. I have learned their ways and am willing to follow my Lord Juwawa in whatever way he leads. I have spoken.'

'So, you think my warriors are weaklings. I tell you now, N'wamanungu, that you may only leave my home when you have fought and killed my champion warrior in combat. Otherwise, your bones will join those of your friend and his wife by the river.'

'I do not fight children, oh Makapaan, but bring three of your best fighters and I will prove that the blood of our common ancestors flows stronger in my veins than yours.'

A bloody but speedy fight, three against one, ensued, after which N'wamanungu stalked majestically down the mountain. Juwawa was allowed to continue his journey in peace.

Chapter 16

A new home

They were nearing their destination, *Zout Pan Berg Dorp.*
'Zout pan' means a flat expanse of ground covered with salt.
The Boers harvested the salt pans nestled at the foot of the
Zoutpanzberg mountain range, hence the name. The settlers
built their houses, dug a water race from the river to the
township and, most importantly, started building a fort. The
town square was a hive of trade. Large piles of white tusks
glimmered in the sun begging to be bought by the highest
bidder. Raw cotton lay in fluffed up mounds projecting the
same message. Stiff and stretched animal hides stood in
bundles stacked throughout the quadrangle, pouring out their
misery in their death smell.

Traders displayed needles, forks, knives and spoons,
inviting anyone for a sewing lesson or dinner. Colourful
fabrics, lace ribbons, hats and women's fopperies squeaked
with small voices, adding colour to the kaleidoscope of goods
to barter. Would-be apothecaries spruiked their recipes for
cures, promoting blue and brown bottles labelled for any
ailments, genuine or imaginary.

The more affluent farmers lived in whitewashed houses
boasting glass windows squinting in the morning sunlight.
The poor made do with the open frames covered with calico
dipped in bees wax. Carpenters and other tradesmen were
spoiled for choice as they purchased timber of all sorts such
as tambuti to make doors, doorframes and beautiful furniture.

Yellowwood was the most sought-after wood. Sawmen reported that these trees were so tall that a person needed a ladder to climb to the lowest branches which could be up to twenty metres above the ground.

***

Gertina and Juwawa sat holding hands in a litter carried by six of the strongest and fittest *Knopneuse*. Juwawa refused to have her ride on the wagon saying that it was 'too bumpy for the bambino'.

Juwawa set up camp about a mile and a half away from the new settlement. In the distance was the silhouette of Hanglip, one of the highest points of the Zoutpanzberg mountain range. To the new settlers it served as a beacon of freedom, reminding them of their release from the oppression of *die verdomde Engelsman*. But for those already living there it served as a stronghold with an unmatched vantage point as they waited nervously to see what influence these strange-looking people would have on the community.

Senhor Albasini and Gertina led the way with two wagons. One was laden with trade goods and the other carried the church windows, doors and pulpit that Juwawa had dismantled in Ohrigstad, fulfilling his promise to bring these items north for the new church free of charge.

***

After a six months journey, Gertina was excited to see Lucas and Ella again to share the good news that there would soon be a little voice calling *Oma* and *Opa*. Ella would start to knit booties and Lucas would start to carve toy oxen for the boy to play with. Senhor Albasini and Gertina had no doubt in their minds that the child would be a boy.

When they met at the front of the house, there were tears of joy and many hugs but, as they entered the newly built home which still smelled of linseed oil, candle wax and dung, Gertina and Juwawa's enthusiasm was dampened. None other than Stephanus Schoeman and his third wife sat, grinning like Cheshire cats, waiting to share in the inevitable cup of coffee and Ella's baking.

Juwawa looked at Gertina as a silent question passing between them. "Is this the moment to share our good news?' Gertina nodded her approval. Juwawa stood up, cleared his throat and proudly drew Gertina to his side.

'*Vader en Moeder*, we have an announcement to make.' He saw the joy of anticipation in the older couple's faces and had time to notice the sour pursing of Schoeman's lips. 'We are going to have a baby and we will call him Antonio Augusto.'

Before Lucas and Ella could say anything, Schoeman ordered his wife, 'Come! Let's go.' To Senhor Albasini he said, 'You won't have any trouble raising another woodcutter and water carrier, will you?' referring to the curse Joshua had put on the Gideonites in the Old Testament.

Lucas exploded! 'Get out of my house immediately, 'Snotklop'. Not everybody thinks as you do. It seems you have not read the New Testament. Have you forgotten about the Man from Galilee? We need unity, not strife. You have bad breath. Get the hell out of my house!' Lucas jumped from his chair and ushered 'Snotklop' out of the door by the scruff of his neck.

***

A week later they left the town to go and settle on João's farm. The soft pink, blue and mauve late winter sky spun an early blanket over Hanglip. Gertina couldn't help but think of the mountain. To her, it looked as if the lip was sulking, questioning the disturbances below. Still gazing at the town disappearing in the far distance, she allowed herself to form a judgement.

What she had seen and heard in the township brought Sodom and Gomorrah to mind. Greed, debauchery and strife were prevalent. She quickly changed her thoughts so as not to turn into an imaginary salt pillar. No, Senhor Albasini was her Abraham and she would serve him as helper, not as a pillar of salt. Any sympathy that she may have still harboured for Schoeman disappeared when he insulted her husband and child. She looked at Juwawa who had got out of the litter, preferring to walk. His hands were clasped behind his back and she heard him muttering, '*Snotklap*, the son of a bitch. Lower than snake shit!'

***

'I have a surprise for you,' Senhor Albasini said when he brought her early morning coffee.

'Juwawa, you never cease to surprise me.'

'If you can still fit into your blue taffeta dress, I'll wear my wedding outfit. You will be meeting the rest of my adopted family later this morning.'

'I see. How should I wear my hair?

Senhor Albasini looked at her and replied, 'If you could wear it down, it would please me very much.'

The whole party travelled east past Hanglip, crossing several rivulets and eventually arrived at the end of a mountain range.

'That is *Luande Piesangkop* ('place where wild bananas grow') where we will live. It is my new headquarters but I have arranged to have a townhouse built in the *Dorp*. Nearby I will have my agent and good friend Casimir Simoes in charge of my trading. I spoke to your parents and bought the section next to ours to build a small house for them. Then you can visit any time you like and attend *Nachtmaal*.

'*Kommandant* Potgieter has also given permission for Josekhulu and Lya to stay with you on such occasions. The *Kommandant* was adamant that I not bring more than three of my impis into the township at any one time. They will not be allowed to carry guns either, but there are means and ways to go about that. Opposition has already come my way, saying that Zoutpanzbergdorp is a settlement for *Voortrekkers* only. You can guess who doesn't like me?'

Gertina laughed at Juwawa as he mimicked Stephanus' habit of stroking his nose. 'Thank you for taking care of my parents,' she said.

***

At the foot of Luande, Gertina clasped her hands to her face because she could not believe what she saw. Against a backdrop of rich vegetation and hundreds of scattered, thatched-roofed houses stood the whitewashed wall of a fortress, impressive in its height and design. She also saw two burnished cannon barrels taking their defensive positions on the terrepleins, one to the east and one to the west.

A wide corridor of cobbled stones led up to two massive wooden doors which were rolled open by *Knopneuse* in traditional dress. The buggy stood waiting for them. Two magnificent black horses, muzzled in red with ostrich feathers as headgear, waited patiently to transport the precious cargo.

They transferred from the litter to the buggy and, as soon as Juwawa took the reins, the procession started.

Young jacaranda trees bursting with pride stretched their necks above oleander bushes parading their last flush of autumn bloom in soft hues of white, cream and pink. They, too, wanted to see the newlyweds. A lonely, wrinkled boab tree guarded the fort and all its comings and goings.

The orphans of Senhor Albasini came *en masse* to welcome him and his bride. On cue, the impis formed the guard of honour. Behind them stood the older warriors, their wives and then the children. Drums rolled and *Bayete Inkosi* resounded in deep thunderous voices.

On either side of the forty metre-wide road, the young impis performed their war dance and showed off their shiny muscled torsos. Shields made from zebra skins mesmerised the eye and their feet stamped to the beat of the drums and the ululations of the women.

These people had never seen anyone with such pale skin as Gertina's. They relayed this information to those who could not see.

'Her hair looks like ripened corn, and the eyes - they look like the sought-after blue beads. She is tiny like the *chinonie* bird (a very small bird found in the region, which the inhabitants never killed).'

As they entered the gates, Gertina saw her future home flanked by a smaller building, both of them surrounded by wide verandas. The house was more significant than any place she had ever seen. Three steps led to a wide-front stable door featuring an ornate brass knocker.

It was too much for Gertina to take in. On reaching the coolness of the veranda they saw Herr von Marnecke, the architect, standing at the front door. He looked smart in breeches and a red velvet waistcoat with a fob watch hanging from his pocket. His round face broke into a broad smile when he took hold of Gertina's hand and brought it to his lips.

'Dear Senhora, I hope the house will be to your liking. Senhor Albasini came to see me in the Cape about a year ago and instructed me to build him something that would please the beautiful *Voortrekker* girl he was engaged to.'

Senhor Albasini was bursting with pride as he looked at his Tineka. He was sure she would be pleased. João addressed Herr von Marnecke in German, 'Excuse me, sir. Would you mind giving us a moment of privacy while I carry my bride over the threshold?'

He swept Gertina off her feet and carried her into the interior which was dark and cool after the hot afternoon sun outside. He put her down so gently and with such reverence that Gertina burst into tears spontaneously.

'Are those tears of joy?' Juwawa asked.

'Of course, you silly man. I saw the message you wrote on the tiles.'

Delighted that she had noticed, João said, 'Let's read it together.'

Neemt het mensch soals hij is,
En weet ook dat gij niet almal behaagt.

(Accept somebody precisely as they are and acknowledge to yourself that you don't please everyone either.)

Gertina giggled and said, 'That will teach some of the visitors a lesson. The self-righteous will have to think twice before they call you an *Uitlander* or a *Porra*.'

A table that could seat at least thirty people dominated the dining room. The aromas of the cook's excellent cooking drifted from the kitchen. Gertina asked, 'Did *Meneer* von Marnece bring his wife as well?

'No, why do you ask?'

'I see the table is set for four. Do we have another guest coming?'

João laughed and said, 'I had thought you would have noticed by now.' He shrugged his shoulders and said, 'It is my mother's tradition. I always have an extra space set for an unexpected or uninvited guest. You will be surprised how often it happens that weary travellers who might not have had a meal in days will be your guest and it is always my pleasure to provide a meal for them.

'I did not want to name the farm before you came, but I would like you to give it some thought. Basque tradition has it that your house must face east to greet the sun and have a name. Otherwise, it does not belong. Will you think of a suitable name?'

'Oh, I remember. You had six places set at Magashulaskraal. We were altogether five. I waited and waited for *Mevrou* Albasini to appear!' She gave a delightful chuckle, 'And now I am *Mevrou* Albasini! I think we should call this place *Goedewench* (A Good Wish) to anybody visiting us. What do you think?'

'Excellent. I'll have it carved in wood to hang at the entrance.'

Thus the tradition of Albasini hospitality commenced, facing Darkest Africa and promoting co-operation and interdependence. The Albasini *Skans,* as it became known, brought refuge and rest to whoever needed it.

Chapter 17

Zoutspanzberg

Antonio Augusto Albasini was born on 10.10.1853 and, by 1864, another three children swelled the family. The midwife, Anna van Rensburg, a relation from the Potchefstroom district, visited Gertina each time to help deliver her babies. Gertina also suffered a miscarriage during this time.

Anna brought her three-year-old son Nicklaas to fraternise with the boisterous Albasini children. He was known to be different. He was an unkempt-looking child with a high forehead, a permanent frown and piercing eyes that looked far and beyond, but never at you. He spoke in riddles but the grown-ups made light of it. Anna thought the change of scenery would benefit him but one night the little boy woke everybody with ear-splitting screams.

Gertina rushed to him and entered the bedroom where he sat on his mother's lap, screaming and pointing in the distance. His eyes were wild and, in-between screams, he said, 'Fire. Fire, fire, fire! Run, Ma, run. I see a church looking at me with hollow black eyes. Stop, stop the boulders. They are noisy, they make the grass go flat. They are big rolling pins and they have shooting guns fastened to them. They go pop, pop. I smell smoke.'

The little boy cupped his ears with his hands. Sobbing, he said, 'Ma, I taste salt, lots of salt,' and, just like that, he closed his eyes and fell asleep.

In the morning everything was back to normal and little Niklaas played with the other children but retained a frown between his eyes. Good manners prevented any gossip, but word did get around and the *Kappie Brigade* whispered about the incident with a mixture of puzzlement and derision.

***

Zoutpanzbergdorp flourished. In 1855, two hundred pounds of ivory was exported. One thousand eight hundred souls occupied the district. In Pretoria, the new town, the settlers haughtily referred to the village as the 'most lawless of their colour in all of South Africa'.

Others said they were hooligans, hobnobbing with the Buys families who were 'eager to put more milk into their coffee', hinting that they preferred to mix with the locals. These settlers were regarded as fugitives who took up hunting elephants and selling the ivory. In 1867, *The Transvaal Angus* mentioned that the town was a 'thorn in the flesh and a moral cancer in the body politic'.

Disaster struck when their leader Andries Potgieter died on 16 December 1852. Pieter, his son, succeeded him but, sadly, Pieter fell into a crevasse on a punitive expedition against Makapaan in 1855.

João and N'wamanungu helped in the attack. When Pieter fell into the crevasse, N'wamanungu, fearless and under enemy attack, dropped into the opening to retrieve Pieter's body. Pieter Potgieter was the only casualty of the expedition.

***

Schoeman's boots were squashing in the muddied street leading to the church in Zoutpanzbergdorp. The red clay oozed around his ankles. 'Damn,' he said. What a pity he had not brought an extra pair of boots. He tried to shake the mud off while holding his umbrella in place. He heard a horse-drawn cart drawing near and had to jump out of the way to avoid looking like a red-spotted crow from the muck which splattered onto his new pinstriped trousers and black tailcoat. It wasn't a question of if but when he would take over the leadership. He would make sure that there would be order in this unruly mecca of ivory.

Schoeman hurried to the half-built church to attend the funeral. It was opportune that he was on his way to the *Oude Dorp*, Zoutpanzbergdorp, when news of Pieter's unfortunate death reached him. He picked up *dominee* Murray from Rustenburg to give Pieter his last farewell because there was no *dominee* resident in Zoutpanzbergdorp.

He offered to do the obituary and was to be a pallbearer. Therefore, he took exceptional care in his outward appearance. Looking his best would win over the admiration of the ladies and their votes but, most importantly, he wanted to impress the widow.

He had given particular thought to the obituary. It was a disguised political speech destined to inundate the leaderless community's ears with ideals of independence, autonomy, good leadership and a soon to be an independent Republic.

He thought it a pity that the widow, Elsje, was pregnant otherwise he could have asked her to marry him sooner. Perhaps he could convince her that he could be the perfect replacement for Pieter and take up the post next to her as the next leader.

The proceedings went smoothly. Afterwards, the family and good friends went to Casimir Simoes's house to enjoy an array of savouries, cakes and milk tarts.

Schoeman was slightly annoyed that the gathering was held at Casimir's house because he knew that the very successful trader in the community was Albasini's friend. When João and Schoeman saw each other at the gathering, there was no acknowledgement of the other. Schoeman was too occupied with the widow and Albasini regarded Schoeman as scum, part of the riffraff.

Albasini was hurt and sulking because no mention had been made at the service of his participation in securing a victory over Makapaan. Even worse, there was not even a whisper of N'wamanungu's heroic deed.

When the two men did lock eyes, Senhor Albasini's were those of a dead fish. He kept staring until Schoeman dropped his gaze and walked away. Only the zig-zagged smirk under the copper fronds of his moustache indicated Schoeman's displeasure.

Schoeman approached Elsje and held her hand, holding it a trifle longer than was necessary. Mustering a most sympathetic look he said, 'Elsje!', letting the word hang in the air like a teardrop about to fall.

'*Uit respecte*, I will come and help you sort out the matters of state. I have already started to collect money for your husband's gravestone. The father of your unborn child,' his voice quivered, 'and my very good friend,' he paused for effect and continued, 'deserves more than a wooden cross in God's acre.'

Elsje started crying and Stephanus quickly took a new white handkerchief from his breast pocket and wiped the tears away tenderly. He nearly hugged her but thought that it might be perceived as inappropriate. Instead, he put his hand on her shoulder in an unnoticeable caress. 'Don't worry, my brave warrior. Having lost my third wife, I know what you must be going through. I'll take care of everything.'

***

The people of Zoutpanzberg were devastated but not for long because, after many *Uit respecte* speeches, lots of coffee, many promises and the odd peach schnapps, Schoeman was elected *Kommandant-Generaal*.

The *Kruis Vlag* (Cross Flag), which his mother had embroidered with white thread to symbolise the purity of the exodus and '1838' to commemorate the start of the Trek, was hoisted with much fanfare, including volleys of gunfire alternating with the boom of cannon fire. The proceedings etched Schoeman's name in local history. His ultimate goal was to be president of the ZAR, the *Zuid Afrikaansche Republik*.

A man of many talents, Schoeman moulded the town to his own rules and regulations to consolidate his power. The church bell had to be struck at eight every night, overruling the staunch church elders' belief that the *kerkklokken luiden niet vir troost en hoop, maar vir geen gekijfen of remoer.* (The church bells should be rung to comfort and give hope, not to stop noise after eight.) No pigs were allowed to run in the streets. A new law restricted elephant hunting from 15 June to 15 October each year. Anyone caught breaking this regulation faces a penalty of 500 Rixdollars.

***

Courting Elsje proved an easy task except for one stubborn idea which thwarted his plans to marry her at the earliest convenience. She wanted an ordained minister to marry them. Communication over any distance was difficult and visiting *dominees* were few and far between. While on a hunting expedition, however, he received an urgent letter from

Albasini to tell him that all the letters that he, Albasini, and both Potgieters had written to the Governor in Inhambane had eventually brought good news. Father Joaquim de Santa Rita Montanha had arrived at *Goedewench* with delegates to negotiate treaties of peace and trade.

The wheel of fortune was still spinning good luck for Stephanus. Father Montanha was indeed an ordained minister, albeit a Catholic, but Elsje did not have to know that.

Schoeman also decided that his wedding day would be the perfect opportunity to change the name of Zoutpanzberg to Schoemansdal. The honour of having a town named after himself made him feel good. Schoemansdal sounded fresh and empowering, especially to his ear.

Father Montanha was only too pleased to assist but the *Kappie Brigade* whispered behind cupped hands that Schoeman's hospitality could not hold up to that of Senhor and Senhora Albasini. They said that João had gone out to welcome Father Montanha to *Goedewench* while the *dominee* was still several miles away. Senhor Albasini came with two wagons, the first the Father had ever seen in his life. It was also the first time in two months that he did not have to sleep in the open because Senhor Albasini offered him the elevated comfort of a tented wagon and a feather bed!

On reaching *Goedewench*, Senhora Albasini's beauty and graciousness overwhelmed the visitor. He sensed a deep understanding between the Senhora and her husband and realised it was exceptional. As he was soon to discover, everything ran smoothly in the Albasini household.

He was deeply affected by the Senhora's humility when, on arrival, they were greeted with a ritual that was well known amongst guests at the *Skans*. Young girls were dressed in calico shift dresses. Their headwear, which consisted of multi-coloured scarves wrapped around their heads, lent a certain jolliness to the situation. They brought small enamel bowls of hot water and white towels for the entourage to freshen up. The Senhora made Father Montanha sit down on the veranda and proceeded to wash his hands and feet herself before drying them in a Christ-like manner.

Father Montanha also learned that Gertina had taken it upon herself to give Bible readings and explanations to whoever wished to attend early in the morning. *Pikaninis* and little girls attended, perhaps not so much for the religious teachings but more to stroke her long corn-coloured hair. It was something they all wondered about and discussed at the evening campfires along with great stories of Juwawa's bravery.

Gertina was also on call for any medical emergencies. She treated wounds with Holman's ointment which her mother Ella swore by. Juwawa taught her to place a small amount of powder on a snake bite and set it alight. The explosion removed the poison, saved a life and strengthened the belief that Juwawa's magical power had been passed on to Gertina. Beestings were treated with warm turds. Her soft voice, compassionate heart and a biscuit for good behaviour completed her efforts.

Senhor Albasini also introduced the *dominee* to Dr Leingme who had fallen into disfavour with the Portuguese government because of his liberal ideas. The doctor found sanctuary with Juwawa who was now in the throes of helping the doctor build a hospital at Elim, about eight miles from *Goedewench*.

Everybody at the dinner table agreed that the doctor was a Godsend to all of the inhabitants of Zoutpanzberg. Doctor Leingme praised Senhor Albasini and told Father Montanha about Monsieur and Madame Junod who were so excited by the Senhor's dictionaries. Twenty-three native languages were neatly bound and organised systematically. The Junods added this valuable asset to their own dictionaries which were quite limited by comparison.

When Schoeman and his followers welcomed Father Montanha with a rifle salute and cheering, he knew that it lacked finesse. He noticed that the soldiers were wearing blue moleskin pants from Albasini's shop. The *Porra* had outwitted him by anticipating that the soldiers' white breeches were unsuitable for Zoutpanzbergdorp's red clay.

***

The Schoeman/Potgieter wedding took place soon afterwards at Waterberg. It was a three-day feast of merriment, high spirits and peach brandy. Whole oxen sizzled and crackled on revolving spits over barbeque fires while guests, inspired by rhythmic sounds of violins and squeaking concertinas, danced from three in the afternoon until daybreak.

It was more than Senhor Albasini could bear when, as custom would have it, the gentleman, being 'Snotklap', stood in front of the girl he wished to dance with and clapped his hands on her knees three times. He then asked her to dance, at which point she was not meant to refuse.

On the first set of dances on the last day of the activities, Schoeman sauntered up to João and said, 'I see you don't partake in the dancing or the drinking?'

Joao squinted at him and replied in a droll voice, 'Dancing is not to my liking anymore and, to quote, "I like liquor and its taste, its affects and that is just the reason I never drink it".'

When Schoeman asked Gertina to dance three times in succession on the last day, Senhor Albasini intervened midway on the last of the three dances and said, 'Gertina, we are leaving.' He also turned to Father Montanha who was nearby and said, ''Pater? You are welcome to come with us if you so wish but we are leaving NOW.'

***

On the journey home Gertina felt neglected. João's attention was divided between the all-important Father Joaquim de Santa Rita and little Antonio. Gertina did not take a liking to the Father because she did not trust him. She shared Elsje's wrath when they realised that Stephanus had cajoled Father Montanha into replacing his usual frock to wear a suit to give

200

the semblance of a minister. Gertina did not like his shifty eyes and regarded him as somebody who did not have high moral standards.

The *Kappie Brigade* was partly to blame because they had told Gertina that Father Montanha had been very eager to accept an invitation from Andries Potgieter and João to visit Schoemansdal to further diplomatic ties between Portugal and the Boers. Apparently he'd had an affair which resulted in a child. Gertina read between the lines when João told her that the Father was quite happy to stay in Schoemansdal for a long time. João also mentioned that the Father had said that the girls in the little village were very pretty but João had picked the prettiest.

She did not like his beady eyes and, every now and then, she saw him take a swig from a hip flask. She also noticed that he offered some to João on several occasions but her husband kept his promise not to touch another drop of alcohol after Antonio's birth.

Antonio had not yet been christened as ministers were so far and few between. Gertina decided that no matter what, she would not let a Catholic priest baptise their children.

***

Father Montanha returned to Inhambane and the district of Zoutpanzberg was left shepherdless. It took a good ten years before Gertina was able to get her seven children baptised by a good (Dutch) Reformed ordained minister by the name of Nicolaas van Warmelo.

Dominee van Warmelo and his wife Josina were welcomed by the destitute families of Schoemansdal who were deprived of spiritual food as well as guidance on what was morally right or wrong. *Dominee* van Warmelo saw it as his calling to serve these people. His wife supported him whole-heartedly and was known to have the kindest heart. They were the first occupants of the manse that was specially built for a minister by Schoeman, right next to his own house.

It was a very sad day when Josina was taken to heaven. Gertina and Senhor Albasini consoled van Warmelo. João made sure that the letter *Dominee* van Warmelo wrote to his mother in Holland to tell her the sad news was taken post haste to Delagoa Bay.

The couple's six children, were all baptised by *Dominee* van Warmelo. Tradition was followed and, although baptised long after he was born, the oldest son was named after Senhor Albasini's father, Antonio Augusto - 10/10/1853.

The children that followed were Zusanna Elizabeth (25/2/1855) named after Gertina's mother; Maria Machdalena (27/12/1856) named after Senhor Albasini's mother; Martha Machdelena (9/7/1859) named after Gertina's grandmother; Lucas Willem (29/5/1859) named after Gertina's father; Gertina Pitronella (8/4/1867) named after Gertina herself; and Hendrika Maria (1/9/1869) named after her mother's sister.

The baptism ritual did not follow the normal procedure. Because João was a Catholic he was not allowed to stand at the front of the church with his wife while his children were baptised. Elder Grobbelaar was elected to stand with Gertina at the baptismal font and repeat the appropriate vows. Senhor Albasini stood in the back row and solemnly affirmed the vows by nodding his head in approval. He was adamant, however, that each child be given two names, as was the custom in Portugal.

Chapter 18

Good news but rising problems

Senhor Albasini realised the importance of a postal service and set about implementing one. Portuguese soldiers ran the service from *Goedewench* to Lorenço Marques. The Senhor offered a salary out of his own pocket and provided accommodation and meals for the soldiers. They, however, took his goodness for granted and, more often than not, got drunk on his excellent port and abused his hospitality. Others deserted or were mauled by wild animals and killed.

In late December 1857, João opened the post and could hardly contain himself. He rushed out of his office and sought Tineka's company. He took hold of her around the waist and did a merry dance, all the time brandishing the document in his hand.

'Tineka! Tineka! *Oh, minha palavara*! Oh my word, you won't believe this. The postal officer has just brought me this letter and guess what? They have made me Vice-Councillor of Portugal in the Transvaal. What an honour! What an honour!'

He sat on the *riempies* coach that stood on the veranda. He sniffled as he used the back of his hands to mop away small rivulets of tears that followed the creases around his eyes. Gertina called Lya and asked her to bring coffee and the little pastries that João loved.

'All my letters have not been in vain, Tineka. Portugal will not be sorry. There is a great future for this district and your people. Get those invitations rolling. We will have a spectacular New Year's celebration.'

He folded the letter carefully and went to his office and wrote to the Governor-General of Mozambique.

I have no doubts about accepting the position and, in humility, I shall do anything that will be advantageous to my nation.

People from far and beyond arrived in buggies, on horses, donkeys and wagons to attend the celebrations. Father Montanha said a prayer in Latin and everybody agreed on the 'Amen.' As custom would have it, Tom Albach performed the incredible feat of grabbing an ox by its horns and turning it on its side, holding it down while the count to twelve was called. Bonfires were lit and a salute of gunshots and fireworks called 1859 into existence.

João Albasini, clad in his blue uniform, stood to attention while the shield was hoisted into position on the arch above the big wooden gates and the Portuguese flag was raised. Those who were familiar with the words sung the Portuguese anthem. Guests stood to attention out of respect but some stayed tight-lipped.

Proudly perched above the *Goedewench* sign, the pot-bellied shield signalled that visitors were now entering the residence of:

VICE CONSULADO DE PORTUGAL
NA REPUBLICA AFRICANA MERIDIONAL

The guests chanted, '*Hoor! Hoor*! Happy New Year and Blessed New Year'. They threw their hats into the air and moved forward to congratulate Senhor Albasini and his wife.

There was no dancing because Gertina did not want to have a repeat of what happened at Schoeman's wedding. After that incident, Gertina noticed that her husband's right eye twitched when he was under stress or whenever anybody mentioned Schoeman.

Schoeman did not attend the fun and games which happened at regular intervals at *Goedewench* and he never received an invitation to New Year's Eve celebrations. Even if they had invited him, he would not have attended because he focused all of his energy on politics elsewhere. Schoemansdal was sorely neglected and became an orphaned child of his ego.

***

'Close the gates! Close the gates, Mr Albasini, I beg you.'

An anguished cry came from the entrance of the *Skans*. Senhor Albasini rushed out to see what the commotion was all about. He saw Chambers, a former British soldier and fellow trader who had married a Boer girl just as he had, come riding into the *Skans* at great speed. He looked terrified and once again pleaded to have the gates closed for his safety.

206

Chambers was known to be a kind soul and was well-liked among the indigenous tribes because he saved the life of Chikovele, the son of a Tsonga chief. When an elephant was about to maul the chief's son, Chambers shot it and saved the boy's life. In a second incident, a poisoned arrow hit the same boy. Chambers acted quickly and sucked the poison out of the wound, once again saving Chikovele. The Tsonga venerated these acts even more so because the boy was the oldest of Chambane's sons.

Juwawa blew his whistle which, by way of different tones, sent out particular messages. He issued the necessary order and the heavy wooden gates were closed. Extra guards appeared on the fort's walls manning the cannons. Some of the impis were armed with rifles while others had their spears and assegais ready to defend *Goedewench*.

On a given signal, Juwawa was able to amass two thousand of his best impis within minutes to gather in the *Skans*. Another signal called up women and children to come and operate the pulley systems which hoisted wooden puppets above the *Skans* wall. The enemy then thought the puppets were warriors and wasted their spears. Meanwhile, Juwawa's troops, hidden in the bushes, could encircle the enemy and have a comfortable victory.

'Come quick, Jan.' The Shoemandallers had christened him *Jan Kombers,* the *Die Taal* version of John Chambers. 'Come, my friend, come into the house and tell us what you are afraid of.'

'Senhor Albasini, as you know, things are not looking good in Schoemansdal. We are only about 250 able men. Some, as you know, are not the most desirable and don't have the same loyalty as the core group. Everybody has become so slack. Because of negligence, the Venda have taken advantage by keeping guns and ammunition after the hunt. Schoeman did not want to pay a fair price for the ivory. The situation is dire. We estimate that the Venda own at least 300 guns. Living in their stronghold, we have no chance of chasing after them. It would be suicide.'

He stopped for a while to catch his breath and acknowledged Gertina who already had a small basin of hot water and towel ready for his use. Chambers plucked his sweat-drenched hat from his head and clasped it to his broad chest, kneading it like a kitten looking for comfort.

'*Kommandant* Schoeman and I quarrelled. He wants to take the cannons that you secretly returned to us away from Schoemansdal. Imagine, he wants to use it for his defence in a civil war he is planning. Outrageous, selfish and with no regard to the people who voted for him to become *Kommandant-Generaal*! Schoeman said, "I will lynch you," and, Mr. Albasini, I swear to God that Schoeman gathered the most vulgar gang and sent them after me.

'I fled as quickly as I could and they will be here soon. You're the only person I could think of who would help me. I have given orders to Dina to pack our belongings. Her brother David and Jakobus Lottering are also leaving Schoemansdal. If we could stay here while things settle, I will be most grateful.' He paused. 'I'm done with the wild Zoutpanzberg district. I promised to take Dina with me to England.'

The cannons in question were called *Ou Grietjies*. One belonged to Schoeman and the other to Senhor Albasini. Senhor Albasini had agreed to keep Schoeman's *ou Grietjie* (the cannon Schoeman had used at the battle of Bloedrivier) until they finished building the fort at Schoemansdal. With the animosity between the Venda and the settlers deteriorating further, they agreed that, under cover of darkness, the cannons be removed and be replaced by fake copper pipes. In the event of an attack, the cannons would be vital for the defence of Schoemansdal.

On Juwawa's whistle-command, the fort's guards fired a few warning shots which dispersed the lynch-mob. Juwawa immediately sent a contingent under Monene to go and help Dina, John's wife, and bring the party safely to *Goedewench*.

*****

That evening a greatly distressed N'wamanungu came to see Juwawa.

'My friend, what is the matter?'

'Ah Juwawa, you have told me about the traitor that you read about in your book. I think you called him Judasiwe.'

'Yes, Judas Iscariot. The one who betrayed Jesus. Yes, yes. What about him?'

'Inkosi, we have a traitor in our midst. My spies have told me he keeps company with the Venda dogs. He drinks their beer, lies with their women and wants to become a Mavesha, a G-string, spineless weakling. He drinks from the same calabash as we.'

'Speak up, N'wamanungu!' Juwawa ordered. 'Who is this Judasiwe you talk about?'

'It is the ringhead.' He knew that the news would upset Juwawa. He shook his head and the betrayal of one of Juwawa's trusted inner circle gave him a grey parlour. He threw down his spear and said in a clear voice, 'It is Monene,' and, as an afterthought, he added, 'Inkosi.'

Senhor Albasini suddenly realised why his calculations did not match when he did an inventory of the gunpowder and lead.

'Also, we have an interesting visitor to see you when you are ready, Juwawa.   Davhana has come to ask for your protection.'

Senhor Albasini was taken by surprise. 'You mean to say Davhana, the Venda chief's oldest son?'

'Exactly, Juwawa. His youngest brother Makhado is the father's favourite or, should I say, he was because they say that Davhana poisoned his father to become chief before Ramabulana made Makhado the chief. Makhado sent the

210

message that he would sew Davhana, while living, into a wet cow hide and let him hang from a tree. He would collect the juices in a clay pot to place onto Ramabulana's grave. Davhana also said that you must be careful because Makhado says it is the white man that killed his sister. He is after your blood too.'

Senhor Albasini had much to think about before he could reply. He thought about the ants that his spies had told him about so long ago, ants who were looking for greener pastures and travelling with their houses drawn by oxen. João also thought about the other ants who lived in the well-protected stronghold of the mountain Hanglip. They also looked for greener pastures, except they lived in their huts. They regarded the other ants as intruders, especially when their leader, the one with the red hair, wanted them to pay toll tax. Thirty-eight chiefs agreed to pay five head of cattle or five elephant tusks or twenty tiger skins each. In addition to this, they had to pay a goat or a sheep or four pickaxes for each dwelling in their villages.

The Venda, who were very shrewd businessmen, nodded their heads in agreement but thought and did otherwise. The chief amassed a strong force to oppose the ants with their pale skins and wide-brimmed hats. Senhor Albasini knew there would be trouble when the legionnaires of such different cultures clashed.

Juwawa looked up at N'wanamungu and said, 'Interesting, interesting. What do you think, my advisor and friend?'

'Let's call a meeting tomorrow and see what the other chiefs have to say.'

'Thank you, I'll see you in the morning. Make sure Davhana gets food and a new hut to sleep in.'

N'wamanungu answered, 'The G-string refuses to go away from your office.'

'Well, then, he will have to wait until after our meeting tomorrow.'

João did a quick calculation and realised that, if he had support, he could have a force of about 5,000 men.

***

Gertina watched through the window and thought that João was still the most handsome man she had ever met. The slightest hint of grey brushed his temples. He still wore his lush, ebony curls tamed in a short ponytail with a neat leather tie, just as he had when she saw him many years ago.

No wonder I get flustered every time he smiles at me, she thought. His gentleness always amazes me. The way he told the stories of how he killed two lions at the same time and the favourite, how he made out to be a mad jackal and killed a wild dog, always had audiences begging for more.

Antonio, the spitting image of his father, would stomp his foot on the imaginary dog, imitating Juwawa, dusting his hands on his pants in mock victory. 'Got you, you bastard!'

Gertina admonished Antonio, 'Don't use that word, it is not gentleman-like.'

Antonio would bow down with a twinkle in his eyes and copy his father and say, 'So sorry, Senhora, I mean it from my heart, but a real man,' he would then pause, 'needs to say words like that to get rid of his aggression. If you choose, my dear, you don't have to listen.'

She admired João and respected him because he had kept his promise. After the uproarious celebration of Antonio's birth, Gertina had, in her gentle way, admonished Juwawa on his behaviour. Consequently, he vowed that he would never put a drop of drink to his lips again, not an easy task when the habit of imbibing was the custom to dumb the effects of the milieu in which they lived.

Gertina looked at her husband and thought, 'Yes, your Daddy is a strong-willed, intelligent man and the bravest of them all. I have seen his courage. I have seen how he manages to lead the *Knopneuse* into battle with the odds against him. They always return home victorious and bring the wounded enemy for me to look after. Extraordinary. I can't believe how he manages it. Invariably the enemy gets persuaded to assimilate into the stronghold of the Juwawa clan. They come to live here in the hills around Luamando so that your father can give them protection. We all live in fear of the Venda.

Perhaps the only ones who don't fear them are your pa and N'wamanungu.'

***

Juwawa was deeply disturbed. On top of the Monene problem, news reached him that there has been another murder on one of the settler's farms. It saddened him and he feared for the safety of Tineka and his children.

The early morning mist had already cleared from Luonde while Juwawa stood on *Goedewench's* veranda and waited for his *ringkoppe* to come to the meeting.

Juwawa stood under the Chinese berry tree and looked at the tiny purple flowers which rained down continually on the floor, whirling away in fruitless purpose. He wondered if his existence was also fruitless.

The tree was a pest but gave such wonderful shade that he was loath to cut it off in summer. The poisonous berries that fruited from March to August reminded him of the troublesome Venda - always there, always watching his back. Living on such a knife's edge, he had to be vigilant and cautious about their actions which were a deadly threat to all. The fruits of the tree were many and so were the Venda. He would have to find a way to live with these weeds. Just like the tree, they could not be axed because the problem would just surface again. He had to think about how he could use the

Venda's expertise and let it give shade rather than poison. He admired their business acumen and they were excellent strategists.

The beautiful aroma of coffee roasted in big heavy-based copper pans on open fires filled the air. There was a bumper crop that year but that was no good. The inhabitants of Schoemansdal drank coffee as an elixir, consuming it at any available opportunity but, sadly, they were leaving the ill-fated town, having been deserted by their leader. Dr Marthinus Eyssell, the only physician in the settlement, found it hard to cope with the number of people falling sick with malaria, typhoid and trypanosomiasis (African sleeping sickness). Their isolation threatened inbreeding and insanity. Officials were corrupt. Looting, lawlessness and constant raiding between Africans and Europeans took the main stage.

The immense number of elephants slaughtered had diminished the herd's population. Casimir, his friend, told him that one of the English merchants alone had shipped out over three hundred weight of ivory in one year, equivalent to more than 350 animals. Together they had estimated that 200,000 pounds of ivory were exported each year, equal at least 2000 elephants killed per year. Most of the tusks were used to make billiard balls which were in high demand. Even Juwawa was awaiting an order of billiard balls made from the tusks of two prize male elephants he had shot. No wonder his traders were coming home with less and less ivory!

His thoughts turned back to the Venda and he sighed, 'It is such a pity that the Venda did not take to the habit of drinking coffee. That would solve the problem of the surplus beans crackling away on the open fires.'

He heard the familiar bantering of the young girls sweeping the yard. They shooed the geese and ducks to the pond and chatted and laughed in the safe environment which he had created at the *Skans*. A happy crowd, Juwawa thought, as he walked briskly to the chair and waited for his team to arrive.

The chief *ringkoppe* arrived one by one, each donned in his regalia. Some still glistened with droplets of water and smelled of Gertina's caustic soda soap after having a compulsory dip in the wine vat that stood at Juwawa's rondavel-office. Juwawa instilled strict hygiene rules - no-one was to see him if they had not cleaned themselves.

Of the twelve that usually met, three were absent on caravan trading duty and Monene had accompanied John Chambers back to Schoemansdal. Eight of his *Ringkoppe* saluted him with *Bayete Inkosi* and sat on their haunches.

Juwawa opened the meeting. 'As you can all see, I am wearing the skin of the fleet-footed leopard and the skin of the lion. The lion has strength and courage but we will need the stealth and the mystique of the she leopard, too.'

'Ehbo, ebho, Inkosi.' They were all aware that it needs one red bead to spoil the whole string. (Shangaan proverb.)

'You all know that Monene has been my most trustworthy general to fight the enemy but, sadly, we have a worm in the healthy-looking pumpkin.'

216

The chiefs clicked their tongues and their looks became even more grave. Some held their heads in their hands while others swayed their heads from left to right to indicate their dissatisfaction with the situation they were facing.

'The young branches always need to rest on the old ones of the fence. I now need advice from you, my respected and loved warriors. As a young branch, not ever having had anybody be disloyal to me, I need to lean on those who have seen treachery before to advise me on what to do.

'Times are changing. I find myself a warrior, not a trader anymore. For us to survive, we need support. I have a *Bakhua* of high rank in the Transvaal government coming to visit me and perhaps we should join forces to fight the Venda, especially Mashau who robs me of my sleep.'

The indunas nodded their heads and started to talk among themselves.

Juwawa could see N'wamanungu growing excited as he waved his spear in the air indicating 'death' as the only option. After some deliberation, one of the other indunas stood up and said, 'Why don't we let Monene come back to us. We will give him wrong information and let him fall into the trap. We have the advantage that he doesn't know that we know. We can do that when he brings the Englishman's wife safely back here.'

Another spoke up with a dry comment, 'If somebody is a sly hypocrite, you have to think very carefully and outwit him by being even more hypocritical.'

Gertina barbequed a goat on open coals and the women made stiff *pap* (maize) and *matoto,* a sauce made of ground peanuts, spinach and chili, to be served to the men.

The young girls took the food to the meeting in big woven baskets lined with banana leaves. They carried the steaming *pap* in three-legged pots and left them in the semi-circle for the assembly to enjoy. The leaders were in deep thought and did not even look up at the young girls who paraded themselves subtly as possible wives.

The *indunas* moulded the *pap* into stiff balls and dipped it into the sauce, eating without their usual gusto. They refused the customary mugs of brandy because they were making an important decision. They convinced N'wamanungu that stealth was the best option. After deliberating for a long time, they came up with a solution and presented their idea to Juwawa.

'Thank you, my clever men. I see I have many she-leopards who can hunt as one. I advise caution and patience with your plan. We will put it into action immediately. Send the spies to Mazula who has been waiting for a long time. Mazula is thirsty for Monene's blood, his wives and his cattle.'

N'wamanungu waved to the young girls waiting in the shade of the bamboo bushes. 'Now you can give us the drink that fires up our bellies.'

The girls took their time, provocatively swaying their hips before pouring the brandy leisurely from small caskets into the tin mugs. Showing all due respect, they lowered their

218

heads and made a half curtsy before offering the mug on an outstretched hand supported at the elbow by the other.

Chapter 19

Honour before a retreat

Gertina and the young girls harvested the feather down from the geese and used it to stuff the new eiderdown they were making. It was the happiest time of the day when she was in in the big sitting room with Juwawa after all the children had been sent to bed.

The corn storks lay like short, fat, glowing pokers in the fireplace. Juwawa took down some nearly-dried venison sausages and speared them on a two-pronged wooden stake used for barbequing. He cooked the sausages as a special treat for the two of them.

She was about to start beating the muid bag to ease the down into the eiderdown when Juwawa said, '*Meu amor*, my love, I have good news for you. I would like you to prepare the guest quarters for a very special guest.'

'My word, we have just cleared out all the stuff Carl Mauch left in your office where he did all the experiments. You know Maria was very disappointed when he did not give her the fossilised bat. I think she was half in love with his blond hair and broad shoulders. Maria is such a serious girl. She says she also wants to become a scientist and explorer like him. When Dr Mauch explained to her that the fossil had to go to the museum in Berlin she understood. You'd better put some money away that she will be able to study in Berlin.'

Senhor Albasini chuckled and said, 'Yes, he asked me how much it cost to build the wall of the *Skans* and I told him as much as it needed to keep my family and the *Knopneuse* safe. Do you know he thanked me so many times for what we did? I was quite embarrassed. After all, I sent him away with only nine porters and Karl Trichardt's directions to the ruins in Mashonaland. On the other hand, he gave me valuable information on how to prospect for diamonds and I will make a study of that shortly.'

Gertina asked, 'Now, tell me, which interesting person is coming to visit us next? Will they also stay as long as Herr Mauch?'

'No, definitely not. The man's name is Paul Kruger. He is about your age, only reads the Bible and believes the earth is flat. He killed a lion at a very young age and is popular with his peers. He wrote me a letter asking if he could meet me in person. He wants to discuss the Schoemansdal situation and noted that he is sad to say that the town, *het n slegte reuk'* (has a bad odour). He signed the letter *Kommandant Generaal van die Zuid Afrikaansche Republiek.*(Commander in Chief.)

'What's more, I already like this man. His birthday is on the same day as Antonio, 10 October. I want you to make milk tart and koeksisters. I have put new cured hams into the smokehouse and I have two gin bottles in the cellar.

'He must leave here with the understanding that, in my capacity as Vice- Councillor of Portugal, we will give him full co-operation and help him to get a route to the sea. There is even a possibility that we may move back to *Cologne da San*

Luiz at Magashulaskraal. My men are tired of fighting. They want to go back. It would be easy to establish a route from the Transvaal to Lourenço Marques. They think of a railway but the Junods and Herr Mauch told me about steam coaches. It would be a viable option from Pretoria to the Bay but not from here to Sofala.'

Gertina had nearly finished feeding the down into the eiderdown and was looking at her handiwork. 'Perhaps I can put this on his bed. Do you think he would like this lovely light pink with the sea-green paisley motive? Would it be too girlish for him?'

'You know what, *meu amor*? Kruger's tastes are uncomplicated. The blue and white eiderdown in Antonio's room will do nicely. Put fresh oranges and nectarines in a bowl, add a Bible to the bedside table and you will be fine. Ah, don't forget the spittoon. Kruger doesn't smoke but he does chew tobacco.'

João liked to know as much as possible about friends or foes before he met them. He stood up to put some more husks on the fire and looked at his wife who had pleased him in so many ways.

'How quickly can you finish sewing up that quilt?'

Gertina saw the glint in his eyes and said, 'When you ask me like that, it doesn't need finishing. Shall we try it out ourselves?'

***

222

Gertina dressed in her blue taffeta dress and Senhor Albasini in the uniform he always wore at an official engagement as they awaited the arrival of the *Kommandant-Generaal* of the Transvaal. Usually, João was keen to show off their beautiful crockery and impress guests with Gertina's cooking. Alternatively, he might add some other impeccably prepared, wholesome Portuguese dishes like Porco Preto (Portuguese ham) or chicken peri-peri.

On this day he ordered plain table settings and hearty food. Gertina was to use the white damask tablecloths and the pewter goblets. There were to be no crystal glasses, only a knife, fork and spoon. The dinner menu was to consist of roasted leg of lamb (no mint sauce, mind you, that would be too English), roasted potatoes, peas, pumpkin cakes with cinnamon, rice and a good gravy.

'Oh, and Tineka, don't forget to wrap the *Papo Secos* (bread rolls) in serviettes to keep them warm. Fresh fruit for dessert. And my best Oporto port,' he said.

They made a handsome pair as they waited for Paul Kruger. The early morning sun had not yet cleared the frost when they heard the clatter of the horses' hooves on the four hundred metre drive up to the gates of *Goedewench*. An early riser, thought Senhor Albasini, I like that.

The *Knopneuse* guards stopped the contingent. Senhor Albasini saw a nondescript but heavy of stature man who must be Paul Kruger conversing easily with the guards. As soon as Kruger announced himself, he and his contingent of ten men were allowed to enter the *Skans*.

Senhor Albasini did not quite know what to expect but was surprised to see the man who he thought to be Kruger dressed in a warm coat with only two buttons done up. His hair was short and combed to one side with a very distinctive part. His hat left a sweaty rim that made the longer hair at the back stand up stick-like. It looked as if he had not had a bath in a while. The Senhora will remedy that soon, he thought.

The agility with which the man dismounted suggested a late thirties or early forties fellow who looked him straight in the eye and extended his hand for the customary greeting. What surprised the Senhor was the hearty salutation in perfect Portuguese. Not be outdone, Senhor Albasini replied in the *Die Taal,* "*Goeie more, Kommandant.*'

Gertina was about to extend her hand but she was drawn in close and given the customary *boere* hug, as was the custom. '*Goiemore Nig.*' (Good morning, cousin.)

She looked at the two men and wondered if there was a subtle power struggle taking place. Neither man had winced at the more than firm handshake. She noticed Kruger's eyebrows knot together and was unsure if it was a sign of approval or disapproval.

From there on, the conversation took place in *Die Taal.* Kruger said, 'I believe your men's language is closely related to Zulu, which I am fluent in, but as these are serious and state matters I have come to discuss, *Die Taal* will do fine.'

The young girls stood on cue, welcoming the visitors with warm bowls of water and clean white towels.

224

***

With the preliminaries out of the way, Kruger thanked Gertina and cleared his throat to indicate that, as they would discuss matters of state, perhaps her presence wasn't necessary. When Gertina stood up to remove the blue china porcelain cups and plates, Kruger said, 'Please stay, *Nig*. What I have come to say must be heard by both of you.'

'Alarming reports of the dire situation in Schoemansdal have reached my ears. Information of corruption and lawlessness has reached the government. They even told me the presiding judge, Meintjies, was picked up and thrown out of the courtroom so that the culprits escaped without proceedings taking place. I believe you were one of the accused.'

Kruger had a twinkle in his eyes, indicating that he knew precisely how unruly the mob in Schoemansdal were.

'What I would like to talk about is this: we believe that individuals with *n slegte reuk* have treated the Venda unfairly in the sharing of the ivory. Now they sit in their stronghold, Hanglip, waiting to pounce on the already troubled settlers. They are refusing to give back to the owners the guns they used for hunting. Reports specified that the Venda have a great vantage point and innovative tactics. The punitive expedition led by Pretorius and Schoeman realised that to take them lightly is a mistake.

'For your information, that is the nearest I could see Schoeman feel embarrassed because the *Kappie Brigade*

225

concluded that the Venda had made Schoeman and his party a laughingstock.

'I have faith that we do not have to use force to press the issue and wondered if you could come up with other solutions. They say that the Venda possess at least 100 big-bore guns and ammunition. The spies tell me that a two-faced scoundrel who goes by the name of Monene helped with acquiring the arms and ammunition.

'To give you some background, our government has reported that we have a shortage of ammunition, hardly one thousand bullets.

'Schoeman estimated that he could muster 2000 armed men to come and help the Schoemansdal settlement. But the men are sick of war and he could only muster forty-two who were willing to come and help us settle the issue, and even they are dragging their feet. These men are waiting at Marrabastad for my orders.

'Of the 300 able men that were in Schoemansdal, I understand that half have already deserted the place. I have thus come in my official capacity to ask if you will consider the appointment of Superintendent of Indigenous Affairs for the ZAR?'

It was such an unexpected request that Senhor Albasini took a moment before accepting the honour that had been bestowed upon him. For once he would not be an outsider. At last they accepted him as one of Gertina's *Volk*, her kindred. He took her hand and squeezed it slightly.

Joy was surging through his mind but he kept himself in check. Always cautious, he asked, '*Kommandant*, you do not think that there will be a conflict of interest? I am, first and foremost, a Portuguese citizen and their Vice- Council. Of course, I will do anything in my power to establish the best relationships between the two forces. But I have one other question. What will my duties entail?'

Kruger looked up and said gravely, 'I believe contrary to what Schoeman says. You are the best person to handle these affairs in the district. They tell me you speak many of their languages and, if a man can master the language of the enemy, it is the most likely way to negotiate for peace, rather than killing innocent people from both parties.

'For that reason, I am learning the pudding-faced Queen's language. I think they will be the problem. I have included the duties and terms on which we will work with you.'

João nodded his head and said, 'I cannot agree more. I compare the English to the upside-down tree, the boab. They will uproot what we have established in this country and it will look like the upside down tree. Will there be any remuneration for my duties?' João asked.

Kruger stood up and handed Senhor Albasini the contract.

João weighed it in his hand before he replied, '*Kommandant*, I have to tell you that I am in the process of negotiating with the Portuguese government to perhaps move back to Magashulaskraal. When I left the area, I donated that piece of land to King Luiz.

'In the correspondence I have had with them, they have coaxed me into the idea of starting up a colony there. I am responsible for my followers who wish to escape the troublesome Venda and relocate to *Magashulaskraal*. They were happy there.'

Kruger harrumphed at this unexpected disclosure.

'You will get a percentage of the taxes from a quarterly auction held here at *Goedewench*. They also told me that you sacked Vercuil. You employed him as secretary?'

'*Ja*?' Albasini replied.

'He is now the dubious Landdrost of Schoemansdal. I believe that you dismissed him on the grounds of negligence and corruption. Rather than forward the taxes you collect to him, we would like you to pay the taxes directly into the coffers of the state instead.'

'*Kommandant* Kruger, this a big surprise and a great honour. I will discuss it with my wife and give you an answer as soon as possible. May I invite you to stay a few days? It will be my birthday on Saturday and we have arranged a gathering. We like to have some fun. There will be *jukskei* (a game played by throwing the wooden pins of the yokes at a target or stick stuck in the ground) and, of course, the highlight of the day, the young ones propelling each other into the air in a wet ox hide. We will be making big fires so that everybody can barbeque the meat over the coals.

'The women of your nation are such excellent cooks so there will be plenty to eat. I can even tempt you with succulent ham that I have cured in the Portuguese manner and which is in the smokehouse as we speak. You will have a small taste of it at lunch. It is not quite ready yet but there is enough to whet your appetite to stay longer.'

***

Senhor Albasini accepted the position and Paul Kruger opened the festivities by reading from the Bible and said grace twice, as was his habit before the guests could start to eat. The ladies grumbled afterwards and told Gertina that the food was getting cold. Could *Dominiee* van Warmelo please do the honours next time, they asked, because he says grace only once!

After many small barrels of brandy were consumed, a shooting contest was in order. Senhor Albasini overheard one of the young men mentioning casually that they thought Senhor Albasini was getting a bit long in the tooth for such shenanigans.

Albasini walked up to them casually and said, 'I take that as a challenge! Pull the puppets.'

The young men in the crowd rushed to pull the wooden marionettes that peeked their heads out above the *Skans* wall. Juwawa took his double-barrelled sanna, aimed and decapitated the first marionette to dance out of hiding on the rampart wall. To the great amusement of the crowd, he showed that he still had all of his skills, even though more people than just Gertina noticed that the twitching in his eye now extended to a mannerism of his left arm as well. His arm shot forward and waved, seemingly without purpose. Senhor Albasini quickly disguised it by willing his hand to take cover in his pocket.

There was no dancing in the evening. Kruger and Albasini both agreed that it was a habit straight from the devil himself. Senhor Albasini bought Gertina a piano for her birthday. The ornate piece of furniture usually took centre stage in the *voorkamer* but, for this memorable occasion, they carried it onto the front veranda where Gertina and the *jonkheer* Reginald Alphons van Nispen took turns in entertaining the guests. Van Nispen was an excellent pianist and also taught Antonio, who already showed great talent and had outgrown Gertina's expertise and Juwawa's patience.

***

"Wy klommen die berg met sonneskyn,
Ons harte waren opreg en rein.
Klim broeders, klim met goede moed,
Houd God voor oogen, want Hy is goed.
Wy waren nog nie by die krans,

En nog oogenblikke daarna,
Toe bidde sommige om gena. "

(By courtesy of Mrs Biccard, daughter of João Albasini)

We climbed the mountain at sunrise,
Our hearts serene and pure
Climb brothers, climb with good hope
Keep God as your guide because He is good.
We hadn't even reached the Krantz,
When some had started praying for grace.

***

'Ma, Ma. It is a terrible fight. The Venda are hiding in the caves. We have no chance for victory. They are rolling boulders the size of carts down the escarpment. Bullets and spears are pelting us constantly. They use anything for bullets in the elephant guns - broken iron pot shards, nails, you name it. Juwawa has had some victory but *Kommandant* Kruger has sent me to come and tell *Dominee* van Warmelo to ring the church bell to tell everybody to pack up as much as they can. We will be evacuating the town early on Monday morning.'

Gertina saw the fear in young Antonio's eyes and wanted desperately to hug him but, knowing that would be an insult to the young boy, she took his hand and drew him nearer to wipe the blood from the scratches on his face.

'Quick then, have a cup of coffee and run off to the *Dominee*. He will be in the fort.'

'Ma, Pa has sent Josekhulu to come and help you pack *Oma* and *Opa's* things. Pa said that you are to leave without him and Josekhulu will look after you. He also helped me down the escarpment so that we could come and deliver the message.'

The troops started moving back into the town slowly and pandemonium was the order of the day. A cacophony broke loose as pigs squealed as they were yarded and dogs yelped. Anxious cockerels and chickens scampered away into the bushes while children ran to catch them.

Instead of giving a sermon on Sunday, Dominee van Warmelo quoted from Luke 14:5, Which of you shall have an ass or an ox fallen into a pit, and will not straightway pull him out on the sabbath day?

The meagre congregation helped him knock out the church's doors and windows and loaded them onto a wagon. Gertina and Senhor Albasini had offered refuge in the *Goedewench Skans* for those who looked to Albasini and his followers for protection.

Gertina sat at the rear of the ox-wagon and remembered back seventeen years to the time when the settlers refused her husband entry into the town because of his contingent of *Knopneuse.* Now Senhor Albasini and his men were busy saving the lives of those very same people who had judged them.

232

Under the admonition of their drivers, a convoy of ox wagons moved away from the town as quickly as they could. Gertina observed the unthinkable. It seemed so many years ago that she looked at Zoutpanzbergdorp and thought of Sodom and Gomorrah. She remembered the dream of her little nephew Niklaas. He spoke about flames and hollow eyes, and what Gertina saw now made her sad. The church stood like a brave, silent, lonely sentinel, its gouged windows like vacant eyes awaiting its fate.

'Is that smoke I am smelling?' one of the women walking past Senhor Albasini's wagon said with a sob. She tried to be brave and not let her menfolk know about her anguish. They looked back and saw hungry flames devouring the thatched roofs of the houses on the outskirts of town.

Everything they had built up over twenty years had to be left behind. Gertina saw impoverished and fear-stricken women running bare-footed to the front of their wagons to take the lead of the bullocks. Their menfolk and children lay buried in the graveyard which held more graves than sermons preached by *Dominee* Van Warmelo. No one dared to look back and yearn for what could have been. It was, once again, a trek to uncertain horizons.

Gertina had to take *Dominee* van Warmelo's hand and led him away from the grave of his first wife Josina as urgently as his unwilling feet could take him. They had been married for only eleven months and eleven days when Black Water fever had claimed her generous, loving spirit.

His second wife contributed a wreath which she and Gertina had plaited hastily from the newly pruned grapevines, decorating it with herbs as greenery and tiny white forget-me-nots as flowers. Tears trickled down his weather-beaten face leaving white lines on his dirt-caked countenance.

'Josekhulu, where is Juwawa?' Gertina asked.

'Senhora, Juwawa gave me orders to get you and as many who want to stay at *Goedewench* safely there. He and N'wamanungu are following and will meet you there.'

She did not ask about Juwawa and Josekhulu thought that keeping quiet would cause no harm. He would make sure that these people got to *Goedewench* as soon as possible. Juwawa had given him 500 men to protect the wagons.

Gertina's wagon was the last to leave the town. She kept looking for João and the rest of the troops but the lonely road offered only an ominous silence.

***

On arriving at *Goedewench*, she immediately took stock of how many people were now under her care.

234

'Josekhulu, see that you manoeuvre the wagons into the stockade and light fires. Let Lya distribute bananas, coffee and dried beans to each household. Have the girls triple the amount of bread they bake today and offer it to the people as soon as it is ready. I'll take care of my own family and see that they settle. Anyone who needs medical attention, bring them to the back veranda. Make haste!'

By the time everything was sorted, she heard the *Knopkneuse* singing as they returned from the battlefield. Sadly, they were lamenting, ululating at intervals to signal their distress. When she looked out of the window, she saw N'wamanungu hurrying up the front steps carrying Juwawa over his shoulder like a bag of potatoes.

She shouted, 'Oh dear Lord, what happened? Bring him to the front room on the veranda. Lya! Lya, where are you? Bring hot water and the bag Dr Legeime left for us. Tell Wayeshe to bring the medicine men immediately. Juwawa needs immediate attention.'

Senhor Albasini groaned and told Gertina in a feeble voice, 'It is nothing serious, my love. I have just lost a lot of blood. The damn thing is, it wasn't a Venda spear or bullet that hurt me. My jacket got pinned underneath a rock and a smaller boulder left a wound to my forehead. Luckily N'wamanungu saw what happened and they rolled the boulder away. That freed me. They then tried to stop the bleeding but I am afraid the gash is extensive.'

'Stop talking, my dear, and lie still so that I can see what to do.'

Gertina had never been so frightened in her life because she would not have known what to do without Juwawa's guidance. She cleaned the wound. One of the medicine men put snuff into the cut while the others assured the Senhora. 'Juwawa will be back soon to admonish us with his *sambok* (whip). The bones predict that Juwawa will give us orders as soon as the sun rises tomorrow.'

'How many families are here, my love?' Juwawa asked.

'Thirteen,' Gertina answered.

'Mmm, I don't like it.'

'Why?'

'The number thirteen does not sit well with me, you know that. It brings bad luck.'

There was a knock on the door. N'wamanungu said, 'There are two men from chief Makakikiaan here to see you. They refuse to talk to me. Would you like me to bring them here?'

Senhor Albasini tried to raise himself but fell back against the cushions. He felt very weak from the loss of blood.

'What do the spies say? Are they safe to enter?'

'Yes, Juwawa, they have been checked, and they have brought you something from a woman.'

'See that they get food and a place to sleep and I will see them when the Senhora sees fit for me to resume my duties.'

***

Three days later, two very tall, athletic men entered the room and paid their respects. The taller of the two pointed at himself and mimicked, 'From Chief Makakikiaan, very far away from here.'

They indicated that they had something to give to João but they needed proof that he was indeed Chief Albasini. Juwawa understood little of what they said but got the gist that he had to demonstrate his authority. He knew that he was a legend among the natives because of the lions he had killed. He hoped that, if he unbuttoned his shirt and showed them the lion's nails, it would be sufficient evidence. The two men looked at each other and nodded their heads in approval.

'Well, get on with it then.'

The other man handed a piece of wood to the Senhor. To Juwawa's surprise, he saw carved into the wood the word HELP and a letter D.

Chapter 20

Troubled times

When Juwawa had recovered sufficiently, he and Antonio stood in the garden of *Goedewench* and looked around them. Antonio said, 'Dad, you know, from here for the next ninety miles we are only 27 men here at *Goedewensch* against hordes of the enemy.'

Albasini answered, 'Don't worry, my son. We will survive.'

The two messengers who brought the piece of wood spoke a dialect that was not familiar even to Juwawa. Their faces turned sad when there seemed to be nobody who could understand them until one little girl asked, '*Mammie hoekom gee mammie nie vir hom nog 'n kombers nie, hy kry koud.*' (Mommy, why don't you give the man another blanket, he must be cold?)

Senhor Albasini stooped down to pick up the little girl. 'Brilliant, 'D' stands for Dina. Yes, Dina Fourie, married to John Chambers. He is showing us a blanket. It must be Chambers, Jan Kombers's wife, who needs help.' (The settlers gave John Chambers the nickname *Jan Kombers* because Chambers sounded like *kombers*, meaning blanket.)

Gert Fourie, a member of one of the thirteen families who took refuge at *Goedewench*, let out an expletive. He fell on his knees and praised the Lord because Dina was his sister.

Senhor Albasini put men at Gert's disposal immediately and they prepared to follow the two messengers the next day to find Dina and bring her to the *Skans*.

***

When she arrived, Dina was delirious. Her caked hair formed ringlets of mud around her gaunt face and her torn, sludge-dried clothes stuck like stiffened weeds to her body. The only words she could say were, 'Makakikiaan *goed.*' (Makakikiaan is good.)

Gertina came to her rescue. 'Come, dear sweet girl. We have the hot water tub ready. I'll help you get undressed and then take you to rest in the guest quarters. Lya will bring you some clean clothes and broth and some of Juwawa's Portuguese bread.'

When Dina was fully recovered, she told her story to the many distraught observers who warmed their hands at the campfire. She had lost her father who came looking for her. She had seen his initials carved onto a tree trunk on the route. His boots were still hanging from the tree in which he had left the message and the shallow grave nearby had not yet lost its death mound. She lost all four of her children and her husband.

She told of how Makakikiaan's eighty warriors came to fetch her at Sofala. They safeguarded, nursed and fed her, and even swam across the flooded Levuvhu River to fulfil the promise Chambane had made to John. Makakikiaan kept his word of honour to fetch Dina and take her back to her people. She thanked Senhor Albasini that he had rewarded the brave warriors by slaughtering two head of cattle and had provided whatever they needed for their return journey. He sent with them a hatchet for Makakikiaan and the settlers collected money for the benefactors. Gert sent a jacket and hat for Chambane, the chief.

The *Kappie Brigade* said later that Makakikiaan greeted Dina by raising his spear and said '*Juffrou.*' (Young lady.) *Juffrou* was the only word Makakikiaan knew in *Die Taal*. His men repeated the salute.

***

Standing at the back of the campfire, Senhor Albasini was busy translating the story to a visiting Swiss immigrant who had come to work at Elim hospital. His name was John Heinlein. He fell in love with the kind and brave Dina and, after she spent four months recuperating at the *Skans*, Heinlein asked her to marry him and she accepted his proposal. The *Kappie Brigade* told the story of how Dina said, 'John happened to be my first husband's name as well and he was good to me. He was also an immigrant like you.'

Once again, there was something to celebrate. *Dominee* van Warmelo presided at the wedding. It was another *Catolico* and *Voortrekker* marriage.

On this occasion, instead of grabbing a bull by the horns, Tom Albach cut himself a sturdy bamboo reed and entertained the guests and young girls by taking a long run-up and hoisting himself over the six-foot-high *Skans* wall, returning to repeat the incredible feat several times. Each time was more daring than the others, drawing great admiration from the crowd.

***

Schoeman boasted to the authorities that he would be a better candidate to look after native affairs in the Zoutpanzberg district than the *Porra bliksem*.

'*Kommandant* Kruger, I can assure you that there will be no peace in the North while Albasini is there. He is a ....,' he paused to rephrase his original phrase of *Porra bliksem* to 'a two-faced swindler. *Uit respecte*, the Pretoria Rifle Corps, of which I am the President, will go there and mop up the mess you left at Schoemansdal. I reckon we will get about 2000 volunteers to do the job. We will resurrect Schoemansdal from the ashes.'

Kommandant Kruger knotted his eyebrows, put his hand forward for an agreement handshake and remarked, 'Very well then, I wish you luck. I presume you have enough ammunition as well?'

Kommandant Kruger saw the stunned expression on Schoeman's face and turned away, indicating the conversation was over.

Schoeman managed to gather only 42 men. They set out for the charcoal skeleton that was Schoemansdal only to find that Albasini had dug himself into a safe haven at *Goedewench* and was preparing to relocate back to Magashulaskraal near Lydenburg. The Great North dream had become a nightmare.

Never seeing eye to eye, the two men were barely civil towards each other. Senhor Albasini did not allow Schoeman to enter the *Skans and* conducted all business at the gates. Gertina was wise enough to send Lya with refreshments rather than taking them herself.

Late in the afternoon Juwawa stormed back into the house. 'Let's have some coffee to calm my soul. The man is so arrogant it is impossible to come to a sensible arrangement. He wants me to use my connections in Swaziland and get their impis to help fight the Venda. He also expects me to use my ammunition and the ZAR government will pay me back.

'I damn well know they don't have any money in their coffers. Kruger told me that the taxes I collect keep the bottom of their treasure chest barely lined.'

Gertina put her cup down with such force it rattled. 'But how can we go on fighting, using your forces, your ammunition and your resources when our supplies are so very sparse? I have been using curtain linings to sew clothes for the women and blankets to sew pants for the men. We feed them, we clothe them and now they want us to fight their battles for them. Let them fight their own wars. I have had enough! I can't wait for the letter to come from Portugal appointing you Councillor of *Cologne de san Luiz*. We need some reserves when we move. At least the Portuguese government will be paying you.'

'My dear Tineka, let us not worry too much. I have provided for you and will do so even after I have died.'

'Don't talk rubbish, Juwawa. You have the constitution of an ox and won't die in a hurry.'

'I am not so sure about that. We live in a dangerous world. I have many enemies.'

'That is true but you have many friends as well. The *Knopneuse* will never leave you in the lurch.'

'Mmm, I know that, but look what Monene did. He deserted me for greener pastures. We have not been able to capture him. He still raids the smaller tribes, burns their huts and steals their cattle. The *Ringkoppe* have a plan brewing. I am sure they will be able to catch him soon.'

Chapter 21

False accusations

As was his custom, Juwawa met with his *Ringkoppe* to discuss matters of the day. A nasty incident had taken place and Senhor Albasini did not look forward to the execution that was about to take place. He had to show strong leadership and execute the laws of his followers.

After they captured Monene, the *Ringkoppe* jailed him at *Goedewench*. Von Marneke, the architect, positioned the jail near João's office at the back of the house in clear view of anybody walking past.

Senhor Albasini and Antonio were away collecting taxes and left *Goedewench* in the capable hands of one of his favourite indunas, Wayeshe, who was getting on in age. He was to guard the jail and take care of Senhora Albasini and the family.

Lucas, Senhor Albasini's second son, was twelve years old. On that particular afternoon, he was playing the role of 'man of the house' and went out to shoot something for the pot. Returning home without success, he stood the rifle up against the jail wall and went into the kitchen to tell his ma that he had had no luck. They were sitting at the kitchen table drinking coffee when a shot splintered the wooden frame of the window overlooking the back yard. Gertina, Lya and Lucas ducked under the table in fear of another explosion. They were puzzled and, on investigation, found Wayeshe the *ringkop* strangling Monene through the bars of the jail

244

window. Monene had somehow got hold of the gun that Lucas had left leaning against the wall and fired a shot at the Senhora.

***

Senhor Albasini walked to the arena enclosed by thick bamboo. Any matters of state and other important hearings took place there. He had to handle many court cases. João used a few very clever ploys to force the guilty party to speak the truth or get him to admit to being guilty.

Sometimes he drew two lines on the ground about six feet apart. The accusers had to stand behind the line on the right side while the accused and his whole family stood behind the line on his left side. João then pulled his revolver, pointed it to the sky and dared them to jump into the space between the two lines. The understanding was that, if he fired a shot, the bullet would fall back and strike the guilty party!

Another tactic he used was to force Condi's crystals beneath the fingernails of his hand. He dared the accused to immerse his hands simultaneously with those of João's in a bucket of water. If the accused was guilty, the water would change to the colour of blood. The guilty party usually chose to admit their guilt beforehand.

He also had a touch-me-not plant. During an inquiry, João would ask a question and the culprit had to touch the plant's leaves. If the leaves closed by themselves, the accused was lying.

The *Ringkoppe,* who had spies everywhere, usually enlightened João on the matters in hand. João more or less knew the verdict beforehand. But today was different. The matter was the most serious João had ever conducted and would have far reaching consequences.

***

He put on his uniform, draped the lion's skin over his shoulders and buckled his swords into place. On second thought, he took one off and placed it on the table. He would need only one today.

Gertina saw him walk to the alcove. He faltered and turned back to the house but, after sighing and shaking his head, he continued on. She knew about his distress because he loved Wayeshe like a family member. There was no way he could defend the guilt of his trusted warrior who had fallen asleep which allowed Monene to get hold of the gun and fire the shot at Gertina.

At the meeting, it was unanimous that Wayeshe should be de-ringed. According to the other leaders, Lucas was still a child and, therefore, could not be blamed. They demanded that Wayeshe be stripped of his rank. He was no longer worthy to be a part of the elite. He had failed in his duties.

Juwawa, King of the *Knopneuse,* looked at his long-trusted companion and their mutual understanding was apparent. What had to be done had to be done. After the charges were laid and the guilty verdict passed, Juwawa proceeded to insert the point of his sword in between the beeswax ring and the scalp.

Each jab drew blood and with each jab there was a cheer of approval. During the ordeal, Wayeshe stood up straight, accepting his punishment as bravely as was expected of a soldier in the *Knopneuse* army. He walked away to his hut where they knew he would fall on his spear and kill himself, as was expected of him.

When Juwawa walked back to his office he could still hear the leaders chasing the guilty man away as if he were a stray dog, shouting, '*Zuku! Zuka* !' (Go away. Go away.)

Juwawa refused coffee, lunch or dinner. A sombre mood prevailed throughout the house. The absence of Lucas went unnoticed. They later found him clutching Wayeshe's dead hand.

***

At midday an officer of the law made his appearance. It was clear that his horse was hard-ridden because lather was flying in all directions. The young man dismounted and entered at the back of the house where the grief-stricken family was having a meal on the back veranda.

'I am so sorry to disturb you but I am an officer of the court. I am looking for Senhor João Albasini.'

'Speak up young man,' João said.

'I presume you are Senhor João Albasini?'

'That is correct.'

'I have here a letter from Pretoria.'

'Give it, man, let me see.'

Senhor Albasini gave the letter to Gertina to read. He saw Gertina pale visibly and her hands shook.

She looked at Juwawa and said, 'They …' she swallowed, 'they have summoned you to court for the murder of a young boy.'

There was shocked silence at the table.

'This is incredulous. I have never murdered anybody in cold blood. Yes, men have died but it was either in war or self-defence. Who are these dogs who slander my name in such a damnable fashion? I would like to smoke them out and let them rot somewhere on a tree. The whole blooming ZAR army and its empty coffers can come and get me here! Do you understand?'

'Juwawa, calm down, my dear.'

'How can I calm down if they accuse me of murder? Who do they think I am? Low-class scum?'

Senhor Albasini rose from his chair but, when the enormity of the summons sank in, he sat down slowly to give it deep thought.

'My apologies, young man. You must be hungry. Please sit down and share in our meal.'

The young man sat down by the empty space. 'Thank you, Senhor Albasini.'

'I have just lost one of my most trusted friends, so you will excuse me if I am not myself. But, can you tell me, how long have I got before I have to be in court to clear my name?'

'Three months, sir.'

'Very well then. At least I'll be able to bury my friend and grieve on the way there.' There was a moment of silence before João continued, 'I have an errand for you. I see that you have come here in good time. Would it be too much if I ask you to take a letter to my lawyer, Jan Preller? I would like to ask him how serious this matter is. I have been summoned to court, including this one, three times this year. They threw out the previous accusations of slavery and tax evasion because there was no hard and fast evidence. All the evidence provided was on hearsay.

'They must have their ears checked. I know this is a ploy of Schoeman to waste my time and money. Travelling to Pretoria and back, for my health, I ask you? It's an expensive exercise.

Dangerous too. The ZAR wants me to leave my wife and children at the drop of a hat. You can also take my resignation as Superintendent of Indigenous Affairs and tell them to stick it where it belongs.'

'Juwawa, we have a guest and children at the table!' Gertina admonished indignantly.

'Let me be woman! Either that or hell.'

***

After the sadness of Wayeshe's death, Senhor Albasini was glad that he had something else to occupy his mind. He harnessed a mule to drag a plough through an unbroken field and trudged behind in grim determination. He finished the ploughing in record time.

He had his wildest stallion saddled and disappeared into the wild with only his gun and saddlebags. He stayed away for a week and came back dishevelled and looking haggard, his eyes bloodshot and his cheeks hollow.

He stood at a distance from Gertina and said to her calmly, 'Tineka, I am going to break my promise to you this time only. Would you mind finding me that bottle of fortified port our friend Des Nerves brought me when he stayed with us? Please don't bother me. I'll see you in the morning.'

He went into the spare room on the veranda and closed the door behind him.

**

Two weeks later, the same young man returned with a letter from the lawyers saying that the matter was most urgent and that Senhor Albasini should come as soon as possible to prepare a defence. Senhor Albasini could have let the matter go but remembered his mother's words, 'You only have one name; don't soil it.' Out loud he said, 'We'll show the bastards.'

Juwawa blew on his whistle and, within a short time, all his indunas gathered at his office.

'Get the new wagon ready. We will take ten of our *Ringkoppe* and go and show them what an honourable man looks like.'

About eighty miles into the journey, the steel bands of the right rear wheel snapped. Juwawa and his men improvised by tying a chunk of wood to the wagon's back axle as a spare wheel. They plodded back to *Goedewench* to get another wagon but, about ten miles into the return trip, they met a farmer who was willing to do an exchange - a brand new wagon with only three wheels for a rickety old one with four wheels.

***

Senhor Albasini arrived in Pretoria in the evening before the trial, leaving hardly any time to prepare for a defence.

The next morning the courtroom was packed. When the charge was read out, Senhor Albasini rose and said, 'Not guilty.'

He sat in stoic silence as he listened to the evidence. The prosecution argued that Senhor Albasini participated in a shooting contest. They said that he ordered a small *pikanini*, a little black boy, to be brought and put up on the wall of the *Skans* as a target for him to shoot.

Senhor remembered the incident well when the drunken young men challenged him to a shooting contest. At the time he just happened to be looking for an opportunity to try out his new, grooved, double-barrelled gun. Calling for the puppets was an excellent excuse to test it out.

Senhor Albasini jumped up from his chair, burst out laughing and, to the dismay of Jan Preller and his team, firmly and confidently said, 'Your Honour and all present. Those with a clear conscience and those who want to defame me, be assured that I would like to plead…,' he waited to get the full attention of the crowd and then dropped the bombshell, 'I would like to change my plea from Not Guilty to….' he paused again, 'to, Guilty! I'll take the defence from here.'

The audience could not believe their ears and waited in anticipation. Senhor Albasini recalled the date and time of the event and proceeded to explain what had happened that day. Being a great storyteller, he had no problem describing how he had crafted black wooden puppets which were connected by pulleys. When a hostile tribe would attack, the children and women were called to pull the puppets.

Shooting the images, the attackers would think they were real people and throw their assegais wasting valuable ammunition. João's men who were hiding in the bushes could then easily attack the enemy and safeguard the Skans. Senhor Albasini had the court and judges in fits of laughter when he explained how some young men stood in awe when he toppled the first puppet that was drawn.

The judge rapped his gavel several times before he proclaimed the accused, 'Not guilty.' The court adjourned for the rest of the day.

***

Senhor Albasini walked out of the courtroom talking to friends and his team who were still laughing at the ridiculous accusation. He had an uneasy feeling that someone was watching him. That sixth sense of his kicked into action and, when he looked up, he saw Schoeman standing on the steps of the building. His beady eyes shifted from side to side, gauging where and how he would be able to confront Senhor Albasini.

'It was you, you son of a bitch?' Senhor Albasini shouted at Schoeman who stood splendidly dressed in his Pretoria Rifle Club's uniform, a satisfied smirk on his face. Because of the shape of his jaw, Schoeman's bottom lip protruded, leaving him no choice as to smile at his nemesis with tobacco-stained bottom teeth. His head was slightly drawn backwards. He was expecting a blow from the man who was moving forward quickly. The only man he could never goad into an outright fight had now risen to the challenge.

He said, 'How is your Gertina? Does she still have a bad breath?' Then he added the final blow, 'She was quite willing to marry me, you know?'

That was the last straw. Albasini lunged forward, grabbed Schoeman by his buttoned-up jacket and pulled so hard that two buttons popped off. Schoeman's tilted hat went flying and landed in the dust.

Albasini felt the taller man's hot breath on his face. He was nauseous and blind with pent-up rage. With a heavy voice, he spat, 'I'll...I'll *donner* (punch) you! If I have been acquitted of a guilty verdict, I am happy to go back into court and be found guilty of legitimate murder. You scum.'

With a quick movement he pulled 'Snotklap' towards him with great force and head-butted him. Albasini had the satisfaction of seeing the blood flow from Schoeman's left eye spilling over the white shirt which was part of the Pretoria

Riflemen's uniform. N'wamanungu rushed forward and pulled Juwawa away. The other *Ringkoppe* formed a protective circle around Juwawa.

In a clear voice N'wamanungu said to the raging bull in front of him, 'Juwawa! Think! Even the Venda say a clever man cannot surpass the careful thinker. We are taking you home.'

Chapter 22

Surprising news

Senhor Albasini knew why he failed so miserably to contain his temper. He could easily have killed Schoeman and was glad of the intervention by N'wamanungu and his other indunas.

The real problem was that his fortune was depleted by the unnecessary travel to and from Pretoria. The elephant trade had come to a standstill and he had to admit that he could not repeat to Tineka, 'I am rich, very rich'. Instead he could now say, 'I am poor, very poor!'

That was not the only surprise he had for her. His lawyer, Preller, told him that there was a lady from Graaff Reinet asking about the Albasini family and, in particular, Gertina. Mr. Preller gave Albasini the address of the woman concerned and he set off to meet her.

He was pleasantly surprised to find that the lady in question, Anna Sophia, was a relative of the ill-fated van Rensburg trek. Anna was forewarned about the visit and had read about the court case and the hilarious turn of events. Senhor Albasini knocked on the door and an elderly, well-dressed lady opened the door.

'Ah, there you are Senhor Albasini. I was waiting for you to come. I have some very interesting facts to share with you.'

'Glad to make your acquaintance, madam,' he said. The lady took Albasini's hat and coat and hung them on the rail mounted to the wall.

'It is a long story. Come and sit down so that I can explain. I'll make it brief. I was about eleven years old when my family decided to join the Louis Trichardt trek. I am Lang Hans van Rensburg's oldest daughter and it was decided that I should stay behind in Graaff-Reinet. I had to look after a wealthy couple who had taken a fancy to me and promised to pay for my education. They all believed that I was very gifted and felt that the trek option would not be in my best interests. It was only last year that I had a visit from a relative in the Zoutpanzberg district who told me that you were partly responsible for saving two children from the massacre that took place. It was to my great joy that I realised I have two siblings and so I set about tracing them. When your court case was so widely published, I knew I was on the right track and now, Senhor Albasini, I can gladly say that I am glad to be your sister-in-law, Anna Sophia Goodman, born Janse van Rensburg. Let's just say my husband recognised my musical talents and the rest is history.'

Senhor Albasini sat motionless and absorbed the information quietly. 'My dear lady, Gertina, I call her Tineka, will be overwhelmed. You must come and stay with us but I must warn you that we live very frugally. We are means poor but asset rich. We live from the land and very little else. Families who fled from the Schoemansdal fiasco live with us at the *Skans*. I have to look at how to care for these people in the future. I have considered going to the Kimberley diamond fields or leave the district completely and set up a colony for Portugal near Lydenburg.'

Anna was impressed. 'Dear Senhor Albasini, let's visit first and then we can discuss the diamond fields proposition better. I happen to know some of my husband's family, a Sammy Marks who has gone to the diamond fields to make his fortune. I will let Mr Preller investigate and we can take it from there.

'I have been left some means by my late husband which I will gladly share with my newfound family. I have no other family.'

Senhor Albasini stood up and went up to the lady. 'I presume you will have no objection to me giving you a hug. May I call you Anna, sister?'

***

Albasini arrived home in high spirits and there was great jubilation when Gertina was reunited with her sister. There was a sense of hope because of the prospect of making money on the diamond fields.

Plans for a Cologne da San Luiz were put on hold and preparations made to go to Kimberley. With Anna's contacts, Senhor Albasini's *Volk* would go with the Senhor and his family to seek their fortune there.

On arrival at the diamond fields, Albasini was disappointed. Obtaining work for his loyal Knopneuse was no problem but he was regarded as a slave trader and shunned by the community. He took refuge on the farm of Mr Christiaan Dreyer and opened a small shop but to no avail. He had no luck in cards, diamonds or work.

Gertina was in the last month of pregnancy with their ninth child. Juwawa suggested they name the baby, if it was a girl, Anna Sophia. *Tante* Anna would be the godmother although she was getting on in age. Anna Sophia Albasini was born on 10.6.1874. There were no *tantes* of the Kappie Brigade to ooh and aah over the pretty little girl. When Anna could walk properly, her sister Maria Machdelena chose her as a flower girl when she decided to marry Christiaan Dreyer's son.

When the Indunas who had stayed behind in Zoutpanzberg heard about the hardships of their chief, they sent 500 young men to bring him and his family back to *Goedewench*. Five litters and several wagons were sent to carry the family home. Juwawa's *Knopneuse* were to follow as soon as they could.

On João's return he served the ZAR Government as Justice of the Peace and as Native Commissioner. He was also a member of the District Council earning a meagre wage.

Chapter 23

Confrontation and collapse

Returning from one of his tax collecting excursions, Albasini was met by circumstances beyond his control. It was late in the afternoon when he returned to *Goedewench*. Senhor Albasini thought about how quickly his life had passed by. He looked forward to a hearty meal, a soft bed and Tineka's welcoming arms.

Both the trading and the tax collecting he had conducted had gone well. He sold two sets of billiard balls which enabled him to buy Tineka a sewing machine, new bed linen and several rolls of material.

'Anybody home?' he called.

Nellie, short for Pitronella, came out of her room and said, 'Mammie is in your office. She said you are to go and greet her there.'

Concerned at this unusual reception, Senhor Albasini rushed to the office. In passing, he noticed the repairs to the kitchen window and that the jail was empty. They could start again. People were moving back to the district but a new and calmer world awaited them at Luiz. He took the steps two at a time and entered the office.

***

He did not often get the 'evil eye' from his wife but it chilled him to the bone when he did. Gertina could be stubborn and very unreasonable at times. He wondered what he had done wrong this time.

Her neat, trim figure sat upright in the casual chair that he kept for visitors. She sat motionless, her mouth set in a thin straight line and her hands, usually never idle, lay still in her lap.

'What is it, my love?' he asked.

He knelt and took her hands one at a time and kissed each with the tenderness and generous love that he felt for her. He realised he was indeed capable of murder if it concerned her. This brave and industrious woman who stood by him even when the odds were high now looked at him with icy blue eyes.

She withdrew her hands slowly, one by one.

'João? '

The voice was heavy and her eyes unwavering. Senhor Albasini thought, she never calls me João. What on earth can be the matter?

'We had a visitor when you were away.'

'Yea, we have many visitors.'

'It was a female.'

'All by herself?' Senhor Albasisni asked.

'A whore.' Gertina spat at him. 'Adorned in bangles, painted eyes and asking to see you in connection with a contract you agreed to sign.'

'And what was her name, if I may ask?'

Senhor Albasini stood and stepped away from Gertina who continued, 'She says you have agreed to open a bottle store at her institution at Punda. Her name is Maria. I ask you, João, how can you think of a liaison with a woman of that kind? Trading in alcohol when you know what a dislike I have for the fornicators and debauchers? Is it not the same woman I saw at the start of our life together?'

He had not expected this welcome! 'She is a good friend of mine from my pre-Voortrekker days. I saved her life in a terrible fire that burnt her 'institution' to the ground. She approached me again to say that I could do a roaring trade if I opened a bottle store next to her building. I thought,' he scratched his head in confusion, 'seeing that the ivory trade has diminished, my diamond adventure a disaster and the ZAR not paying any compensation, I have to look for other means to support my family.'

He paused to see what her reaction would be. There was still no melting of the ice. 'If this venture goes against your nature, I will not sign the contract and endeavour to look for other means of income. What else did she say?'

Through pressed lips Gertina said, 'Tell me about family in Lourenço Marques.'

João said, 'Shall I order some sandwiches and coffee? I am starving. It is a long story.'

***

He was about to call Josekhulu when the door was flung open. N'wamanungu stood there holding a letter in his hand.

'Very urgent, very urgent, Juwawa.'

'Thank you. Wait outside. Please ask Josekhulu to bring us some food and coffee.'

Senhor Albasini took the letter opener from his desk and opened the envelope which carried the official stamp of the Governor of Lourenço Marques. He unfolded the letter and started to read. Gertina saw the colour drain from his face.

'Swine, they have moved the boundary lines from 23 to 26 degrees longitude. Magashulaskraal now belongs to the ZAR and I have lost my dream. The *Cologne de san Luiz* is no more.'

He was devastated but he had to answer Tineka's question.

'Loving you is like breathing. How can I stop?' Before he could answer her question, his hands flew to his head, clutching it in anguish. 'Oh, my head, oh, my head!'

He saw the dark mahogany desk where he had written so many letters drifting in front of him at a strange angle. The porcupine quills, sharpened and neatly stacked, stood in a holder next to an ornate ink well. It was a present from his father. The last quill he used still balanced on the bride's arms, cradling it as something she valued. He wanted to hold the books lining the walls and tell them how sorry he was that, because of his poverty, he had to tear out the front and back pages to write on. He wanted to glue them back in but the headache was too severe. He thought that he must put on his work coat which hung from the three-pronged rattan stand. But the ostrich feather that stuck jauntily in his straw hat's band quivered in the breeze, signalling him to let go of his head, but he couldn't.

He heard somebody grunt and realised it was himself.

***

Gertina saw things happen as if in slow motion. Albasini's left hand fell from holding his head and the twitching stopped. His left eye looked at her without blinking. His mouth drooped on one side and he lisped his last words.

She rushed forward to bring a chair for him to sit on but was too late. She saw him trying to grab the chair but to no avail. He fell to the floor, his right leg kicking aimlessly in the air as if it was willing the other leg to stand up. Droplets of perspiration sat like fat beads on his face, slowly accumulating into bigger ones that dropped on the faded Persian carpet's intricate pattern.

264

'Josekhulu, N'wamanungu, come quickly, come and help me. Juwawa is unwell.'

The two most trusted friends rushed in to see Juwawa clutching his head.

'What happened, Senhora? Josekhulu asked.

'I have pain in my head. That is all. Please take me to my room,' Albasini lisped through tight lips.

Panic paralysed Gertina's thinking. Josekhulu cradled Juwawa in his arms and carried him to the room on the front veranda.

N'wamanungu said, 'I'll go and call Antonio to be with you, Senhora. When we were on our way back, we saw Dr Eyssell on his way to visit the Bester farm. I will dispatch somebody to get him to come as soon as possible. Would you like me to contact Dr Leingme at Elim as well?'

'Yes, thank you, N'wamanungu.'

She went to Juwawa's room and sat by his bed, wiping his face with a damp cloth. She tried to close his eye but it kept falling open.

'I'm so sorry. I'm so sorry.'

Juwawa wanted to smile but all he could see were the contract's signatures between the ZAR government and The Governor of Mozambique. One of the witnesses had signed in an ugly black scrawl: Stephanus Schoeman.

Chapter 24

Memories

Senhor Albasini never recovered fully from the stroke and remained bedridden for three years. He kept council with his Indunas and reminisced about old times.

They recalled the story of how they helped Modjaji, the rain queen, by ending the harassment she received from Magoro, a hit and run brigand. Juwawa grasped the opportunity to win another ally in Modjadji who was a powerful ruler.

They sent out spies who returned after a month to report on the comings and goings of Magoro's warriors, womenfolk, cattleherds and visitors. Everything was carefully tabulated. It struck Juwawa that the cattleherds (grown and strong men) hardly ever varied in numbers and were always counted in and out when they descended or climbed the spiral path with their herds. The area was prone to heavy mists which sometimes lay low on the ground for days on end. Visibility was almost zero. The mist was always accompanied by a biting breeze and the herd-boys were usually swathed in blankets during their time of duty.

A very simple method was chosen to put a spike in Magoro's arrangements. N'wamanungu, together with fifty specially chosen Shangaans, infiltrated the grazing area of the Magoro herds and, carefully biding their time, overpowered the herders during a heavy mist.

At the usual time, the cattle were gathered and driven home up the path but, this time, by the Shangaans in Venda dress. The sentries discovered the deception too late and Magoro was marched to *Goedewench* in shackles.

Modjadji was informed and given the right of passing sentence on Magoro. She was a peace-loving ruler and only demanded that Magoro behave himself and confine his thieving to his own area. N'wamanungu was never allowed to forget that he had to dress up as a *Muvhesha,* a G-string wearer, in order to win that victory.

The story they liked the most was of the time when João II was born. Makhato, another Venda chief, hated N'wamanungu intensely and offered many wives and cattle to thirty of his best warriors to capture N'wamanungu. They knew there would be celebrations till late in the night and saw it as an ideal opportunity to capture or kill him.

They arrived at *Goedewench* late on the second night of the celebrations and hid in the bushes. The Shangaans were having a Royal party and the usual strict discipline was somewhat relaxed. N'wamanungu's hut was somewhat removed from his subordinates because of his rank and the Venda waited patiently for him to enter his hut and fall asleep before challenging him.

Although still befuddled by drink and tired from dancing, N'wamanungu woke to the realisation that he was in serious difficulties. Undoubtedly there was somebody within hailing distance to assist him but it was beneath his dignity to call for help. In any case, he was not averse to a good fight and had no love for the G-string wearers.

As was the custom, she-goats with kids were tethered inside huts for protection against marauding hyenas and jackals. Such a nanny-goat shared N'wanamungu's lodgings and so he planned his strategy. He untethered the goat and, grabbing his short stabbing spear, shouted to the Venda, 'Suns of dogs and misbegotten sons of drunken fathers, here I come! Be prepared to die for your impertinence! The son of Ngungunyane is coming forth and woe the man who remains within a stone's throw away from me. Here I come!' He jerked the door inwards and pushed the nanny-goat out.

Venda spears rain on the luckless goat while N'wamanungu took them from the rear and created havoc with his short *knobkierie*. They took flight with the old warrior at their heels. They crossed the river and, when twelve of them reached the sanctuary of the forest, the other eighteen lay strewn along the way. N'wamanungu cut off their right ears at his leisure and presented them to Juwawa at the dance.

The indunas remembered the verbal lashing they received from Juwawa when they failed to capture Lwamondo and his witchdoctor Masindi. 'Call yourselves warriors? A flock of women and weaklings! Why I bother to appoint idiots and the spineless as Generals, I don't know. Be prepared in two days' time to follow me personally to teach this Venda dog his lesson!'

It was most embarrassing! N'wamanungu was quick to remind them how he had slung Masindi's fat body over his shoulder, carried him down the mountain and dropped him at Juwawa's feet early the next morning, causing Juwawa to splutter his coffee. N'wamanungu was jubilant because this seemingly impossible feat of single-handedly capturing a witchdoctor who acted as a bodyguard to the chief earned him Juwawa's praise. Lwamondo's power was broken without the witchdoctor's guidance.

Chapter 25

A dignified passing

Lya, always gracious, approached Gertina to tell her, 'Senhora, you need to prepare yourself. Our King is going to die today.'

'Don't talk to me like that, Lya! You know João is a fighter. He won't give up. He has recovered previously, there's no reason he shouldn't do it again.'

Lya bent down on her knees, tears streaming down her cheeks. 'Yes, Senhora, but it has been three years now that he has been lying in bed. N'wamanungu, my husband, said he saw a star move last night. In his culture, it tells us a King is going to die.'

She sighed again before continuing, 'Senhora, please put on your blue taffeta dress. I have prepared it for you. You know that he likes to see you wear it. I have cleaned his uniform and I have waxed the imperial *karos*.'

She resumed her plea, her voice pitched even higher, anxious to convince her mistress. 'Senhora! The pigeons did not eat today. They are listless, there is no flapping of their wings and they just sit. Please, Senhora, don't be caught off guard. Prepare yourself. Don't cry. When a king dies, we don't cry. You cry later when they don't see you. Tell your children, especially Antonio, even if it breaks his heart, not to cry. Juwawa's people will not accept him as the next King if he does.'

Fear gripped Tineka. She turned and went to her room to put on the most beautiful dress she had ever possessed. It had changed her life and her way of thinking. If only she could turn back the clock and give João the assurance that he had been the only one she had ever and would ever love.

Even though João had indicated that he had forgiven her, she still felt responsible for the incident that caused the latest stroke. She remembered when her adopted father, Lucas, invited João for a cup of coffee after church.

'Gertina, that's your name, eh?' João said. Just the soft, prolonging sound of the 'a' in Gertina was a caress in itself. She was in love and didn't even know it.

'It sounds German to me. However, I struggle with the guttural sound. Perhaps I'll call you Tineka.' He continued, 'I happen to have a piece of taffeta to match those charming eyes. Somebody who plays music to touch my soul deserves a reward. Hopefully, you will be able to make a dress for a very special occasion. I hope I can be a part of it one day.'

Her experience taught her to pay attention to what the followers of João said. She needed time. The pain of losing one she so loved dearly and admired greatly made her tread slowly and heavily.

As she took her time she realised that the dress had stood the test of time. Thirty-two years of boundless experiences together with extraordinary events and adventures to be told time and again made her wonder about her future. She and her children were neither here nor there. She couldn't be the

Queen of the *Knopneuse*. How could she? She was a *Voortrekker*. Antonio would be crowned as their next King and little João, her grandchild, would follow him.

She remembered the day João II was born. Juwawa had grabbed the baby wrapped in a blanket and rushed out onto the veranda. He unclipped the brooch, placed it into the baby's hand and closed it softly with his own hand. He greeted his men, 'My bambino, my bambino!' He did a jiggle and said, '*Bayete Inkosi!*' (He will also be your king one day!)

But times were changing. Would anybody ever believe that João existed or that he had a following of 5000 people who worshipped him? Impossible! João had created a nucleus of people, a unique cluster, who survived because of his efforts. What would happen to the *Knopneuse*? How would they survive? João was poor. There was no money left. When he died, the *Knopneuse* would be destitute and leaderless.

Antonio didn't have his father's leadership abilities. He was sickly and little João would live in another era when many Europeans would infiltrate the area of Luonde, Piesangkop. The sanctuary João had created would disappear. The *Knopneuse* would become servants, the very thing João fought to avoid. They would not be able to keep *Goedewench*. Ruins and rubble would greet those visiting Juwawa's grave. English jaws were already wide open to swallow the Transvaal.

She splashed her face with water from the basin and dried it slowly. She dressed with great care. Her arms felt like lead but she forced herself to comb her hair up high and pinned it carefully with the two diamond-studded combs João had given her at Antonio's birth. She looked in the mirror and was satisfied that Juwawa would go to heaven with her image firmly planted in his brain. His Tineka would be his queen, loving and adorable. She would stand by him as she did as a wife and now, in his last hour, as a guest to see him say farewell.

She took the now faded uniform from the bed and brushed away imaginary dust particles. The golden epaulets still looked magnificent but it was with sad anticipation that she realised that the emaciated body of her beloved husband could never fill them with the pride and joy he had carried for this uniform. She eventually left the room, steeling herself for this day that she and all his followers never wanted to happen.

On entering his room, N'wamanungu stood up slowly. 'Senhora, I am glad you have prepared yourself. My friend, my master has asked that only you and I be present.'

Senhor Albasini opened his eyes. The fierce green light had faded but his compassion and love for her shone through. He signed to her. 'Sit down, *cara*, I have little time left.'

João opened his eyes. He turned his face toward N'wamanungu and unclipped his mother's rosary. 'You are to have my rosary. It is valuable. You can sell it and use the money. I always hoped you would accept my faith but, faith or no faith, you served me better than I have served you.'

He pointed to his little finger. N'wamanungu realised that Juwawa wanted him to take off the ring which was the duplicate of Tineka's. His marriage token came off easily and João continued pointing to his head, indicating that he had used reason for his decisions. 'That is for Mamahela and the other sons, Antonio and Francisco. See that they get it.'

Senhor Albasini continued, 'My Tineka, when I spotted Tommy sitting in a tree over-looking the river where your family was murdered, I also saw the iron rims of the wagons. I returned later to claim the iron and had it melted down to be sold. I used the money to buy my first guns and ammunition to start my trading as an ivory merchant. I always felt guilty about it but I have made amends and have deposited a fair amount of money in The Bank of Lisbon. It is for you and Hendrik to retrieve and use as you may need it. Also, look carefully under the lapels of my uniform and you will see that I had diamonds sewn into the woven gold. That is if you should need immediate money. Sammy Marks, my friend and *Tante* Anna's acquaintance ,will be able to help you.'

He pointed to Tineka's ring, indicating that he wanted her to take it off. He folded her hand in his non-paralysed hand. He looked up at her, thanking her with his eyes. He held onto her hand and pointed to the twin rings' inscriptions. *Manus in Manu* was inscribed in Tineka's ring. He gestured at the other ring and asked N'wamanungu to show it to Tineka. She read, *Pari Passu*. He cleared his throat and continued.

'There won't be unity between black and white for many years but my death wish is for you to keep my secret. Time will show that Juwawa, King of the *Knopneuse*, was a visionary. He wished for *assimilato*, for equal rights, for a

274

right to live and for the freedom of slaves. He wished for *Manus un Manu'*, hand in hand, and *Pari Passu*, with an equal step for all.'

He paused before continuing, 'I, João Albasini, have lived my faith. I have experienced the meaning of my name, *God is gracious*. I have left you a letter in one of the breast pockets of the uniform.' He closed his eyes and tears trickled down his temples. He hardened his grip on Gertina's hand and, by force of will, he breathed, 'My Tineka!' He reverted to Italian, '*Solo tua*'. (Only yours.)

Hand in hand, he died.

Gertina Pitronella Maria Albasini, born van Rensburg, sat motionless yet brave, without tears, showing respect and love for her extraordinary husband. N'wamanungu gave back her ring and pocketed the other.

***

N'wamanungu, bent down reverently, unclipped the lion nail brooch from the gold chain around his King's neck. He stood rigid, his jaws clenched, only his big Adam's apple working up and down, showing the inner turmoil and grief that he felt.

He left Gertina, closed the door and went to look for Antonio Augusto Albasini, the triple-A of his name standing for excellence. He would be the next King of the *Knopneuse*.

N'wamanungu shivered slightly as a question crossed his mind, would Antonio be as good a king?

N'wamanungu unhooked the Kudu horn from the yellow wood stand in the entry. He walked out onto the front veranda and noticed that it was late afternoon, almost dusk, a time befitting for a King to die.

The magnificent African sun, heavy with blood, was severed by the Lebombo mountains' jagged ridges. A fierce, red-orange blanket engulfed the charcoal silhouettes of the tall jacaranda trees lining the pathway that lead up to the entrance of *Goedewench*. The guinea fowls stopped screeching their sorrowful message of 'Bankrupt! Bankrupt!'

N'wamanungu had warned Juwawa about these funny-looking chickens. It was common knowledge among his people that you would become bankrupt if you kept guinea fowls in your yard.

N'wamanungu lifted the horn to his lips slowly. The woeful howl of the jackals pre-empted the news. N'wamanungu blew the horn, two short bursts and one long, announcing, 'A king has died.' The sound of lament echoed, carrying the message out over the valley inhabited by a nation, a nation born out of respect, admiration and reverence for a man whose leadership had meshed them into the Mashangaan, a tribe of which to be proud.

It was a tribe that, many years later, adhered to the principles instilled by Juwawa, their King. The mining companies of South Africa acknowledged their work ethic and bravery.

276

Invariably a Shangaan would be chosen as a Boss Boy in the mines for just those qualities.

N'wamanungu, in his grief, noticed the upside-down tree still standing lonely and immovable, a dignified sentinel ready to absorb the history of the next two centuries. It would witness the changes colonisation would bring to Africa, two World Wars, and the rise and fall of *Apartheid*. In time, it would behold the birth and death of another great leader, Mandela, who might never have heard about Juwawa but certainly brought the same ideas to fruition. Could it be that Juwawa was a Mandela born nearly 200 years too early?

The African night dimmed her light on an unsung hero. Far away in the Basque country, a morning sun greeted mothers who were telling their sons, 'There is no 'Happy ever after' but 'Heroes, if they lived well, they died well'.

The letter

(Courtesy of Lynette de Vaal van der Merwe: João "bravest among the brave")

A rough translation from 'Presenças Portuguesa na África do Sul e na Tranvaal durante os Séculos"XVIII e XIX. (I don't know if you want this parte too). Publicado pelo Ministério de Educação, Instituto de Investigação Científica Tropical, Lisboa 1989.'

During my life on this earth I have tried my best to always act justly and wisely, because I would like posterity to be proud of me.

Unfortunately, there are a few things that happened during my life of which I feel ashamed, but my innate honesty and integrity prevent me from keeping them secret indefinitely. I am not trying to excuse myself, but the reader of this document must please take the circumstances and times in which they happened into consideration.

One of the Venda chiefs, Mashau, posed many problems for me. He didn't want to pay taxes so my faithful induna, Wamanungu and I made plans to take him captive.

Three thousand warriors would openly proceed by daylight with me to the foot of the mountain and pitch camp.

Wamanungu and about a hundred of the most courageous and strongest warriors would move along the other side over

*the crest of the mountain, take cover and wait for me to light
a fire, signalling that the attack must begin.*

*Mashau felt secure in his stronghold at the top of the
mountain. He even took a stand on the cliffs and shouted
derogatory remarks to us. When the sun went down without
us starting to attack, the Vendas thought that we were trying
to starve them. Close to midnight I lit the fire and commanded
the Shangaans to storm the mountain. Mashau was rudely
disillusioned when Wamanungu and his men attacked the
village from behind and took him captive when he was not yet
fully awake. They tied his arms behind his back and forced
him to walk down the mountain. He came face to face with me
next to the fire. I was in full uniform. Mashau was defiant and
made derogatory comments. It enraged me and I drew my
sword and touched his extraordinary fat paunch with the
point of the sword to show him who was the boss.*

*Unfortunately, one of the worriers encircling us excitedly
jostled me so that the point of my sword pierced Mashau's
belly. He squealed like a pig, especially when fat and entrails
started protruding from the gash. Wamanungu finished off
with his knobkierrie, this man who had defied us for so long.*

*Another thing that robs my peace of mind happened many
years ago when I was a young bachelor in Mozambique. I
lived in the vicinity of Intamane, at that time I was a big game
hunter and trader. Black refugees sought protection from me,
and I supplied them with game and food during the drought
of three years. They made me their chief and were willing to
work for me as porters in exchange for protection when I went*

into the interior for trading and bartering ivory. They called me Juwawa and would do anything for me.

A benevolent chief of one of the tribes whom I helped during these difficult times gave his beautiful daughter to me as a gift. To preserve peace and not give rise to offence I took the girl into my house. Many of the young Portuguese men in Mozambique took black wives during those years because there were few Portuguese girls available for marriage. By that time, I could already speak a number of black languages and had no difficulty communicating with the girl. She gave birth to two sons, Antonio and Francisco, by me. Later we moved to Lourenço Marques where I was considered a rich man.

However, the lure of new horizons, challenges and adventures was too strong to resist, and I decided to trek into the interior. After I had been wandering around in the interior for months, exploring the possibilities, I went back to Lourenço Marques to say farewell to the woman in my house and my two sons. I gave them my thatched-roof house in which they lived, some rondavels, five cows and four slaves. I made certain that my sons would get the best education possible available in Lourenço Marques at that time.

Although I never spoke about my two sons in Mozambique, I never forgot them. The Boers had higher moral standards concerning relationships between men and women than the Portuguese in Mozambique. My history would definitely have upset them, and they probably would have rejected me. We were interdependent and therefore I decided to keep my peace.

I want to assure my children in both countries that I have loved you equally and I trust that the blood connection between you may be symbolic of the good relationships between the two nations. I have very few possessions and little money left for you to inherit, but may you live prosperously in this part of the beautiful country South Africa that I have helped to tame with hard work and much hardship. This is my heritage to all of you...."

Thanks

I wish to thank the following people:

My husband, Sybrand, for all the encouragement I needed. My four sons, Wouter, Sybrand Jnr., Gideon and Anton van Schalkwyk and their families. A special thanks to Gideon who inspired, cajoled and helped without hesitation. Thank you for designing the cover and refining the title. Anton for his patience in helping me with technical glitches and saving lost data.

A special thanks to my sister-in-law Rhona van Schalkwyk who encouraged me after each chapter to write the next. Her positive motivation was the driving force to help me finish the book.

Ian Hauser, my editor, who corrected my very raw manuscript and advised me on many subjects with a gentle soul.

All the Albasini relatives: My mother, Christina Helena Lombard, my brother João Lombard, Tessa Bevan and the Eyssell family, Vivian Bannantyne, Ian Dreyer, Christiaan Dreyer, Gwyneth Rix, Frans Bijsterveld, Natalie Albasini, Martin Bergh and all the family who inspired me.

Alice Maria Albasini Magalhães provided me interesting facts about the Albasinis in Mozambique.

All my friends, especially Nicolaas Taljaard, Nico Mulder, Marlene Stubbs, Megan Cracknell and Angela Pretorius.

Linette de Vaal van der Merwe, my second cousin, for allowing me to use her book, *João "bravest amongst the brave"*, as a reference book.

John Coetsee, a South African author, who kindly gave me all of his research on João Albasini. He felt that he would not be able to finish such a big task in his lifetime as he was already in his eighties when he contacted me. He said it was too big a task to complete in his lifetime.

Stuart Bradshaw for the very helpful legal advice and encouragement.

Michael Hill from Michael Hill Jewellers who sent me a personal handwritten note of encouragement to write the book, after he gave me some excellent background information on diamonds.

Liz Dimblebey for her advice on handling horses.

UNISA university, Pretoria, South Africa for their excellence in having all the documentation ready for me to use in the very short time I had available to access the information.

University of Pretoria History Department.

Torre do Tombo - Alamida das universidades.

Ana Fernandes - Helping our son Anton who visited the archives in Lisbon translate the birth certificate of João.

About the author

The author, Esma, an acronym of all her grandmother's names (**E**lizabeth, **S**usanna, **M**aria **A**lbasini), grew up on the farm Beja adjacent to Goedewench, the Albasini Farm.

Since Knee-high to a grasshopper, she romanticised the stories told about the legend, her great-great grandfather João Albasini.

Her husband, four sons and friends encouraged her to write down the stories she fondly told at family dinners or social gatherings.

There are many Albasini stories still to be told and time will tell if any more will come from her pen.

 **E. Lombard**

Appendix – Albasini Family Trees

Below is the Albasini family tree outlined in text format for ease of reading in a book with such small pages.

Note that not all family members are included here. Each number indicates the child order for each couple in the tree. And the child of each couple is placed at the beginning of the line.

For example, the outline below shows that João Albasini and Gertina Janse van Rensburg had a son named Antonio Albasini, he married Aletta Albasini and they had 8 children.

For a graphic representation of this family tree, and many other amazing nuggets about Senhor Albasini's Secret, join our Facebook group at:

www.facebook.com/groups/albasinibook

Albasini Family Tree - South Africa

João Albasini's parents were Antonio Augusto Albasini (Italian) and Maria de Purificaçao Garcia (Spanish). Below, the family tree continues, starting with João Albasini.

João Albasini | Gertina Janse van Rensburg
1. Antonio Augusto Albasini | Aletta Snyman
   1. Cornelia | Bannantyne
   2. Gertina | Dahl
   3. João | Susanna de Jager
      1. Antonio Augusto | Beatrix Jansen
      2. Christina Helena | Jacob Jacobus Lombard
         1. Pierre | Venter
         2. João | van Blerk
         3. Japok | Language
         4. Christoffel | Emily de Beer
         5. Esma | Sybrand van Schalkwyk
            1. Wouter | Ruiping Li
               1. Elizabeth
               2. Anja
            2. Sybrand | Kariena Corbett
               1. Simeon
               2. Jesse
               3. Ethan
            3. Gideon | Tineke van Ameyde

1. Lucy Shalwick

2. Sophie Shalwick

3. Jack Shalwick

4. Anton

3. Johannes | Hester Robinson

4. Aletta | Mugglestone

5. Marie | Eyssell

6. Joan | Kruger

7. Susanna | van Vuuren

8. Cornelia | Holtzkamf

9. João | Engela de Bruin

10. Carolina | Bergh

11. Antoinetta | Kopp

4. Antonetta | Kilroe

5. Nicolaas (never married)

6. Aletta | Aldred

2. Zuzanna | Gouws

3. Maria | Biccard

4. Martha | Dreyer

5. Lucas | Meintjies?

6. Gertina | Pittendrich, later de Smit

7. Hendrika | Zeederberg (famous coaches)

8. Anna | Hazelhurst

9. Jacob (diseased during infancy?)

Albasini Family Tree – Mozambique

Here is a very incomplete family tree for João and his liaison in Mozambique, thanks to the assistance from Alice Albasini Malgahães.

João Albasini | Magude

1. Francisco Albasini | Maxequene Albasini

   1. Francisco Albasini | Maria

      1. Amelia | Jose Malgahães

         1. **Alice Albasini Malgahães** | Eugenio Malgahães

            1. Fabio Malgahães | Anon 75

            2. Patricia Malgahães

            3. Rogerio Malgahães

         2. Sandra

References: João Albasini (1813-1888)

JOÃO ALBASINI by João Albasini III – by permission from Gwyneth Rix.

BULPIN, T.V. Die Nasionale Krugerwildtuin No 1. Published for Mobil, Cape Town.

DE VAAL, J.B. (1953) – Die rol van João Albasini in die geskiedenis van Transvaal. Archive Yearbook for S.A. history, 16(1): 1-166.

Lectures No 3. Ernest Oppenheimer Institute for Portuguese studies University of the Witwatersrand Johannesburg 1983: 1-21.

DE VAAL, PHC. (1986) – Die Dorp Louis Trichardt. Kirsten Drukpers, Louis Trichardt 1-28.

EYSSEL, ANTONIO (Bobby), son of Marie Eyssell oral retelling.

EYSSELL, MARIE, (born Albasini), handwritten notes.

IMMINK, R.J. (1979) – Restoration of the Albasini-ruïnes. Article in Custos. March 1979: 13-14.

Hazyview, Mpumalanga South Africa blog for Hazyview & KNP.

National Archives at Torre do Tombo Lisbon.

A history of Mozambique – Marlyn Newitt.

Limpopo Journey – Carel Birkley.

De Zoutpanzbergen en de Bawenda Natie – Johs Flygare.

Valley of the Misits – H Klein.

SanParks – Official website South African History online.

PIENAAR, Dr. U. de V. (1990) – Neem Uit Die Verlede. Nasionale Parkeraad van Suid -Afrika: 1-611.

VAN WARMELO, The Copper Mines of Musina, pp 56-57.

VAN WARMELO, contributions towards Venda History, p 32.

PAMFLET, Schoemansdal, 'n Dorp Herleef 1988, Transvaalse Provinsiale Museumdiens.

Lost Trails of the Transvaal by T. V. Bulpin.

At the fireside by Rodger Webster.

By 'The waters of the Letaba' by A. P. Cartwright.

The Star 20 and 27 June 1925.

O. J. O. Ferreira Stormvoël van die Noorde.

A History of Mozambique - Marlyn Newitt, Published by Hurst & Company London 1995.

Legend of the Lowveld- uncompleted John Coetzee.

Army of spears, page 227 Book II.

TEIXEIRA DA MOTA, A rough translation from: 'Presenças Portuguesa na África do Sul e na Tranvaal durante os Séculos"XVIII e XIX. (I don't know if you want this parte too). Publicado pelo Ministério de Educação, Instituto de Investigação Científica Tropical, Lisboa 1989.'

Printed in Great Britain
by Amazon